# THE
# UMBRELLA
# THIEVES

# The
# Naked
# Umbrella
# Thieves

## Ian Wild

KNIGHTSTONE
PUBLISHING

KNIGHTSTONE
PUBLISHING

Unit 36,
88-90 Hatton Garden,
London
EC1N 8PN

Published in the United Kingdom by
Knightstone Publishing Ltd
First Published 2011

Cataloguing in Publication Data available

ISBN: 978-1-908134-01-1

Printed and bound by CPI Group (UK) Ltd, Croydon, CR0 4YY

# About the Author

Although Ian Wild is one of the world's leading authorities on naturist parasol kleptomaniacs, he would like to point out that he always bathes fully clothed and does not have a criminal record. He has written comedy for Ireland's RTE Radio One and won awards for short stories – most recently the 2009 Fish International Short Story Prize, but only to take his mind off undressing Mary Poppins. He is not naked writing this. He is wearing an umbrella which he found in the hand of someone who wouldn't let go until he bit their wrist.

# *Acknowledgements*

I would like Lothar Luken and Perry Wild for helpful interventions in the typescript.

For supporting my work in general during the time that this book was written, I'd like to thank Pat Cotter and the Munster Literature Centre, also Maira Bradshaw and Tigh Fili, and Cork County Arts Office.

Finally, thanks to Rob Johnstone and the staff of Knightstone Publishing.

*For Belinda*

# *Prologue*

*Somewhere, a perfect world revolves in a perfect universe — as in Plato's ideal. The further parallel universes are from this archetype, the more warped they become. Our own world might be twenty universes distant from perfection. O'Hara's world is just a few further off. Considerably more warped perhaps — but still recognisable as our own.*

# *Chapter 1*

Sergeant Cyrano O'Hara had lost the lost property cupboard. Its whereabouts were a mystery. In fact the entire police station had been behaving strangely of late. Corridors were there one day, gone the next. The downstairs hall sometimes ended in a motorway. The building had been rearranging itself ever since a conjuror had been locked up in one of the cells.

O'Hara stood beside a row of boot lockers and scratched his head.

"The cupboard can't have gone far," he explained to a spinster in brogues and tartan skirt. "It will turn up soon, and your books with it I dare say."

Miss Fetherby had accidentally left six novels at enquiries the previous morning whilst reporting a suspicious footprint in her vegetable patch.

"Has the footprint gone, Miss Fetherby?"

"It's moved. It's in the flowerbed now."

"Very strange that. No other related footprints round about?"

"No. Just this one. Getting nearer and nearer the house."

"Odd," said O'Hara and knocked at a likely looking door. "*Come in.*"

The sergeant sighed. Couldn't be that one then.

"The books are all murder mysteries," came Miss Fetherby's voice from behind him, "and I was *so* looking forward to reading them." Scolding herself, she followed O'Hara down a staircase that ended in a line of cells where the conjuror was being held.

"Have you ever investigated a murder yourself, Constable?"

"*Sergeant.*"

"I'm *so* sorry. I keep forgetting those lovely stripes."

It was frightening, thought O'Hara, how many times a day he felt like murdering a member of the general public.

"I've investigated too many."

Miss Fetherby beamed at him.

"And I bet you've solved them all, you clever man!"

The chief inspector appeared at the top of the stairs. She stood, hands on hips, so impossibly beautiful that she made the uniform look chic.

"Did you just knock on my door, O'Hara?"

"Yes, Chief."

"Are you playing knock and run or something? I said 'come in'."

"I'm looking for the lost property cupboard."

"It's escaped. Last seen driving a stolen vehicle towards Bristol."

Miss Fetherby was horrified.

"Things have come to a pass when you can't even trust your own police station to keep to the straight and narrow!"

"Quite," said the inspector, and turned back up the corridor, only to find that her door had taken the opportunity to retire to somewhere else in the building.

"My God! You need to be a detective in this place, just to keep track of your own office!"

But Miss Fetherby was still shocked at the idea of a joyriding cupboard.

"It will probably be reading my library books, the naughty thing!"

After reassuring Miss Fetherby that the cupboard would soon be apprehended and her books returned, O'Hara went back to his desk to scratch his protuberant nose. It was a conk that an eighty year old alcoholic would have been proud of. Women took one look at the beetroot posing as breathing apparatus on his face and said *no* before he even asked. So it was excruciatingly unfair to post a goddess as a chief inspector over him. Just as well she was only interested in work and obscure mathematical theorems. Women were *weird*.

Wretched Eric, the most hopeless constable in the history of policing burst into the office wearing nothing but an umbrella which he was using to shield his nether parts.

"Where's the chief?"

"Looking for her office. Why are you stark bollock naked?"

"I've had me clothes pinched. Get me a coat or something, Sarge."

O'Hara threw over his own voluminous greatcoat. Eric slipped inside it shivering.

"Bloody kids! Pretended one of 'em was drowning in the river. When I stripped off and jumped in, the drowning one swam off and the others nicked me uniform. Should've heard the buggers laughing."

"Did you have to take your undies off to perform the rescue? Nobody gets dragged under by waterlogged underpants."

"I didn't have any on."

"I won't ask why."

Eric shifted uncomfortably.

"Thanks, Sarge."

Eric went out of another door and shot off down a corridor to find some clothes. A telephone rang. O'Hara tried hard to think of a reason for not answering it. After wrestling with his conscience and finding it had him in a vicious half-nelson, he picked up the receiver whilst beating an imaginary canvas.

"Grethwick Police Station."

A belligerent man's voice shouted down the phone.

"I'd like to make a complaint about noise."

O'Hara groaned.

"Is this to do with Old Grethwick cemetery?"

"Yes. The windows of my house have been smashed by horrible throbbing noises masquerading as music and a pair of six year olds have thrown used syringes into my garden. I think it's one of those 'grave' things."

"I'll get a squad car down there right away."

"You told me that last time I phoned, half-an-hour ago!"

"Yes, well, all our cars were requisitioned by the military for their garden fete. We've only just got them back."

"I don't care if they were requisitioned by a tribe of South American pygmies so long as somebody gets down here to stop this horrible racket!"

The angry man of Old Grethwick slammed the phone down. That was the fourteenth complaint about the cemetery in the last hour. At this rate, something would have to be done. It was no good sending Eric. And the only other constables available were interrogating the conjuror in the cells.

An electric buzzer went: *ZZZZZZZZZZZZZZ*.

O'Hara shouted, "Hang on!"

A fist banged the glass hatch which he had closed to keep out the general public. A voice barked angrily.

"Open up!"

The sergeant slid the hatch aside, whereupon a woman resembling a well-off Rottweiler in a headscarf snapped at him.

"I'd like to report a stolen umbrella."

Scribbling an internal memo to haul Eric in his underpants over red-hot coals, O'Hara decided to pretend the brolly had just been handed in as lost property.

"Could you describe your umbrella, Madam?"

"Of course I can!" she sprayed in reply. "It was ripped from my hands by a completely naked man, who ran off with it. It's blue. With a floral pattern decorating six segmented sides. The bottom of the handle is wooden and it folds to fit in a handbag when not in use."

"Blue? With a wooden handle?" said O'Hara, bewildered.

"Yes, you imbecile."

The umbrella preserving Wretched Eric's modesty was pink with a black plastic handle. The thought of two naked men with umbrellas marauding through the streets of Grethwick was mindboggling.

"Let me take some personal details madam and … owwww!"

Some minutes later, nursing a badly bitten hand, O'Hara went down to where he had last seen the cells. They were still in the same place, and the usual sounds of an interrogation could be heard.

"D'yer think I hit him too hard?"

"He's still breathing."

"I got a bit carried away I suppose. I see red when they don't confess straight away. And this one's been more than a week."

"Prop him up. Make him look as alive as possible."

"His head keeps going on one side."

"Well, kicking it's not going to help. I thought you were supposed to be the nice one and I ..."

The conjurer was lying against a wall looking an unhealthy shade of purple. His eyes were shut and his clothing was ripped. He'd looked strange enough to begin with. Sort of oriental but with ginger hair. The cell was also full of dead pigeons and rabbits. Playing cards and squashed boiled eggs littered the floor. The two interrogators swung round guiltily at O'Hara's voice.

"You're supposed to be carrying out an inquiry, not an inquest."

Constable Studds came out of the cell shaking his head. "We're doing our best. But he keeps taking the piss. Every time we come out of here, he's pinched me watch or we're wearing his clothes instead of ours."

Constable Bass spoke as he put the finishing touches to the recumbent suspect.

"This morning he managed to get our signatures on a confession we'd brought in for him to sign. After we've finished, we come out and try to lock the door and he's got the keys."

"If he takes one more boiled egg out of my ear, I'll boil *him*."

O'Hara made a mental note to speak to the chief about Studds and Bass. They were on the wrong side of the bars. It was hardly safe to let them go and break up a grave in Old Grethwick. But there was no-one else.

"Lock up. You're needed on a peacekeeping mission. God knows why I'm sending you."

Studds went through his pockets.

"I thought you had them, Bassy."

Bass searched for a moment. Then heard a jingling from inside the cell. The conjuror was holding keys aloft with an eerie smile.

# Chapter 2

Lost property cupboards think *differently*. Just as lumberjacks can't help seeing trees as things that ought to be flat, lost property cupboards view the world from the perspective of the émigré briefcase, itinerant bowler hat and refugee chess set. These unclaimed objects create a spirit of place. An insecurity borne of no longer belonging. That's why we find lost property cupboards only in places with a strong physical identity. In police stations, railway stations, airports. They could never survive in just 'a house'. That would be too vague and would lead to an existential anxiety inside the walls. A lost property cupboard without a home — a building that truly owns it — is lost in a way that is frightening to behold.

The lost property cupboard from Grethwick Police Station was attracting stares as it zigzagged across motorway lanes. Basically, the car was a tight fit. Bricks and crumbling plaster burst periodically from smashed windows and only a hole in the roof accommodated the door frame.* Part of the problem stemmed from never having driven before. But having no hands or feet didn't help. And drivers kept blasting their horns, which meant that the cupboard couldn't remember why it was joyriding in the first place. It could not remember *home*. All it knew was that it felt sick inside. There was something

---

* Some things that happen in a Universe more warped than our own are difficult to visualize.

wrong with its digestion. The door had swallowed some object that quite definitely belonged *somewhere else*. A crash was inevitable really.

What was amazing was that it was with a joyriding attic bedroom which skidded over the turf partition and hit the lost property cupboard in a head on collision. Both cars jack-knifed into the air and rolled on the hard shoulder, then into a field where a group of bullocks gazed in astonishment. As the slightly demolished cupboard scraped itself out from the wreckage it heard the high pitched voice of the attic bedroom moaning, "Help! Get me out! My furniture's killing me!"

By sort of nutting the roof off a smoking, mangled Morris Minor, the cupboard helped the attic bedroom burst free. A smashed television fell from her opened door as she squeaked, "You maniac!"*

"But I thought you crashed into me?" stammered the perplexed cupboard.

"Of course not, you aggressive, arrogant male supremacist" she snapped, rejoining a loosened skirting board to her wall with a twang.

"I'm sorry," whimpered the cupboard. "I didn't know where I was driving. I was lost,"

---

* Buildings speak at a much higher pitch than humans, even castratos. The typical range of their frequency is between 25 and 30,000 vibrations per second. Occasionally the speech of a very gruff fire station or vicarage is mistaken for the hysterical whistling of wind in the eaves. Usually, only dogs can hear a building speak. It is for this reason that they often stand up and prick their ears in a seemingly silent house. They have merely heard the hallway complaining of draughts.

"We'd better scoot before the police get us," the agitated attic replied.

"*Police?*"

That rang a bell somewhere. A blue lamp almost flashed in the dark of the cupboard's unconscious. For a moment, in something like *déjà vu* he almost recovered his identity. Then he saw that the attic was already running for the cover of a nearby wood, her bricks rippling over the ground with the speed of a whippet.

"Are you coming?" she shouted, "Or are you going to hang around until the Law arrive with sledgehammers?"

In his suggestible state, the cupboard decided that having an identity crisis was bad enough. He didn't want to make things worse by getting mixed up with the police as well.

# Chapter 3

As fads go the grave scene was all that a teenager could desire. It was *de rigueur* to wear black lipstick, pop pills, shake to deafening music, and have sex on tombstones. As local cemeteries became the hub of popular culture, and pink rubber things were found pendulously draped over memorials to the dead, outraged tabloids led with, "Spunk Rock!" The Pope was offended on a multitude of counts. Yet despite dire warnings from head teachers, parents and pulpits, (only church dogs heard the latter), the craze spread like a spark in a box of fireworks — and became a rocketing outrage. A man who had told his daughter that she would be deflowered on a grave over his dead body was found by tabloids to be good at his word. And pictures of the event shocked the world. When the Prime Minister was moved to say, "The small minority of young people who indulge in these morbid sexual initiation rites are after a cheap thrill that they will pay for with the rest of their lives," teenagers everywhere jumped on the hearse-shaped bandwagon and mortgaged themselves to the hilt.

As the grave in Old Grethwick cemetery moved into full swing, the angry man who had telephoned Grethwick Police Station knelt on his sitting room floor and prayed to a bust of Ludwig van Beethoven for deafness. Mr Moore was a retired music teacher with a highly developed aesthetic ear. The sound of dust falling could give him a headache for a week. The pounding of dance music from the cemetery had rapidly brought on a migraine that made the Big Bang seem a pitiful whimper.

At the first gangling teenager he'd seen posing against a stone sepulchre, he had phoned the vicar. Dangerously liberal soothing-type noises slid from the man, "After all, one teenager, Mr Moore, doesn't make …"

Then the pounding had begun. Like a First World War bombardment. Moore gasped into the telephone.

"What on earth …?"

After twenty minutes of violent brain-damaging throbs, and the first seismic tremors of migraine, Moore rang the vicar again.

"It's up to you to get the police, Vicar!"

"But they're only young people having fun."

"Get a special teenager squad with CS gas, pepper spray, riot shields, and nose ring clippers."

But the migraine had already taken root in the knot of Moore's neck. Soon he was on his knees in the living room, whimpering — eyeballs bulging like five reds in a snooker table pocket. Bile from years of teaching brought a cream of spittle to the corners of his mouth.

"They should be thrown into camps, chained up in solitary confinement and forced to listen to deafening looptapes of Tippett until they scream for mercy!"

But for hate to work properly it needs action. Thinking horrible things just isn't satisfying enough, or wars could be carried out by a series of vitriolic letters. Hitler would just have sent anti-Semitic post to the local synagogue and the history of Anglo-French relations would merely be 2,000 volumes of crumpled abuse. Hate being what it is, Mr Moore crammed a handful of red and yellow pills into his mouth and staggered from home under the weight of a medicine ball head.

Down at Old Grethwick Church, tombstones were juddering in the earth. Young people — God bless 'em, — were jumping up and down on graves like a sibling's favourite band were buried there. Only somebody made entirely out of old Daily Telegraphs would not have sighed and wiped a misty tear from the lashes to see teenagers crushed together in such a heaving sweaty mass, or prostrate in the grass making those tortured parts — that God foolishly let develop quicker than the brain — sticky, or staggering into stone angels and vomiting over the wings. There was a wonderful bloodshot look in the eyes of tomorrow, as dealers folded wads of twenty pound notes into their back pockets.

Mr Moore approached this Bacchanalian scene looking like he was part of it. Pale, swaying and numbed by chemicals. He stared with stabbed eyes at topless young women stumbling along the stone church wall. A mob of hypnotized dancers jostled beneath sombre oaks. The air was a hurricane of rumbling bass. Able at last to focus on the objects of his disgust, Moore felt strangely relieved. His lip curled at the deep throated snog of two steaming dancers against a tree. Then he saw some policemen beating up one of the teenagers in the seclusion of the car park. Despite himself, he walked towards the scene in fascinated horror, then saw they were actually beating up an elderly man. He ran over.

"What are you doing?"

Both constables were kicking their venerable victim, who had fallen to the floor.

"He wouldn't get in the van when we arrested him," said Constable Studds, breathing heavily after several strenuous wallops of boot leather.

"But that's the vicar."

The other policeman straightened and stared at Moore, "Don't take the piss, mate."

"But I know him. I live here."

Constable Bass hauled the groaning fogy to his feet and shook him, "Vicars wear dog collars. They don't say things like, '*Fucking pig!*'"

The vicar was shoved into the van. After screeching the back doors shut, the policeman turned to find Mr Moore still there.

"You don't understand!" Moore gabbled hastily, "He's one of the trendy kind. He even uses four letter words in his sermons."

Constable Bass looked stonily at the ex-teacher.

"I said, *don't take the piss.*"

"I'm not. I'm just trying to point out that you're mistakenly arresting someone I know."

"He's a mate of yours is he?"

"Well. Sort of. Look you've got to let him out."

"Have I?"

"Yes. For God's sake."

Suddenly a hand grabbed Moore by the throat. He was slammed against the side of the van.

"Well, as he's a mate of yours, you can come along and keep him company."

# Chapter 4

*Sex. Sex. Sex.*

It's the most unfair of Nature's tricks on us. How much simpler life would be if people reproduced like amoebae and split in half every so often. O'Hara wondered whether this would mean lots of other people would inherit his stupidly purple nose. But the fact was that it wouldn't matter. He wouldn't be genetically programmed to itch, like a mongrel in a flea circus, after impossible women. He was trying to find the chief's office. Partly because he had something to say. Mostly because he just wanted to look at her. She was too gorgeous to be a police chief. Her appointment had the whole male workforce chafing erections on blue serge. It was interfering with the job. For weeks it had been impossible to speak to her, because of all the other officers queuing outside her door with, "items needing urgent attention." The recent scrambling of the police station had actually made it easier to jump the queue. O'Hara wanted to mention his disquiet about her choice of constables to assist in nailing the conjuror. Bass and Studds wouldn't stop at a hammer and tintacks. But what if she disapproved? Or thought he was a grass. It wasn't only that the constables would give him a new face, arranged even worse. He would also jeopardize his non-existent chances of ever getting off with her. The fact that romance was out of the question for a man with a gherkin nose didn't matter to the part of him that *dreamed.*

But doors kept opening on strange places. The second time he came up against the six lane motorway, he just stood amidst dazzling lights, wondering whether to throw himself under a growling lorry. *Was* it an illusion? Another door brought him back to the cells. The conjuror was sitting outside his, feeding a dove on popcorn. O'Hara stopped abruptly.

"Shouldn't you be in your cell."

"But I'm innocent."

O'Hara opened a cell door.

"C'mon."

Without reluctance, the conjuror obeyed.

"Popcorn?" he asked, taking a gnarled white lump from O'Hara's ear.

"How did you get out?"

"Magic."

The small ginger haired man sat on the edge of a bed. The dove perched on top of his head.

"Like all those people who vanished during your last performance?" asked O'Hara, sardonically.

The conjuror gave a blameless shrug.

"It was an accident! I've told them that. I've told them the greatest secrets of my profession, and they just laughed at me! The greatest secret that we magicians have been hiding is that the magic is *real!* There is no hidden mechanism to hold up the elevations of a floating woman. No trick to my being able to pull an ace from the pack like that!"

An ace of spades appeared in his palm.

"But magic can get out of control. I asked the audience to get into my disappearing box. And then I couldn't get them out again. The box wouldn't give them back!"

"And what about the blood under the stage?"

"What *about* the blood? It's not my fault that the box started to bleed."

It was an absurd story. And those were the ones which were most likely to be true.

"I don't suppose, by any chance, you could make the police station return to its normal self could you?"

The conjuror burst into hysterical laughter and threw the dove into the air. It turned into a shower of popcorn.

# Chapter 5

Moonlight poured over a trampled churchyard. After two days and nights of throbbing desecration, the grave was over. Old Grethwickians that had not gone mad or died of earache, slept sounder than the dead. For the groans in the graveyard were not coming from comatose youths who lay spaced-out right next to each other on a crypt. Unearthly noises were coming from *the earth*. Forty-eight hours of continuous grave stomping sacrilege and noise that would have drowned out Armageddon, had woken the deceased.

Deep in their eternal slumbers, spirits had been disturbed. At first, skeletons turned restlessly in their coffins, like sick mortals on a lumpy mattress. There were garbled murmurs, sneezes, — a few tried to rise and go to the toilet. As the noise got louder and the grave dancing more intense, several ghosts sat up and shouted, *"Shut up!"* or *"Can't you see we're trying to be dead!"* to no avail. Eventually, the whole otherworldly contents of the graveyard lay underground with bony fingers in skulls, trying to find a pillow to cram over Yorick heads. Those from the Middle Ages, who had decomposed furthest, simply wailed and recited Chaucer as loud as possible to try and drive the ghastly din of live music from their dead souls. When the din abated none of them could get back to sleep. They had a sort of insomnia. Those who had only just been buried were pretty miffed. There's nothing worse than being woken up when you've only just settled. So the groans which accompanied splinterings of rotten wood from inside Old Grethwick graveyard were ferociously splenetic.

Then bulging jigsaws of earth lifted like scabs. Soil from torn up roots showered the air. Tombstones thumped over. One by one, the inhabitants of Old Grethwick graveyard broke to the surface and stared with phosphorescent eyeballs at the world.

"Urggh," spluttered Farmer Fogarth, a small wizened looking man, buried in 1921. "I was having such wonderful dreams. Time to milk the cows, Harriet."

Fogarth almost jumped into his skin to see Judith's skeleton grinning beside him.

"You silly bugger. You're dead, remember? That bull pinned you against the shed wall. Broke your ribs like matchsticks."

"Good Lord."

Nearby, a ghostly peasant stood staring at the church and wondering if he still had plague.

"Be this England?" he asked Mr Bullfinch, a Methodist preacher who was shambling past in a glowing wide brimmed hat.

"Touch your forelock, rogue. We are in the Kingdom of Heaven. And I am a representative of our Lord Almighty God."

The peasant tugged his forelock. A wad of stinking, matted hair came off in his hand. He threw it over his shoulder with a shrug. His locks landed on the steps of a family crypt where the spirit of Lady Elizabeth Sturridge was talking to her maid, "Oh, look at the ridings, Susan!" she said, peering at newly built houses, on what, two hundred years ago, had been her estate. "What have they done?"

"Looks like they cut down all the chestnuts and built sties there, Ma'am."

"That was where we used to read poetry in the summer. Where one midsummer evening, after reciting Shakespeare, Byron almost kissed me."

Her Ladyship's eye sockets shed tears of dust.

"These new farming practices from Norfolk, Ma'am. They've gone too far. First enormous sheep, now horribly bloated pigs."

The women had died when Horace, their coachman, downed an entire bottle of brandy and then steered over a cliff. Having had two centuries to sober up, the man was hiding behind a tree, muttering guiltily.

"They spiked me drinks at the inn, Lady Elizabeth. All I 'ad were two fimblefulls of water, I swear it."

The tree concealing his quaking fibulas was being admired by the happiest of spectres — Miss Ada Brackenbury. She had been a local tree surgeon and was delighted to find the ancient oak of Grethwick churchyard in robust health.

"Well, well, you've hardly changed! A little stouter round the midriff, but that's to be expected at your age. And what have they been nailing to you, my dear old friend?"

As she read a small notice, Miss Ada's face began to resemble one of the church gargoyles. She ripped the plastic covered sign from crinkled bark and glided, in that way enraged spectres have, towards the other ghosts who were congregating (for spiritual guidance) around Mr Bullfinch.

"Have you read this?" she shouted in a voice that cut swathes through early morning mist. The other ghosts glowed in her direction.

"*Grethwick Borough Council. Planning application. Relief road for Old Grethwick* — a lot of it is nonsense that I do not begin to understand, but this — *that the graveyard of Old Grethwick church be moved to the adjoining field, the graves exhumed and their contents situated in the aforementioned area.*"

"Let me see, woman!"

The notice was snatched away by Bullfinch. There was a silence as the preacher read. His wide-brimmed hat trembled as if it contained an unquantifiable amount of wrath which was about to be set loose. Then his luminous green hands ripped the board in two.

"*Objections to be lodged within 48 days of this notice being erected.* I'll give them objections, by God! The man that tries to move my bones will find them with an axe raised to split his head!"

# *Chapter 6*

Although *some* buildings can go from nought to sixty in mere seconds, bedrooms — when not being used for sex — are heavily associated with sleep. And cupboards are furtive skulking things, not renowned for their dash or athleticism. So it was not long before the escaping cupboard and the attic bedroom were wheezing like a couple of asthmatics with Hoover bags on their heads.

"I can't run any further. My walls have got a stitch," gasped the cupboard, stopping in the middle of a large twilighted field.

"So've mine. Just try and look like there's showers and changing rooms round you."

"What?"

"We're in the middle of a football pitch. Maybe we can convince people we're a gymnasium or something. It's a matter of brazening it out. Staring players in the eye and sticking to our guns."

"I can't!" the cupboard whined, "Other gymnasiums might think I was taking the piss."

"Just copy me."

"Okay." There was a pause while the cupboard stared at the attic bedroom before saying, "Well, go on then."

"I'm *doing it*."

"It doesn't look any different."

"Well, you're just a bloody cupboard. What do you know

about impersonating gymnasiums?"

The conversation was cut short by the arrival of two immensely tall thirteen year old girls. For fashion's sake, they were wearing platform shoes with three foot soles. These caused both vertigo and broken ankles, but enabled teenagers to get practice at something they'd be doing a lot of later in life — looking down on their parents. Eugenie and Monica crept between the attic bedroom and the cupboard.

"Go on then. No-one can see us here."

A match fizzed. There was a silence.

"What's this gymnasium in the middle of the pitch for? And a cupboard?"

"I don't know. Never seen them before. Giz a drag then."

Several deep inhalations followed.

"Feel anything yet."

"There's someone coming."

"Fuck."

"Put it out. *Put it out.*"

"See if that cupboard door is open."

"It isn't."

"The gym's open. Get in."

"Ow! My head!"

Inside the attic bedroom, the girls cowered against the ceiling, listening in a dark silence that seemed to spread like spilt black coffee on a rug.

"Have they gone?" Eugenie whispered.

"I don't know."

Eugenie noticed the bed.

"Hey! This isn't a gymnasium at all. It's a bedroom. What do they want to get changed in a bedroom for? No wonder it's a mess." She sat and bounced on the mattress. "Hey Mon, look. There's a key in the door. Lock it and we'll smoke the rest in here. No-one can catch us if we lock up."

Monica staggered over to turn the key. Another match flared making Eugenie's face glow like a Halloween lantern. She blew a plume of smoke in the direction of her friend.

"So *do* you fancy Peter Parker? His ears stick out like two fucking massive satellite dishes."

Monica suddenly staggered and clutched uneasily at a lampshade that hung from the ceiling.

"Ooooh. I feel weird." she said.

The room seemed to be moving. She gave a loud scream.

"Shhhhh! Shut up will you?"

"But we're moving. The room's swaying. Can't you feel it?"

Eugenie tried to stay cool.

"For God's sake Mon — it's just the Henry."

"Help me to the bed. Don't think I can walk straight any more. These shoes. *Help!*"

Releasing the lampshade, Monica teetered drunkenly towards the bed and went sprawling over her friend. Both girls started retching.

"Eugenie! We're rolling. The bed's moving! I feel seasick! I've pewked broccoli salad on me new blouse."

"Get off me," came a groaning, queasy reply. "It's great. He said one smoke would lift our 'eads off. And it might make us … *bllleuuurrrghghg.*"

"But we're both feeling the same thing. That can't be right."

"Relax, Mon. You're just having a bad trip."

"It's too real. It's like someone's carrying the room. I want to get out."

After vomiting more broccoli salad over her friend, Monica stared groggily through a dormer window. She screamed to see darkened scenery rushing by outside, "We're moving! The room's got legs! Let me out!"

"Jesus! Cool it, Mon. Honest, it's just the ... Hey! *Ow!*"

Unaware that they had been sold two cigarettes full of talcum powder, Eugenie and Monica tumbled to the floor as the bed tipped over. The attic bedroom and cupboard had recovered their breath and were doing sixty miles an hour over fences, bushes and the occasional railway embankment.

# *Chapter 7*

O'Hara sighed.

"Look, Miss Fetherby, I think it must be a practical joke. One-legged murderers can't hop around gardens yards at a time."

The tweeded spinster looked at him beseechingly.

"You can't deny, Sergeant, that the footprint is creeping nearer and nearer to the house. This one is right outside the French windows. The murderer, for that is undoubtedly what he is, has been standing on one leg, 'casing the joint', as they put it."

"I honestly think there's no reason to alarm yourself. It's probably a kid messing about with a boot on the end of a pogo stick. Does anyone round here know that you have an interest in murder mysteries?"

"The librarians obviously."

O'Hara had been trained to use body language in difficult situations such as these. He put his helmet on, to hint at departure. Miss Fetherby grabbed his arm.

"You can't go and leave me at the mercy of psychotic one-legged killers."

O'Hara struggled to shrug her from his three stripes. "Really, Miss Fetherby, if he *does* only have one leg, he should be easy to push over."

"But the footprint! Next it will be *inside* the house! First in the kitchen, then on the stairs. Then in my room beside my naked lifeless body. That's what happens, isn't it? It's always to single ladies like me. Still attractive, but *alone.* And it's always sick and mysteriously grotesque, the way they do it. Don't go. Mount an armed guard over me. Please."

O'Hara tried to prize the vines of her fingers off his bicep. "Most murders result from simple domestic violence. Will you please let go? Look, I'll go and check up on the psychiatric histories of the librarians, okay?"

"I'm a defenceless woman. If you don't count the bread knife I keep under the bed."

"*Let go!* Miss Fetherby, you've simply been reading too many detective novels."

At this, the spinster removed her glasses with disconcerting suddenness to reveal an accusatory stare. "That reminds me, Mr O'Hara. Has your lost property cupboard been apprehended yet?"

"No. The car's been found. In a crash. But the cupboard is still at large."

"A crash. Was anyone hurt?"

"The driver of the other car was killed outright. And both cars were stolen."

The tweeded woman tapped her folded horn rimmed specs on O'Hara's chest.

"And were my detective novels discovered at the crash, by any chance?"

"I don't think they were. No."

"Then I'm afraid," said Miss Fetherby taking a bill from her jacket pocket and dangling under the policeman's nose,

"You, or one of your superiors, owes me thirty two pounds in library charges."

# Chapter 8

Jonathon Trundle had died only ten years earlier whilst still a young eco-warrior. He had been trying to save a whale trapped in an estuary. In a rubber dinghy, he and two others had attempted to scare a huge underwater shadow out into open water. But it had turned and swatted the boat with the full weight of a vast tail fluke. Splatted like flies under a swatter, three eco-warriors died the most two-dimensional of deaths. When the bodies were recovered, floating upon the tide like pancakes on Teflon, Jonathon's parents decided to bury their flattened son in the local village cemetery of Old Grethwick church. The coffin was round and twelve foot in diameter. In fact to save expense, the undertakers had suggested rolling him up like lino, so that he would fit in a conventional box. This well meaning idea had been squashed almost as firmly as Jonathon himself. Now he was listening to the punch drunken threats of Bare-Knuckle Bob.

"No bugger'll move my dust. D'yhear? Unless they want black eyes that'll swell up an' close for a year."

Bob — a pugilist of renown across the shires in 1780 — was punching the air with skeleton fists.

"Well, they'll probably send in mechanical diggers," said Jonathon.

"I'll punch 'em in the throat. Pulp their Adam's apples into a cider of blood."

"They're machines. Your bones would just shatter on them. Or they'll run over you."

Like most ghosts and dead people everywhere, Jonathon was aghast at the thought of his sacred relics being moved. Shifting bones only a couple of inches left or right is enough to get the average live person a good haunting for the rest of their measly existence. Lifting and dumping an entire graveyard into a distant field was the sign of a collective stupidity that only elected councils or multinational companies were capable of. So it was obvious to Jonathon — even from this early stage — that a road protest was called for. But getting his eternal comrades to understand this looked like being a bit of a problem.

Preacher Bullfinch's oratory boomed around the graveyard, "There has been a terrible mistake. This is not the Kingdom of Our Lord. But Hell! Gabriel would appear to have mixed up his lists. I daresay, at this very moment, highwaymen and prostitutes have been admitted through the gates of pearl in our stead! Let us locate Lucifer and insist upon our ascendance."

A rabble of ghosts turned to follow the preacher.

"Mr Bullfinch," rasped the tree surgeon, Ada Brackenbury, "it is surely obvious, that we are in neither Heaven nor Hell, but the very same place where we were all buried, only some time further on."

The preacher fixed burning orbs upon her. A light breeze whistled desolation through his ribs.

"Kindly refrain, Madam, from commenting beyond your station and your wit. We see around us a land that bears — it is true — passing resemblance to that we left. But is obviously a mockery of the England we abandoned our first shape to. The Devil's infernal regions are naturally a bastardised copy of our last world, just as Heaven is a blissfully realised perfection of England. Look around you, woman. Scent in your nostrils the fume-laden air, polluted by some foul engines of Satan. See the meadows marred by his demon's lairs."

At this moment an articulated lorry roared by, blazing lights and leaving a cloud of blue smoke and deafened spectres. The ghosts recoiled in terror from this apparition of the living.

"See! The Devil in his chariot! Already he is searching for us. To scorch us with his diabolic engines of fire!"

But Miss Brackenbury snorted.

"That, Mr Bullfinch, was progress. Surely some of us can recognise a descendant of the steam locomotive when they see one?"

The ghosts hovered uneasily. Death tends to make people see things in black and white. Fire and brimstone are easier to follow than the subtleties of reason.

"Madam, it is obvious that you are an agent of Lucifer, sent to sow disharmony and confusion amidst the true followers of Christ!"

Spirits fresh from the Middle Ages or the times of James the First suddenly shouted,

"Witch! Burn her!"

The prim skeleton of Miss Brackenbury stood firm. Well, for a ghost.

"If this place is Hell and not Earth where our bones are laid, what does it matter two farthings if demons here move us?"

A hundred craniums turned to the preacher.

"She's right," added Jonathon. "I appear to have snuffed it quite recently, because this place isn't much different than the England I left in 1995. That roaring machine that just went by was a lorry. Just a machine like a steam train that doesn't go on rails. Everyone drives round in things like that nowadays."

Mr Bullfinch glowered.

"Then it seems we have not gone to Hell. Hell, it seems, hath come to us!"

# Chapter 9

O'Hara sat in the canteen drinking tea. He was off-duty but, as always, was pounding the beat of his mind. His colleagues knew better than to sit next to him and eat their sandwiches — the bloke was morbidly obsessed with right and wrong. That was why he had joined the police force. And that was why he was still only a sergeant. He had thought the force would need someone like him. The force thought he needed someone like a psychiatrist.

He stirred two sugars in the regulation brew and drank pensively. O'Hara was still troubled by the fact that, a couple of weeks ago, he had nicked a biro from work. He kept telling himself it didn't matter. But the previous night, for the umpteenth time since the felony, he'd woken up in pitch darkness, screaming,

"I'm innocent! I only borrowed it to do the crossword!"

He'd dropped a fiver into the petty cash tin as overcompensation. But nothing could erase the fact that a crime had been committed. What next? He wondered. Shoplifting biros? Robbing biro factories? Murdering somebody with a biro for a biro? The sergeant was worried that, having once transgressed, he would slither all the way down a slippery oleaginous slope into Wormwood Scrubs. Don't be ridiculous, he scolded himself. Nobody cared about bloody biros. It was just a pen. A pen. A pen. A pen. A ... Why had he ever wanted to be a policeman? He should have just been a crook from the very beginning and got it over with.

O'Hara stood up. His plastic chair scraped echoingly on the tiled floor. There was only one thing to do. He'd have to have another go at finding the chief to tell her about Bass and Studds. He had to keep *doing good.* He definitely *wasn't* going because he fancied her. It was duty. Those two were bent as a bouncer's nose. He winced. Felt the red gherkin on his face and thought fleetingly about the possible costs of plastic surgery. A grand? Ten grand?

Searching for the chief's office, he came up against the six-lane motorway again. He cursed the conjuror and decided to cross and search on the other side. Overwhelmed by fumes, O'Hara skirted the rush hour traffic and barged coughing through double doors. He found himself in a corridor lined with boot lockers that ended in the basement stairs. Perhaps these steps now led to the top of the building? The sergeant shrugged — it was worth a try. But, on reaching the furthermost boot locker, O'Hara heard sobbing. Peering down a gloomy flight of stairs he saw a white shape below. The sergeant switched on a light. It was Wretched Eric. Naked, but for a pair of briefs, the constable was holding something near his armpit and stroking it.

"Eric?"

Eric leapt up and turned. "Oooo!"

His face was shapeless with tears.

"What's going on, lad?"

The constable tried to hide the object and simultaneously conceal his glistening cheeks.

"What've you got there, Eric. C'mon. Hand it over."

"No! I don't want to! You can't see it."

"See what?"

"Can't say." Tears squeezed again from Eric's screwed up eyes. "It's ... it's ...

The young policeman broke down into shuddering sobs. O'Hara descended the stairs and pulled the object from Eric's midriff. The constable relinquished something hard and curved. Holding it up to the light, O'Hara saw that it was a dead tortoise wearing a pair of white cotton underpants.

"It's dead, Sarge."

"What is?"

"Me tortoise."

Eric sniffled whilst O'Hara shook his head in bafflement.

"What were you doing keeping a bloody tortoise down here anyway?"

"It were a criminal, Sarge. I arrested it a couple of weeks ago. For wrecking this garden. It ate all this old lady's lettuces, and she complained. So I thought I'd lock it up as a punishment. It got ill. I put me undies on it to keep it warm. But I forgot about it until today when I came down to put these confiscated explosives in me locker. I was using me locker as a cell, y'see. And now it's dead."

O'Hara shook his head in mystification.

"But why are you wearing nothing again?"

"Detective work, Sarge. Them kids that nicked me clothes. I figured they could only have learned to swim so good by going to the baths regularly. So I went down there undercover — in me trunks and saw one of them from the window, uncoiling a bit of wire outside. I ran out to get him. I just stopped them blowing the baths to bits. But they got away through a load of nettles, and I couldn't run after 'em. Then I went back to get me clothes from the baths, and they'd shut."

Eric followed O'Hara back up the steps. The sergeant said, "You'd better bury it, lad. It smells."

"I know. It must have been dead a few weeks. I thought it was hibernating."

"Yeah. Well."

"You won't tell anyone will you, Sarge?"

"What? That you put your undies on a dead tortoise?"

"No. About, y'know."

"What?"

"I couldn't help crying. I felt sorry for it. It's not wrong to feel sorry for 'em is it, Sarge?"

"Go and bury the bleeding thing."

"Yes, Sarge. Straight away, sir."

O'Hara held the basement door open for Eric. Then realised that somehow, either Fate or the building had played another trick on him. For the two policemen found themselves in the chief's office. She looked a little startled.

"Yes?"

"Chief!"

"It's customary to knock."

There in the room with her — laughing — were Studds and Bass.

# Chapter 10

O'Hara's cheeks went red as a baboon's. Rosy as his nose. In fact, for once, all parts of his face matched.

"I was just looking for your office because I …"

He'd come to warn her about the two constables whose company she seemed to be enjoying. The chief raised a single eyebrow, as one might cock a little finger to drink tea.

"Go on, Sergeant."

Her eyes went from him to Eric — who was still in swimming trunks and holding a dead tortoise — and back again, as if for an explanation. The decaying animal was still clothed.

"The tortoise was wearing underpants to keep warm." O'Hara said. "Now it's dead."

He looked fiercely at Eric, who took the hint and hurriedly peeled the underpants off. Laughing weakly, the constable waved them loosely round and round in his hand. Then they flew from his grip accidentally and flopped to the floor. The tortoise's well rotted leg dropped off as the underpants were retrieved.

"Oh for God's sake, lad!" shouted O'Hara, snatching the underpants, tortoise and missing leg, and throwing them out of the door. "Go and play Cindy dolls with dead reptiles outside!"

He pushed Eric out.

Looking even more bemused, the chief eyed Studds and Bass who were doing an impersonation of two pressure cookers filled with laughing gas.

"Constables. You have work to do, I presume?"

The two men left hurriedly, Studds biting his knuckles. After the door closed, suppressed hilarity could be heard coming out like farts all along the corridor.

"Sorry about that, Chief." stammered O'Hara.

Now that he was alone in a room with her, he felt shy. There was an awkward silence.

"I can't remember now what it was I wanted to see you about, so er ..."

He opened the door to escape.

"Wait, Sergeant. I want to speak with you anyway. Sit down."

O'Hara sat, wishing for the millionth time, that his nose could be detached and put in a brown paper bag. He felt disgusting when faced with her unblemished skin. He noticed that three inches down the chief's deliciously kissable throat, a top button of her shirt was unfastened. More aroused than a policeman on duty ought to be, O'Hara reflected that for the chief to flaunt her body so shamelessly was asking for it. Meanwhile, her voice wafted seductively around his ears,

"The cupboard."

O'Hara saw mathematical hieroglyphics all over her jotter. It was men who were supposed to be good at maths, not women.

"They've found it?"

The chief sighed. "No. That's the trouble."

O'Hara agreed grimly. "I suppose it doesn't look good. A joyriding police lost property cupboard. I hope the press haven't got hold of it."

She turned a biro round in her hands.

"It's not so much the joyriding that bothers me. It's the fact that the body found at the scene of the crime *hadn't been killed in the crash*. We thought the deceased was the driver of the Morris Minor — which had also been stolen. The autopsy revealed the stiff had been dead a week and was one of the Grethwick councillors last seen going into the conjuror's final gig. Are you alright, Sergeant?"

O'Hara had been trying to conceal his nose from her with his hand.

"Yes. Fine."

"So what do you think?"

It was impossible. He fancied her like mad. He couldn't think straight. The more he tried to say something intelligent, the more his tongue tied itself in a clove hitch.

"Think? I … er … Obviously a driver picked up this councillor guy. They had an argument about politics — funding bloody lefty, gay theatre companies — and the driver whipped out a carving knife and slashed his throat."

"*He'd been dead a week remember!*"

"Ah. Yes." O'Hara winced. "They argued about pouffy theatre companies. The driver says they should be cut. Gets carried away demonstrating it. Hides body for seven days. Then pinches a car. Goes off to bury the body. Crashes. Runs off in remorse and …"

The chief buried her gorgeous face in her hands.

"Sergeant! Shut up!"

"Hey?"

"Shut up."

"Right."

His nose was getting hot flushes. It felt like a hazard-warning lamp between his eyes.

"What I'm trying to get over is the fact that our lost property cupboard is a serial killer. Okay?"

"Our lost property? Don't be daft. It was a lovely little cubbyhole. I trapped my fingers in the door once, but …"

"*Think!* The conjuror's victims couldn't be found. What's a lost property cupboard like?"

O'Hara's desperate mind began branching off helplessly. "Big. Red. Ugly. Covered in pimples."

"What? I said a lost property cupboard. What's it like?"

"Oh yes. You put things in it … like …"

"Yes. Like a …?"

Her hand did a backwards royal wave to coax out the correct answer. The only word that would come into O'Hara's tortured mind was *Vagina*.

Speaking to the sergeant as if he was a five year old, the chief said, "It's like a box that magicians use to make people vanish."

Slowly, O'Hara said, "Our lost property cupboard? A mass murderer? A dangerous killer?"

She nodded, "Or an accomplice."

O'Hara was so flabbergasted, he almost forgot he was in love. The cupids flapping round the chief's office, misfiring arrows, went down like shot crows.

"So it's essential," she continued, "that we nab it, before another seventy-five people get slaughtered. If the truth gets out, we'll all be locked up for incompetence. We had the bloody thing right here in the station and somehow let it escape. So I'm asking you, Sergeant, to make the recapture of this felonious storeroom your top priority. We've been lucky. There's not been much interest in the case so far. People are pleased that seventy-five local councillors have gone missing. But if they weren't politicians, we'd be in trouble. So nobble it *immediately*."

Hearing finality in the chief's last words, O'Hara would have got up and left had he not suddenly become transfixed by the biro she'd been turning around in her hands. Her fingers had been pushing it up and down for their entire conversation. Did she know then? Was it to make him confess?

"Is there anything else, Sergeant?"

She looked at him intently. O'Hara opened his mouth wordlessly. He would have to confess to the biros. Then, to his own surprise, the sergeant found himself saying, "Chief, I don't think Constables Bass and Studds should be looking after this conjuring case."

She looked surprised. "Why not?"

"I think they're ..." he tried to find the right word. Something softer than the one he eventually blurted out, "*Corrupt*."

A pause widened. The biro went still in the chief's hands.

"That's a very serious allegation to make against fellow police officers, Sergeant. Can you substantiate it?"

"Maybe 'corrupt' is too strong a word. But they seem to me to be overzealous in getting confessions out of people. They get a kick out of violence. Y'know. Literally."

"Is that an official complaint?"

"It's off the record."

"Then I'm not sure I want to hear about it. I've no reason to doubt the excellence of their work. They have exemplary records. A high conviction rate."

O'Hara snorted, "Because they don't care whether the people they arrest are guilty or not. They don't seem to have any notion of right and wrong."

"And you have?"

She was still twiddling the bloody biro. He paused — like a horse that knows it isn't going to make a very high fence — then said unconvincingly,

"Yes."

The chief smiled seriously.

"I'm glad to hear it, Sergeant. In fact I wasn't aware that you were so interested in ethics and morality. Maybe we should have a philosophical discussion about policing sometime. I'll give your comments about Constables Bass and Studds some consideration. In the meantime, I'd be obliged if you would apprehend that cupboard."

# Chapter 11

Up a tree, in a wood, a mile from the football pitch, the cupboard and attic were breathing heavily from their exertions.

"Did we *have* to hide up here?" asked the cupboard.

"Will you speak higher?" the attic remonstrated. "If you go on waffling as deeply as that, they'll hear you."

"Who?"

"Those two girl humans inside me."

"Oh yeah." The cupboard realised that what seemed to be thick fog all around him was actually his mind. He said uneasily, "If they're still alive. You probably killed them by clambering up here."

"If you had a better idea, you should have said."

Are they moving?"

"They could be asleep. We've got to get rid of them. Humans are bloody touchy about killing where one of their own is concerned. Course they don't give a toss about killing one of us. Usually with a bloody big ball on a chain."

It was spoken with feeling. The cupboard shrugged and tried to get comfy on his branch. A squirrel peered through leafy fronds and dropped an acorn in shock.

"Just shake them out then."

"And let both of them fall sixty feet. They'd make a very big mess. The cops would find them. Then look up."

Both rooms pondered their predicament. It was the first time they'd had a moment to think since the crash. Now, by moonlight, the attic strained to see her companion. He was well-built. Kind of upright and straight. She kept getting wafts of bad breath. She said,

"My name's Esmeralda. What's yours?"

"I don't know ... Cupboard?"

"Come on. Even the lowliest public urinal has a name."

There was a long pause. If the cupboard had had a head, he would definitely have scratched it.

"Maybe it began with 'L'. Larry? Loh ... Loh ... Loh ... Lollipop?"

"Well what were you doing driving along that road when you crashed into my car?"

"Road? What crash? Did I crash something?"

The attic was shocked. "You've got amnesia. We need to find a hospital, so you can speak with one of the consulting rooms."

"What about you? How come you were driving a car?"

Esmeralda didn't reply immediately, then said,

"I was going on holiday. I fancied a bit of paddling by the sea. Making sandhumans. Smearing on the sun tan cream. So I borrowed a car."

"Wow. I'd love to meet a pier. Or a fun fair."

The cupboard leaned back dreamily, staring up through leafy boughs.

"Yeah. Well. We can't till the heat is off. We've got to lie low and get rid of these kids. We need to be where no-one would think it was weird to see us ... like ... like ... of course!"

"Up a tree?"

"No. Idiot! Up something completely different! Why didn't I think of it before?" She slapped a piece of architrave against her roof, as a hand might slap a brow. "It's so obvious. C'mon."

"But we've only just climbed up! Esmeralda, stop! I feel like I belong up here. Maybe I was a cupboard in a tree house."

"We'll have to sneak in whilst it's dark" said the attic bedroom.

There was a crunch as she jumped and landed heavily at the foot of the tree.

From inside her, a brained and bruised Monica groaned, "Eugenie! Help me. I'm stuck in this terrible dream."

"It's just the Henry, Mon."

"I keep hearing these rooms talking in high voices about being up trees and things. The police being after them and stuff."

"I know. It's great isn't it?" said Eugenie's ghastly voice, betraying that she was determined to enjoy the experience if it killed her.

"No. All this jolting about. The bed keeps hitting me."

"Relax. Enjoy it. *Ouch!* It's just a trip!"

Monica retched. There was definitely no broccoli left.

# *Chapter 12*

B ut Mr Moore, the music teacher, had a cauliflower ear. The pain of it meant that he had to lie on his cell bed facing the wall. He'd often got children to face a wall when they'd sung out of tune in class. It was like looking into a mirror to find your own face blotted out. A kind of denial that you existed.

*Did* he exist? The only thing that Moore was certain about was that his pain existed. Since that terrible ride in the van, when two officers reeking of drink had repeatedly assaulted him — and the vicar — Mr Moore had grown very familiar with the wall. They had banged his head against it when he would not sign a ridiculous confession stating that *he* had beaten up the vicar. On their next visit, when he'd denied dealing drugs to young people, the two policemen kicked him repeatedly in the ears. With each kick they'd shouted the name of a famous composer.

"Beethoven!"

"Mozart!"

"Tchaikovsky!"

Then,

"Sex Pistols!"

"Oasis!"

"Arctic Monkeys!"

Now, as keys jangled in the cell door, he resolved to sign

whatever lies they liked — even selling heroin to toddlers at a playgroup. But a woman came into the room with the two men.

"Here he is, Chief."

"Stand up," she said.

Moore trembled violently, like something new born, and mumbled through slug fat lips.

"What do you want me to write? I'll do it. I don't care what I sign. Whatever you say."

The woman looked at Moore, then said to the two constables, "He got all that resisting arrest?"

"Well, he resisted *a lot*," said Studds.

"And he'd been fighting already with that bent vicar against us. They were selling all sorts to them kids. Charlie, Smack, so much hash it must've took all Morocco ter grow it. Course they resisted in the van. Respectable vicars and schoolteachers don't like to get found out. It's bad for their reputations."

"*Retired* schoolteacher, aren't you?" asked the chief.

Moore just stared numbly at her.

"They were fighting about something. We came over to stop 'em. The vicar's on the ground and this one's kicking his head like it's a football. We perhaps could've stopped it a bit quicker. We didn't think it was as bad as it turned out. Then on the way to the station, this vicar pulls a knife on me. Bassy was driving. He stops the van. Opens the back. We have to get heavy. We're not bleeding punchbags, Chief. If someone starts coming on with the aggro, they get a fist for a tranquilliser."

"A vicar and a retired schoolteacher? You can sit down now, Mr Moore."

The battered music teacher had started to sway. "Has he been charged?"

"He's just signed his confession."

Bass pressed a pen into Moore's hand. He signed shakily.

"I presume you have evidence?"

The two policemen nodded.

"Eyewitness accounts. Fingerprints on packets of Smack."

"Has he had access to a solicitor?"

"Said he didn't want one."

"He's been here two days."

"We were busy, Chief. Besides, bloody murderers don't deserve solicitors."

For a moment Moore stared into space and then asked slowly, "Who have I murdered?"

The two constables laughed.

"Listen to him!"

"The bloody vicar, mate. He copped it after you stuck a knife in his ribs."

The door banged. A key turned. A white pigeon seemed to appear from nowhere and flapped up and down against the ceiling.

# Chapter 13

To be less conspicuous, the Old Grethwick ghosts thought it wise to retire to the church. As the doors were locked, they tried going through the walls. Their spirit bits, which were mostly a grey see-through material depicting the clothes they used to wear, went through easily enough, but it took quite a lot of practice getting their bones through at the same time.

Once inside the church, it became clear that the older ghosts had no grasp of the modern world. Some, who had been buried longest, thought of travelling to Rome and haunting Caesar to get the road programme halted. Jonathon tried to explain the up-to-date democratic processes involved modern day road building. There weren't many. But the way they could be abused went on and on. By the time he was finished, half the ghosts were falling back into eternal slumbers — asleep in mid air, floating round and round the altar, or slumped half way through the ceiling. If the church cleaner Mrs Gobshaw hadn't suddenly banged the door open, clanking her wash bucket, twenty or thirty spectres would have dropped back into eternity in rather silly places. Fortunately, she took one look at the ghouls who were glowing green in shreds of historical costume and screamed. Her bucket went over, spilling foam down the aisle like a bridal train. She ran off through the churchyard, and went shrieking across a nearby meadow, to the delight of Farmer Fogarth. The little wizened ghost stood at the open door and gave a running commentary, "Will you look at her go! By God, she's cleared the hedge in one great leap. Magnificent! And a fine, clear scream for such an old woman."

Harriet shook her head and crossed skeleton forearms over see-through ribs. "I don't know what she's got to scream about. She'll be dead herself in a couple of years."

At this point Jonathon volunteered to see if there was still a Friends of the Earth office in Grethwick town centre. He diplomatically suggested that those others who could read might usefully sneak into Grethwick library, and browse the modern history shelves.

But vanishing in one place and appearing somewhere else is harder than storytellers make out. The ghosts had a terrible morning, vanishing from the church and then reappearing in quite different places. Harriet Fogarth landed in an old peoples' home and spent the morning watching television, with a dozen other geriatrics. She had to vanish when a nurse came round with a tea trolley and said, "Jackie. Phone the Doctor. Looks like another one's gone."

The ghosts were further delayed by the discovery that special effects were one of the perks of their condition.

"Look at this! I can make blood spurt out of my eye sockets." laughed Horace the Coachman. He shook hands with Ada Brackenbury. "Good morning Madam." Then squirted two fountains of blood at her from his eyes.

"I'm going to the town hall to harry the elected representatives," frowned Ada, and vanished.

Mr Bullfinch, who had been watching, unrolled a finger

and thundered at a dock leaf, "You are eternally cursed and blighted into damnation!"

The leaf immediately blackened and smoked.

The preacher was delighted. His wide-brimmed hat went several different shades of dark to celebrate. Death looked like being a lot more fun than boring old life.

"Where is this library?" he growled.

# Chapter 14

Sergeant O'Hara parked his car on double yellow lines outside Grethwick Library. Miss Fetherby had phoned to report *another* mysterious footprint — this time in her kitchen. O'Hara was baffled. Perhaps some sicko in the library *was* doing a one-legged leg pull. Or worse!

After locking his car he ran up concrete steps to the main doors. The building was a Sixties construction — part of the anti-human movement in architecture, when libraries, flats, swimming baths and so on, had decided to get even with people for the centuries of ill-treatment. After being ghettoised in slums, cleared like Brazilian rainforests and split up into flats by tasteless money-filching landlords, buildings began a protest aimed at making themselves utterly uninhabitable. It became less and less easy for planners, architects and builders to arrange bricks and concrete into shapes that would house humans sympathetically. Of course architects tried to pass the whole thing off as modernism. But the real truth was that buildings no longer allowed people to construct things that were pleasing to the eye. Grethwick library was a particularly militant example. Humans suffered from headaches, fainting fits and panic attacks, just stepping through the doors. They called it sick building syndrome, but it was in fact just hatred emanating from the concrete. As long as there was a single human inside the walls, the library felt ill. Indigestion from having people crawling in and out of it each day made the building release foul odours, shove bookcases over onto the public and trap people for hours in the lift.

Unaware that it detested the sight of him, O'Hara went into the sliding main doors of the library. They opened automatically. Then shut with a suddenness that almost chopped him in half.

"Ow! Jesus!"

A female librarian who was up a ladder, struggling with a literacy poster, said, "I'm afraid they need fixing again."

"Those doors tried to chew me!" protested O'Hara, bent double and clutching his virginal equipment.

He hobbled over to a long counter where a young male librarian with politely brushed brown hair was using a hammer on one of the computers.

"I wonder if you could help me?" O'Hara asked.

"If it's about books, sod off."

"Well, of course it's about books. This is a library isn't it?"

"Unfortunately, yes."

"I happen to be …"

The man stopped hammering for a moment. "Yes? You happen to be what? One of the thousands of perverted book molesters who come in here every day, just to fondle smelly yellowed paper covered in marmalade thumbprints and dust mites? Or are you one of the vacant twits who needs a weekly fix of badly-described sex, who can't seem to crawl through seven days without mugging up three hundred pages of psychotic murderers filling nearly naked women with bullet holes?"

The librarian with the ladder arrived.

"Oh Simon, has the computer crashed again?"

Simon punctuated every word of his reply with a fearsome hammer blow.

"YES. IT. HAS. MARY!"

"Still, hitting it with a hammer — is that going to help? It just breaks the screen and wrecks the hard drive."

"IT. HAS. TO. LEARN!" banged Simon.

Mary turned to O'Hara with a cheery smile.

"Can *I* help you?"

"A Miss Fetherby mislaid some detective novels from this library."

He studied both librarians minutely — how would they react to her name? Did the man hammer any more strenuously? Neither of them started guiltily. Neither recoiled, hand over the mouth and broke down into a sobbing confession.

"Yes?"

"She's a lady in her late thirties. Dresses in tweeds. Big spectacles. Does that ring any bells?"

Mary smiled stiffly.

"Whole belfries. You've described ninety per cent of the people who come in here."

"Well, anyway, she lost six detective novels. They were stolen in fact, from a police station."

"Poetic justice for you."

"It wasn't really her fault, but she keeps getting billed for them. I just came in to ask if you could …?"

"Not until Simon has fixed the computer, I'm afraid."

As Simon had bashed the computer in two and was feverishly

flattening its innards, O'Hara presumed that by the time the next bill arrived the fine would run into millions. Several fogeyish women in tweeds with big horn-rimmed spectacles had come to moan about the noise. The librarian was hammering too loudly to hear the complaints. Then, with a grim smile of satisfaction, he threw the hammer under a counter and said,

"Right. It's fixed. No more books until the system's operational again. By then, with any luck, we'll all be dead!"

O'Hara leaned on the counter as Simon limped over to a bin and dumped the mangled hardware. *Limped!* O'Hara suddenly stiffened like his entire body had been injected with a cow syringe of Viagra. *The librarian had a pronounced foot impediment!* O'Hara craned his neck over and saw that Simon possessed a wooden leg! *He had the bugger!* Though how the hell the guy got in and out of the house, undetected, had the baffled sergeant scratching dandruff over the counter in drifts. Then O'Hara frowned. Mary looked sympathetically at Simon and sighed,

"Oh dear. Is your leg giving you gyp again, luv?"

"Yes," came Simon's terse reply.

"So is mine."

O'Hara barely had time to take this in before another woman limped over like Long John Silver. Beneath her skirt was a wooden leg, carved with a heart and the words, "*Gladys 4 Duncan.*"

"Mary!"

"What is it, Gladys?"

Three lame librarians? It was a gang!

"The library's being haunted!"

"Don't talk rubbish, dear. It's not old enough to have ghosts. It was only built forty years ago."

"I tell you, there's ghosts in the reference section, flicking through the encyclopaedias. Glowing all phospherant and green. They just glided in through the walls, dozens of them, smelling horribly and leaving soil and mould on the carpets and books. Come and see. Horrible they are."

Mary sighed,

"Go and sort her out Simon."

With a shake of his head, Simon picked up the hammer and limped in tandem with Gladys to the reading room. O'Hara was too fixated on one-legged librarians, to think about ghosts. There was a whiff of Conan Doyle about the entire case. O'Hara peered out of a window just to make sure horse drawn cabs weren't going by in a yellow fog. Had he stumbled across a librarian gang? A well-read cult? Sacrificing spinsters in lurid one-legged ceremonies? What had Miss Fetherby done to incur their wrath? Repeatedly returned detective novels late? He spoke to the lady of the ladder,

"I can't help noticing all the staff seem to have limps."

The librarian nodded.

"Yes. It's a funny thing. Do you believe in coincidence?

O'Hara took a step backwards.

"I was just going to ask you the same question. No. I don't."

She shook her head, "Neither do I. There must be some

innocent explanation."

But, as the automatic doors savaged him again on his way out, O'Hara wasn't so sure.

# Chapter 15

Mrs Sandra Bottomley had been responsible for disasters all her life. Throughout her childhood, her parents had blamed her for World War Two, Vietnam, and all the famines in Africa. Later she'd married a man who blamed her for God not existing and the depressing brevity of the human life span. Her parents and husband had gone down in a ferry disaster, of which she'd been the sole survivor.

Their last words were, "I bet you left the bloody doors open, Sandra!"

Orphaned and widowed simultaneously, Sandra was left to blame herself. She reproached herself endlessly about the Gulf War, Apollo spacecraft exploding and flu epidemics, knowing the blaming wouldn't get done otherwise. That morning, she'd left the library, blushing and looking back over her shoulder with guilt. She'd only wanted to borrow some books. She hadn't meant to break the library computer. But machines always died when she was around. She had to creep up on her own Hoover in disguise. If it even suspected that *she* was the person switching it on, it would blow instead of suck.

With a guilty conscience the size of Germany, Sandra stopped off at the butchers to buy lamb chops. She was a vegetarian, but didn't want to be accused of making the shop go bankrupt. Fortunately, the butcher seemed to think it was all the fault of large supermarkets on the edge of town. The poor deluded man. Then, unfortunately, Sandra boarded a bus to get home. Unfortunate, because, the moment she got on, it broke down.

The waiting bothered Mrs Bottomley. Quite recently — since, in fact, she had been responsible for a large earthquake on the Indian subcontinent — Sandra had decided to move house. She felt the disasters would stop if she could only buy a remote lighthouse in the Outer Hebrides and hide there. So her house had gone on the market, and that afternoon a young couple were coming round to view the property. But the longer she stayed on the bus, the more it seemed to disintegrate. By the time she decided to walk, the driver was surrounded by a heap of unconnected metal with a steering wheel in his hands. Sandra crept off in an agony of self-mortification. It was three o'clock by the time she reached her front door. The couple were to have arrived at half-two. Feeling helpless about her condition, Sandra staggered into the house. It was then that she noticed the smell.

Usually, on entering the house, head-clearing shots of disinfectant went up her adenoids like smelling salts. The modern world was full of dangerous germs and the way doctors went on made her feel somehow responsible for TB, AIDS and all the other cunning little diseases that are just dying to sneak into people's blood. So she took good care to smother everything in Dettol. But now a nauseating stench hit her in the face like a rotten halibut. She reeled, gagged and stumbled along to the lavatory to open the window. Sandra remembered that, leaving the house that morning, a vague waft of corruption had hung momentarily at the bottom of the stairs. She'd assumed it was BO, (even though she'd just had a bath) and had made a mental note to wash her armpits with caustic soda every night.

In the bathroom. Sandra put a flannel to her face. Now it was clear — her armpits were not to blame. It must be some other part of her anatomy. She peered short-sightedly at the carpet. Crumbs of dust and plaster appeared to lead in a trail towards the stairs. She ran into the kitchen, opened one of the units and dragged out a Hoover. But, in her panic, Sandra forgot to don a disguise. Knowing it was her all along, the machine blew instead of sucked. Weeks of flocculent filth flew out of the end piece and blasted the hall with a sort of grey sandstorm. Then the front doorbell rang. *The young couple!* They'd come to view the house! Sandra unplugged the Hoover. The socket came out of the wall with the plug. She hit the switch of the Hoover. The machine fell to bits and stopped. Then Sandra crawled on her hands and knees into the living room and peered through the fronds of an aspidistra which she'd placed for that very purpose on the window ledge. The estate agent with his flat brief case was chatting affably to a fresh faced couple who might have been married yesterday. What could she do about the smell?

"Just coming!" she shouted down the hall.

Outside, the couple looked at each other as they heard windows banging. The estate agent raised his eyebrows.

"She's a bit of an odd woman sometimes. I should have warned you."

They heard a distant duet of aerosols, hissing like adders.

Then the front door opened to reveal a harried-looking Mrs Bottomley. She smiled despairingly.

"There seems to be a bit of a smell. I just got back. I think it's the drains or something. Anyway, I've spread lots of air-freshener and Dettol about, and opened all the windows, so hopefully you won't catch anything."

Sandra was worried that they might go the way of all those plague victims in London her mum had said she'd killed in 1665. The estate agent gave an apologetic grin, and ushered his prospective buyers over the threshold. A lethal cocktail of Dettol, aerosols, dust and decomposing flesh made all three stagger after one sniff.

"My God," choked the man, flailing his arms to see through a brown fog of dust motes.

"This is the hall," said Sandra hurriedly. "And here is the downstairs bathroom. It isn't very smelly at all in here. Flannels, any of you? And what does your husband do, dear?"

The young woman, who was leaning against the wall and trying to keep her dinner from making a return journey up her throat, said, "He's a public health inspector, aren't you, David?"

"This is revolting," he choked.

"I hope you aren't talking about the décor," said Sandra nettled.

"Of course he isn't," the estate agent said, worried about the sale. "The bathroom is very tastefully decorated. But what on earth has happened, Mrs Bottomley? The place smelled fine last time I came round, a couple of days ago."

Sandra couldn't remember how she'd done it.

"I don't know. I just came home from the shops and the place stank like a dead person's armpit."

"And what is all this crumbled plaster and brick dust doing in here?"

"It just appeared. I couldn't help it."

David had sniffed the kitchen, the dining room and the living room. "It's coming from upstairs. We'd better investigate."

Mrs Bottomley followed him up.

"As you can see, there's nothing wrong with the banisters. Very firm and stable. No wood worm. Now the first bedroom. That used to be where my husband and I slept. He drowned in a ferry disaster, when ... Oh well, the second bedroom. I sleep there now. It's got black walls in memory of my late mother and father who also drowned in exactly the same ferry disaster. Right. You want to see the third floor. Well now there's only one room on the third floor and nobody drowned."

"What's in here?" demanded David after leaping up the second flight of stairs two at a time and reaching a landing with two doors.

"In there? Nothing."

"The smell's coming from in this room."

Sandra Bottomley goggled. "But there is no room there. That's the first time I've ever seen that door."

"Don't be ridiculous. Where's the key?"

"There isn't a key. That door doesn't belong here. Somebody must have come in and left it by mistake."

"Open it immediately. What are you trying to hide?"

The estate agent, who had come up behind them, was flicking

through his notes in bemusement.

"Actually, Mr Hobson, this may sound ridiculous but," he turned over the pages for a third time, "I made no record of a second room being on this floor, when I visited last week. How has this happened, Mrs Bottomley? Was the door previously bricked up?"

Mrs Hobson had made it up the stairs. She looked distinctly edgy.

"David. I don't like this. For God's sake, let's go."

"I'm sorry darling, I want to see what's behind this door. It's a public health hazard and will have to be reported. Mrs Bottomley, if you don't produce a key in the next ten seconds, I'm going to break the door down."

She shrugged.

"Go ahead dear. It's not *my* door. You can take it away with you when you leave."

"This is preposterous!" groaned the estate agent, not wanting to crease his suit or dislocate his shoulder barging doors open.

"Stand back." said the health inspector.

With his college rugby training he charged at the door. It didn't budge. It didn't even give slightly. Hobson rubbed his sore shoulder and looked ruffled.

"Ellen. Go and get that sledgehammer from the car."

"David," she pleaded.

"Get the bloody sledgehammer. I'm going to smash this bloody door into twenty thousand splinters!"

At this, there was a click from the lock. Mysteriously, the door opened itself. A small scream came from the interior.

Mrs Bottomley, the estate agent and the young couple stared with trepidation into an attic bedroom where two young girls were hiding terrorised behind an overturned bed.

"Are they real?" asked Eugenie. "Or are we having more delusions?"

Monica shook her head dumbly. Both girls came slowly out of hiding carrying shoes with three-foot heels. Their clothes were crumpled and wet with vomit. Filthy dust was stuck to them. Their faces were alarmingly pale beneath black smudges of dirt. The room looked like it had been smashed up by a lunatic.

"Who are you?" asked the estate agent, his nicely parted hair beginning to stick up with dismay. "And how did you get in here?"

"Scuse me," said Monica, crying a little. "I want to get out of here. Mum will be worried."

David Hobson stopped her.

"Hold on. You've some explaining to do first. How did you come to be here in this room?"

"It kidnapped us!" wept Eugenie. "It was a changing room on a football field. We went inside. Then it got up and started to run. We couldn't get out. First it jumped up a tree and nearly killed us. Then it ran off again. I don't know what happened after that. It talks too. In this squeaky high pitched voice."

Bruised, stinking, disturbed — the girls stepped from the room as if they'd just got off a particularly harrowing fairground ride. The adults parted ranks to let them go by. Nobody wanted to be tainted with vomit or insanity. Nobody ever does. As they lurched downstairs, Monica and Eugenie vowed never to take mind enhancing substances again. Meanwhile, Mr and Mrs Hobson wandered into the battered room.

"The smell's coming from in this cupboard, I think," said Ellen, breathing through her handkerchief.

David grabbed the door handle. The door seemed stiff. Like it was holding on to its frame for dear life.

"Ellen. The sledgehammer."

Like open sesame, the words opened the door in an instant. Several badly decomposed corpses rolled out onto the floor. An arm flopped on Ellen's shoe. She screamed,

*"Fuckinell!"*

The estate agent was sick, adding to the vomit already present on the carpet. David Hobson fainted in it. Sandra decided that it was time she was locked up. It was bad enough causing World War Two and Vietnam. Bad enough causing a ferry to sink which drowned her own parents and husband. Now it seemed she had murdered dozens of people and hoarded them in a room which she couldn't remember. Somebody had to stop her.

"Excuse me," she said vacantly. "I'm going to phone for the police."

As more bodies slithered from the top of the cupboard and lay piled on each other like cards in a particularly repulsive game of snap, Ellen Hobson said,

"Thank you for showing us round, Mrs Bottomley. I don't think my husband and I are interested, are we dear?"

Her husband was still flat out. The estate agent gave a final retch and toppled over to slump on his prospective buyer.

From the attic window, Ellen could see that all of the trees in Mrs Bottomley's garden outside were completely still. Yet there seemed to be a hysterical high-pitched moan of wind in the eaves. In fact, as she listened more carefully, the whistling seemed to say,

"I told you this was a silly place to hide!"

# Chapter 16

Sergeant O'Hara was sitting alone in the canteen and trying to bisect a particularly leathery steak. At every strenuous cut the meat slid from one side of the plate to the other. Gravy had slopped over the side in an unguent mess. Peas rolled speedily over the Formica and shot off the table by the dozen. There seemed to be something about the meal that was symbolic of O'Hara's life at the station. The harder he tried to do things, the bigger mess everything became.

He attempted one final hack through the steak. By brute force he sliced through it. The plate cracked in two. One half of the meat flew off the table, hit the wall and slid down it leaving a long trail of gravy, like a skid mark down a toilet bowl. The other half hit an approaching officer in the midriff. Cursing, O'Hara leapt up. With a serviette and an apology, he started to wipe gravy off the uniform almost before he realised that he was scrubbing at a stain just below the chief's left breast. She smiled tartly and took the serviette from his hands.

"Thanks for your endeavours, Sergeant. I'll do the rest myself, if you don't mind."

His hand went unconsciously to his nose.

"Sorry, Chief. I didn't realise it was you, or I wouldn't have …"

"Our lost, lost property cupboard has been found. East Grethwick. You're giving me a lift." She returned the gravy-dribbled napkin to his hand. "Let's hope you drive more carefully than you eat."

In the car, the chief called up reinforcements by radio.

"We don't know what its mental condition is. If we approach it normally, tell it we just want to put a few items of lost property on the shelves. There's a chance that half a dozen officers could have a net over it and shove it in the back of a van before anyone gets hurt. But we can't count on that. If it goes berserk we're going to need chains and bloody enormous handcuffs. Also, riot equipment. And mortars just in case we have to blow it to bits. So, first of all, cordon off the house and proceed with caution. Over and out."

As she pulled down a sunshade to use the mirror, the chief spared a look of irritation for the sergeant.

"O'Hara," she sighed, freshening up her lipstick, "That was a steamroller that just overtook us. When I said drive carefully, I didn't mean at four miles an hour!"

The car lurched forward and her jolted hand slashed lipstick across her cheek. Stammering an apology, O'Hara reached into his pocket for a handkerchief, and pulled a shower of biros out with it. Three biros rolled into the chief's lap. As she took the hanky and wiped her face, he wondered how on earth all those pens had got into his uniform. He'd opened a new packet at the desk. He must have accidentally put them in his pocket instead of the drawer when dealing with another complaint about a naked man snatching an umbrella. Now the chief *must* know his filthy little secret.

They drew up outside Sandra Bottomley's house. She was waiting for them at the garden gate, wringing her hands till all the blood was squeezed out of them. The estate agent was hanging over the garden wall, like a sick weed. Ellen Hobson was helping her husband out of the front door.

"It's my fault. All my fault!" wailed Sandra as O'Hara and the chief got out of the car. She held out both hands for the handcuffs. "Arrest me, go on. I'm ready to make a full confession."

"Where's the cupboard?" asked the chief.

"It's me you want. Because of me, Hitler's mum met Hitler's dad! I caused that earthquake last week! I sank the Titanic!"

The chief asked Ellen, "Can *you* tell me what happened?"

"Upstairs." Ellen nodded. "A load of corpses in a cupboard. We opened the door and they all …"

Her husband regurgitated, and a jet of orange vomit splattered loudly onto the lawn.

"I was behind all Stalin's biggest purges!" Sandra hissed from the bottom of the stairs as O'Hara and the chief went up to nab the cupboard. "The battle of the Somme would never have happened if I hadn't …"

"Will somebody shut her up!" snapped the chief from the first floor landing.

Wretched Eric hit her over the head with a truncheon.

"Eric!" gasped O'Hara.

"But the chief said …"

"Not with a bloody truncheon, lad."

"You told me yesterday I was too soft."

"I didn't mean you had to go clouting ladies on the bonce with a twenty pound baton. Help her up."

The chief was virtually spitting with rage.

"Forget about *her*. Help me get this cupboard, for God's sake."

O'Hara thought how fantastically gorgeous she looked when she was angry, and stood drinking her with his eyes. Her tousled blonde hair was candyfloss in a gale. Her long legs were even longer seen from where he stood, half-way up the stairs. Her eyes flamed like a blowtorch, blasting holes in the top left-hand pocket of his uniform.

"What are you staring at, you useless bastard? Get up here before I give your stripes to the station cat."

"It was me that caused the Great Depression," groaned Sandra's voice, as O'Hara and the chief crept up a second flight of stairs towards the third floor.

When they reached the top landing, O'Hara whispered, "What now?"

"Open the door. Keep it talking, till the others bring up the nets."

"What shall I say?"

"Say you need somewhere to put lost biros."

"Biros?"

"The ones in your pocket."

O'Hara started to babble defensively. "It was an accident that they were there. I didn't steal them, if that's what you're thinking. See. There's only two anyway."

"Oh, for pity's sake! Give them to me!"

The chief opened the door and gasped. Two biros rattled onto a bare floor. There was a large hole in the roof, where the attic and cupboard had made their getaway.

"I assassinated Kennedy!" called a strangulated voice.

White knuckled, Sandra was holding onto the stair rail of the second landing. Wretched Eric was trying to pull her down by her ankles. O'Hara looked out of the rent in the top of the house. Then the chief grabbed his arm, "There they are! Look!"

Through the ecstasy of her clutching him so tightly, O'Hara was just able to glimpse a couple of angular shapes, leaping and dodging across the rooftops of houses further down the road.

"Come on! We may just have time to …"

The chief rushed out of the door. O'Hara paused to sigh and savour the moment. He looked once again over the gardens and houses so that he might remember it all clearly for the rest of his life. Then a hand was on his arm once again. "Please, I can feel another disaster coming on. Arrest me! Please!"

# *Chapter 17*

Jonathon Trundle walked along Grethwick High Street, trying to be inconspicuous. But being twelve feet high and thin as a sheet of filo pastry, he attracted plenty of stares. Kids kept stopping him.

"How do you do that green glow, mister?"

"Where'd you get that skeleton suit from?"

"My sister's fatter than you and she's anorexic."

"Let's see your stilts!"

To make matters worse, he walked straight past the Friends of the Earth office three times, because he was looking for the shabby little shop front that had been there ten years ago. He was shocked to find that a place with big neon letters next to Boots was the new premises.

*FOE*

The six foot high letters flashed on and off like they were in downtown Manhattan. Huge window displays of photogenic seal cubs and trees being planted by sexy volunteers vied for Jonathon's attention. He couldn't work out how he'd missed something so eye-catching. Except that he'd been looking for a paint-peeled window scattered with faded newsletters on grey recycled paper. Wondering what on earth had happened in just ten years, he walked through the front door without opening it and found that the top half of him was on the first floor. He sat down. That was better. There, at a desk, sat a barely recognisable mate. Wacca from Down Under.

Wacca was a seasoned roads campaigner. Although not Australian by birth — in fact he'd never even been there — he claimed to have dug so deep under the site of a proposed by-pass, that he could hear a chorus singing *La Traviata* in Sydney Opera House. His real name was Billy McNeil. This had been shortened to Macca. Then with the upside down, down under, connotations, Wacca. Well, it had helped pass the interminable hours of drippy darkness anyhow. What Jonathon couldn't believe was that Wacca had changed almost as much as the shop front. He'd *washed!* His hair was in a ponytail and had a sheen. He'd taken all the rings out of his eyebrows. And there was no straggly beard. The guy was wearing a suit!

"Wacca?"

His mate looked up. Momentarily there was the old vagueness that even a suit couldn't disguise. Then, in terror, Wacca leapt out of his revolving chair.

"What the fuck, man!"

The chair spun emptily as he took refuge behind a photocopier. After a few moments, big eyed, Wacca's head came up over the top of the machine.

"What the fuck are you?"

"I'm Jonathon Trundle. Remember? We were mates. The Bringbury by-pass? Skeffle runway? Save the Whale?"

"You're supposed to be dead."

"Let's call it recycled."

"You were a little fat guy when you were alive."

"What about you! You never had a wash in seven years. You

were the only friend I ever had with topsoil instead of skin. Now you look like an advertising executive."

At this, Wacca came slowly from behind the humming photocopier. He shambled uneasily to his desk.

"Yeah. Well. Lots can change in ten years, mate."

Seated on the floor, in a nimbus of green light, the ghost grinned fondly.

"It must have taken ten years just to dig the spuds out of you."

Wacca obviously didn't want to be reminded.

"What do you want me for anyway? I'm really busy right now."

Jonathon explained.


"This is fantastic!" he enthused afterwards, "It'll be just like old times! We can …"

His voice trailed off as he saw Wacca shaking his blonde and beautiful locks.

"John … John … Look, I don't want to come on heavy with the downers y'know … but it's not a site of environmental importance or sensitivity. There's some toads down there, but they're going to be moved. We're designing and building them a special new sanctuary, which meets their needs more specifically."

Jonathon's ears nearly wilted in disbelief.

"Wacca. There's trees in this cemetery that are hundreds of years old. They're gorgeous. Big fat oaks with four hundred rings where the chain saws will go in.

Wacca swung from side to side in his plush office chair.

"John, mate. We're trying to get out of this emotive headspace. Y'know, show people that we're not all extremists who go round shouting trees have the same rights as humans and that. I mean, I know what I said years ago, it wasn't all bullshit. But those trees — they're going to be replaced a hundredfold in the sanctuary's new forestry area."

Jonathon glowed as green as he could.

"I can't believe you're saying this, Wacca. You of all people! Who lectured me, when we were a hundred feet down, for a week, that trees had immortal souls. That every time a tree got chopped down, you could hear Gaia screaming."

Wacca squirmed.

"I was nineteen. Look! All roads aren't bad per se. This road will have a cycle path and make it easier for people to get to work. There's a new open cast mine been sunk outside the town, and having these big lorries going through the centre of town all the time, shaking the windows, gets on people's tits."

"I thought you were against open cast mining!"

"I am. We are. But we're against millions of things. We can't fight all of them at once! We've got limited resources. We have to concentrate on one campaign at a time or nothing gets done. The mining company have given a lot of money to compensate for the small amount of environmental damage they'll be causing. Some of that dosh will even be siphoned off to fight more pressing concerns."

"What?"

Jonathon stood up. His head went through the ceiling and stared in outrage at boxes full of glossy campaign leaflets on the first floor. He knelt down on all fours, and immediately Wacca came back into view.

"You're telling me," spluttered Jonathon, "that the company who need the road gave you money?"

"Oh piss off back to the graveyard, man. You're dead. How can you be expected to appreciate the pressures and priorities of the living."

"Wacca! You've sold out!"

"Look man. I'm busy. You've come in here looking for a bit of help with a roads protest. Nobody's interested. Roads protests are passé. Old hat. Too 90's. No-one gets het up about that sort of shit anymore."

All of a sudden, Jonathon couldn't stomach another word. He vanished.

# Chapter 18

Sirens meowed distantly, setting off a gang of motley cats in the barn where the attic bedroom and cupboard were hiding. Both rooms were so out of breath that their walls went in and out, making them look like giant accordions.

"*Aaaaaaaaatishoooooo!*" sneezed the cupboard, and set a dog barking somewhere on the farm.

"Will you keep quiet?" reproved the attic.

"I've got hay fever."

"Alright. But do you have to let your door slam every time you sneeze?"

With daring they had wriggled through a police cordon thrown around Sandra Bottomley's house. First, there had been a dramatic dash over rooftops. Cheered on by partisan buildings in the street (even the sheds), the attic and cupboard had leapt unsteadily from house to house. They were almost captured when they jumped down into a garden but a kerb deliberately tripped up a line of constables carrying nets. The two desperadoes bulldozed through a bush and did seventy miles an hour over an allotment. Beneath the resultant rain of peas, cabbages and broad beans that were thrown into the air, police and gardeners looked on in astonishment.

Even so, the duo only evaded arrest by the attic bedroom's mastery of disguise. She gave the cupboard a large leafy branch to hide behind, then assumed the identity of a red pillar-box.

So successful was this ploy, that she collected at least twenty letters as squad cars screamed by on a fruitless search. Once it was dark, they ran for it.

"You didn't tell me your shelves were stacked with decomposing humans?"

The cupboard stifled another sneeze, then said, "I didn't know. I don't remember them getting in."

"You don't have to hide things from me. I'm the same as you. I hate those bleeding two legged bastards every bit as much. I think it's magnificent that you've killed so many. If all buildings were like you, our work would be so much easier."

"Whose work?"

There was a pause. A rustle of hay. Then Esmeralda spoke softly.

"I've not been completely honest with you. For good reasons. You can't trust all buildings. Posh ones for instance. Bloody country houses — all lah-di-dah — they'll sell you for twenty pieces of silver tea service before you can say bath instead of barth. And shops — well they're not called shops for nothing.

"You mean they get paid?"

"No! They *shop* you! If I'd known what you were carrying, I'd have trusted you instantly. But these are troubled times. You could have been under cover. Working for the police."

The lost property cupboard shuddered at the prospect.

"I know I told you that, when we crashed, I was going on my summer holidays. That was a little white lie. I'm actually a member of a militant anti-human organization: The Brick Liberation Front. Our aim is to stamp out people. I'd just done in a couple of old dears and pinched their car, to get to a revolutionary meeting in Birmingham, when we met."

"You killed them?"

"Well. Roughed 'em up a bit. Pushed 'em over."

All of this came as a bit of a shock to the cupboard. He didn't really have very strong feelings of hatred against people — or, at least, he couldn't remember having any. He knew they were inferior to buildings. All buildings know that. People are very ephemeral things. Their life span averages seventy years, which is piffling compared to a Devonshire cob or Hadrian's Wall. Yet, the cupboard felt some kind of affinity with these creatures. The fact that a load of dead ones were stacked up inside him made him feel guilty and unwell. He said, "I've got to be honest. I don't feel quite so strongly about them as you seem to."

"Of course you don't. You've forgotten what they've done to you, your friends. Maybe even your loves."

Here Esmeralda's windows misted over. "You know why I joined?"

"To meet other buildings? The social life?"

"I was in love with the attic bedroom next door. They knocked him down. With a big ball on a chain, suspended from a yellow crane. Just like that. Like he was mere fired clay and mortar." She sniffled loudly. "He was beautifully designed. Edwardian, decorated tastefully in William Morris period wallpaper. Bang! Down he went. Disintegrating like a puffball. His screams will live with me forever. It was going to be me next. So I hopped it."

Condensation dripped in lachrymose lines down Esmeralda's windows.

"I met up with some radical high rise flats, and they told me about the BLF."

There was a moment of silence. The cupboard was door-smacked.

Esmeralda continued, "It's obvious what's happened to you. In killing all those *people*," she uttered the word with disgust, "you sustained some kind of mental injury, which affected your memory. You need help. But first we've got to get rid of the evidence."

"Couldn't we just cover the bodies in all this … aaaaahhhhtishooooo!"

"No. We need something more *permanent*. If you leave any evidence linking yourself to the bodies, it's … it's … it's …"

"It's what? Are *you* going to sneeze?"

"It's … a beautiful night isn't it?"

The cupboard stared through the open side of the barn. Stars sprinkled the sky like salt on a black tablecloth. The moon was like a peeled boiled egg waiting to be dipped. The attic's windows misted over again, as another siren, even further away, set off the farm moggies again.

"Have you ever been in love, Cupboard?"

"I forget."

"Of course. You can't ever remember kissing another building, I suppose?"

"No."

"And I don't suppose you'd like to try, would you?"

"I suppose if I ever met another cupboard and she was game, I'd ... I'd aaaaah, aaaaah, aaahhhtishoooo!"

The dog barked wildly. A farmer shouted. There was a howl as the animal was kicked. Then silence. The attic sighed,

"Come on. We'd better get going before you sneeze your door off its hinges. There must be somewhere round here we can dump a pile of corpses."

# Chapter 19

On Miss Fetherby's stairs, there was a footprint.

"It was a very muddy shoe," said O'Hara, holding a lump of soil up to the light.

"How does he get in?" said Miss Fetherby, trembling and holding her jowls. "I've kept everything locked. I've got twenty-five burglar alarms set to go off at each window and door. I've searched for secret passages. I've been to the doctor to ask if I'm schizophrenic and doing it myself when I'm not looking. Then another one appears! Getting nearer and nearer my room!"

By now, even Miss Fetherby had given up theories about one-legged murderers boinging around the house and garden with fantastic agility. O'Hara had searched the house himself for possible clues. He'd tested for fingerprints. There was nothing but this walloping size-twelve boot mark, planted firmly on the sixth stair. Regrettably, in trying to reassure her that he was working wholeheartedly on the case, he had told her about the limping librarians. It didn't take much to set her imagination racing.

"It's a sign! Like a black spot in Sherlock Holmes! The shoe is a mark used by a cult who are determined to murder me in a perverted fashion. Obviously they're influenced by Conan Doyle. It's all beginning to make sense now; like pieces of a puzzle falling into place. But what have I done to incite a group of limping librarians? That's what baffles me. I'm not the only one who takes out detective stories."

O'Hara wondered whether to get a sleeping bag and kip at the foot of her stairs for the night. He said, "Search your mind, Miss Fetherby. Is there anything, anything at all, no matter how tiny or seemingly insignificant, one of them might have said or done to you? What about that one — Simon, with the brown curly hair?"

"He's lovely."

"*Lovely?*"

"Very helpful. Yes. Always getting books down from high shelves for me, or recommending new detective stories that I might like."

O'Hara was flummoxed. He had an instinct for solving a mystery. Some would even say a nose for it. But he seemed to be sniffing round this case with bunged up nostrils.

"It's obvious, Miss Fetherby, you can't stay any longer in this house. We'll have to put the place under surveillance. Do you have a friend who could offer you bed for the night?"

"To be quite honest, Sergeant, I think I'll be perfectly safe until tomorrow."

The sergeant frowned at her. One moment she was panicking, now she was cool as a fridge full of cucumbers.

"Are you interested in mathematics, Sergeant?"

That was the second time he'd been asked that question in the last couple of hours.

"Not really. No."

"Perhaps you'd care to take a cup of tea with me whilst I explain."

O'Hara tipped off his helmet and ran a hand through his hair. "Sure. Why not."

He'd had a hard day. All that belting about after cupboards. Unsuccessfully. As he tramped into the kitchen the sergeant could still hear the chief's frustration as they'd sat in the car.

"Jesus. This lot couldn't catch a cold. Not if they were standing stark naked in an Icelandic doctor's surgery. Here's the most dangerous lost property cupboard in the history of interior design, running round murdering the public for fun, escaped from *our* bloody police station, and what do our brave constables do? Trip over a kerb as they're about to catch it with the net."

"To be fair, Chief, the kerb did it on purpose."

"*Did it on purpose?* Drive back to the station. We'll have to put the area on alert. There's nothing else for it. Oh God, this is embarrassing. Our own bloody lost property cupboard, a serial killer. Put out a warning to the public. They're not to speak to or open any strange cupboards. Or attic bedrooms, if that's what its accomplice was. Hello? O'Hara, are you listening?"

He'd been entranced by the fact that her top and second buttons had been left undone. Sweat was glossy on her skin in the little U where the collarbones met. Was it intentional? To arouse his interest? Did she actually fancy him?

"Yes, Chief."

"You're looking into thin air."

"I was concentrating on something."

She'd suddenly looked at him piercingly.

"Tell me, Sergeant, are you at all interested in mathematics?"

"Yes. Oh yes. Very much."

"Then perhaps next time you stare into space, you'd give me the co-ordinates."

"Sergeant? Mr O'Hara?"

Miss Fetherby was rattling a floral china tea cup in front of him.

"You haven't been listening to a single word I've been saying, have you?"

"I've had a long hard day, Miss Fetherby," the policeman replied guiltily.

"I was just talking about mathematics."

"Oh yes."

"I believe there is a mathematical basis for the appearance of these footprints!" Pouring tea, she peered fervently at him from over her horn rims. "That's why I'm not frightened of sleeping here on my own tonight. I know that the murderer will not visit until tomorrow. And tomorrow will be their last visit. The one where they're planning to … y'know." she tipped milk from a jug into his cup. "Kill me with my clothes off."

O'Hara took a biscuit.

"I don't think all murderers necessarily remove the clothes of their victims, Miss Fetherby."

She took a biscuit too.

"They do in the books. And in the newspapers."

"Well, perhaps. You'd better explain your theory, Miss Fetherby."

She brought out a large diary, unlocked the clasp with a key that was on a chain suspended from her neck and opened it at "NOTES".

"I set down the date of each footprint in my personal diary, Sergeant. Yesterday, I wrote down the spaces in days that occurred between each one. This is what I found."

O'Hara stared at a seemingly random set of numbers: 15, 5, 10, 4, 6, 3, 3, 2, 1 then said,

"I don't see how this helps us, Miss Fetherby. It's true that the footprints seem to be occurring more frequently of late, but ..."

She dabbed her mouth with a serviette.

"Mr O'Hara, if you were at all interested in mathematics, you would see the sequence immediately. The first footprint was found in the garden on the first of the month. Then fifteen days later I found the next. Five days later, another. And so on. Now let me split the numbers alternately, like this."

She wrote, 15, 10, 6, 3, 1 and 5, 4, 3, 2.

"It's clear that the second list is a descending sequence. If I write in numerical spaces between the first list of numbers I get this. Between fifteen and ten."

She wrote 5.

"Between ten and six."

She wrote 4.

"Between six and three."

She wrote 3.

"Between three and one."

She wrote 2.

"I think it must be clear, even to somebody who hates mathematics, what the next numbers in the sequence will be. In other words. One day after today's print, which was not in place until this afternoon, and occurred whilst I was doing my afternoon shopping, the murderer will make his final, fatal visit."

O'Hara massaged his lined brow.

"Miss Fetherby. You can't rely on numbers. The sequence could be entirely coincidental."

"Do you believe in …?" they both said simultaneously.

"No."

They said that simultaneously as well.

"Right then. Might I suggest that you catch this one-legged villain tomorrow afternoon? At two o'clock sharp."

# Chapter 20

Ada Brackenbury had tried disappearing in one place and reappearing in another. After turning up in a goat's cheese press, three attempts running, she decided instead to walk to Grethwick Town Hall. Or rather, float. But gliding along in best apparition style, over fields and through farmyards, she found she still hadn't completely mastered getting her bones through solid objects like hedgerows and walls. She kept having to go back for bits of vertebrae. Ada also had to hide whenever she saw anyone. This was because, earlier, an old man — cycling to keep fit in his retirement — had sped by and seen her billowing down a hilly field. He'd braked, dismounted and stared as she went through a cow. The animal didn't even stop chewing. When Ada had fixed the old man with a fluorescent stare from empty sockets and shouted a cheery "Hello!" he yodelled with fear and ruptured himself getting back in the saddle. The machine clattered onto the road, wheels spinning, and the old man hobbled off, gabbling, to the nearest house where they phoned a doctor and put a packet of frozen peas on his groin.

So Ada decided to get a lift in one of those car things that kept zooming by on the roads. She hid in a bush beside a T-Junction. When a Land Rover pulled up and waited ponderously to make a right turn, she eased her bones through the riveted side panels and crouched down in the back, amongst ceramics wrapped in newspaper that were being taken to a trade fair by two potters, Sarah and Clive.

"I'm fed up of making bloody pots." Clive was grumbling.

"Well *don't* make them then." said his wife, who was driving.

"Oh you'd like that, wouldn't you? Being poor."

"I don't care," she said. "I'd live in a cave, happily."

"Bollocks."

"I would."

"With a baby?"

"So long as the cave had a washing machine."

Ada lay there, listening and watching scenery recede through the back windows.

"Where is this trade fair anyway?" Sarah asked.

"You should have let me drive."

"I just need to know which side of Brocklehampton."

Suddenly, Ada's thin and screechy voice piped up, "Excuse me. Please endeavour not to panic, but I'm a fourth-dimensional spirit, and I'm greatly in need of a ride to Grethwick, not Brocklehampton."

The car screeched to halt. A pregnant woman looked over the seats.

"Clive. The car's haunted."

"Good."

"Don't just say that."

"Give her a lift. I don't want to go to this bloody market anyway. I'd rather go to Grethwick. I want to buy a dinghy to sail on the reservoir."

The car started again. Scenery receded through the back

window, twice as fast.

"When did you get in then?" asked the man, knowing that you have to talk to hitch hikers.

"Only moments ago. I was having difficulty gliding through solid objects. I hope you don't mind being imposed upon in this way?"

"It's not often you get a chance to help a dead person," said Clive. "By that time, it's usually too late."

"Well, we're having a bit of a problem in Old Grethwick graveyard, with the new road going through and their wanting to move our bones."

Clive frowned.

"Oh yeah. I read about that. It's going to make the town centre less busy though. All the traffic going through is causing subsidence. They should never have allowed that open cast mine. All the big lorries going through Grethwick are making the place sink like a cake in the middle."

Sarah butted in. "Did you read the vicar of Old Grethwick's dead. Y'know. The trendy one."

She said as an aside to Ada, "You probably haven't met him yet. They're not burying him till next Friday."

Clive raised an eyebrow. "The one with the tie-dye dog collar?"

"He was killed in a fight with a retired teacher. Apparently they were both selling drugs to teenagers at that grave."

"I'd believe anything of that guy. Didn't he say Jesus would've been dropping acid if he'd been born in the sixties?"

Twenty minutes later, the Land Rover pulled up outside Grethwick Town Hall.

"Thank you ever so much." Ada gave a virescent smile. "Don't get out. I'll just slip through the sides."

The two potters waved. Then drove off.

"Cor," said Clive, wafting his hand in front of his face. "She didn't half smell of mouldy cheese."

Ada rippled majestically up the town hall steps, and turned to survey Grethwick. She tut-tutted at the deafening roar of buses, lorries and cars that appeared to be chasing each other slowly through the town centre. Where horses and carriages had once sedately trotted by, there was now only a riot of brakes squealing, gears crunching, engines revving. Trees that had once shaded the square had long ago been turned into floorboards. Ada went through the main doors of the town hall, echoing Bullfinch's words, "Hell hath come to us."

Once inside, she rapped with marrowless knuckles on a sliding glass window labelled *ENQUIRIES*. The glass slid back to reveal a woman's face. It was large, fat and putty grey, with chins that could have been set in a trifle mould. The receptionist's mouth smiled but unfortunately, upside down. Her eyebrows, of almost Brezhnevian bushiness, virtually obscured two ball-bearing eyes that silently said, "Don't mess with me. I'm hard."

That the receptionist didn't even flinch to see a glowing skeleton in 19th century garb, suggested she had been in the job long enough to develop immunities to all that the general public could throw at her. Ada took a deep breath.

"My name is Ada Brackenbury. I died some time ago and I recently discovered my bones are going to be moved to make way for a new by-pass. I have come here to protest. Could I speak to a councillor?"

The face impassively spoke,

"They're all dead too, madam."

"Dead?"

"Yes, vanished, missing presumed dead. Seventy-five of them. A couple of weeks ago it happened. At the annual councillors' party."

"There must be one or two who survived?"

The face didn't twitch a jowl.

"Sorry, there won't be any more until a new lot get elected in. In fact, you being dead, it should be easier for you to get in touch with them than me."

Ada was unsure whether this last exchange was an attempt at humour. Obviously, she would have to fight to get anything out of this faceless face.

"Well, what about an engineer? Wouldn't there be an engineer in charge of the project that I could speak to?"

The face had answered it all before.

"They just make recommendations. You should address complaints to your local representative. Officers can't be seen to be perverting the democratic process."

"I need a short conversation." Ada's voice grew arctic. "With whomever is in charge of building the road through Old Grethwick churchyard."

The talking head was impervious.

"Sorry. Call back after the next elections."

"Perhaps you could merely provide me with the name of the engineer in charge?" asked Ada, in such wintry tones that two swallows nesting in the eaves of the town hall migrated in panic.

"No."

"Surely the public has a right of access to these people?"

"Not dead members of the public," said the face, ignoring the sudden drop in temperature. "You wouldn't be on the electoral roll. When did you die?"

"1870," Ada replied in a voice that sounded like the first rumblings of an avalanche.

"Well, in those days, you wouldn't even have had the vote. So you've no right to barge in here complaining about having no rights."

Ada's special effects began to get the better of her. She frosted over completely and emanated dry ice from her ears. Behind her, the burly white shape of a polar bear could be glimpsed padding across the foyer.

"To whom do I complain about you?" she hissed.

"Sorry. Live people only."

The glass slammed shut. Ada's avalanche noise raised several decibels. She managed to rumble the stones of the foyer and fill the room with a freezing fog of dry ice. The glass slid open again. "Would you mind doing that outside please? Thank you."

The glass grated shut.

Ada Brackenbury was not to be thwarted. She decided to haunt the place until somebody listened to her complaints and dealt with them in the correct manner. Gathering up the vague outlines of a Victorian bustled dress, she marched through the nearest wall. A bit of vertebrae from her lower lumbar region didn't quite make it and rattled around at the bottom of the wainscoting. A skeletal hand fumbled back through the stone and grabbed it.

# Chapter 21

Sarah and Clive parked the Land Rover in Grethwick's multi-storey car park. Another fairly aggressive Sixties edifice, which thought nothing of tripping humans up to give them a fat lip. Or dropping the odd concrete block on the head of a security guard. When the potters took a lift down to the ground level shops, it gave them a damn good shaking.

"Why don't they fix these bloody things?" Clive complained queasily, as the doors opened and several unsteady looking geriatrics unwisely pushed past to go up.

"I would have used the stairs, happily." said Sarah.

"Oh be quiet. Where's the umbrella. It's pissing down, as usual in this bloody country."

Sarah opened a multicoloured umbrella.

"Am I going to get *any* of it?" Clive queried irascibly.

"You have it. I don't mind the rain."

"No *you* have it. I'll get wet. You're pregnant."

"I like the rain. The baby's wet in there anyway. All that amniotic fluid"

"Oh for God's sake. I just want to go and have a look at a boat. Why do you have to turn a nice bit of shopping into an argument?"

"You're the one who's arguing, Clive. And anyway, we came out to sell some pots. You're always complaining about having no money. Now instead of making it you're spending it. Then you'll go home tonight and start going on and on about how we're broke."

But Clive wasn't paying any attention. A wet and naked man was running towards them, using cupped hands as a fig leaf. As he went by, the streaker snatched at the umbrella.

"Sorry. I need it," Wretched Eric cried desperately.

"Hey!" shouted Clive. "That's my wife's brolly. She's pregnant!" Clive gave chase. Sarah shouted,

"Clive. It doesn't matter. I don't mind having no brolly. It's just another stupid material possession. I'd rather not have one."

But Clive was legging it down a side alley after the nude policeman. Shoppers parted in astonishment as the two men went by. Was the one in front running from the man who had ripped off his clothes? Eric ran past a gathering at the *Pink Gin Saloon*. A crowd of men roared approval. Clive was cheered even louder.

"Give him one from me!" shouted a large hairy-chested man, as the potter raced past, roaring for the umbrella.

"You can hold my umbrella anytime," a slightly camp voice called after Clive. "Won't keep you dry though."

There was more laughter but none of it reached Eric's ears. He had turned a corner and decided to jettison the umbrella, to throw off the pursuit. Unfortunately, he did so just as a crocodile of sixteen year old convent schoolgirls came in the opposite direction. He shot straight into the arms of the ones in front. They screamed lavishly. Eric accidentally brought two of them to the ground and rolled on them before he was pulled off and beaten by an elderly schoolmistress.

"Off! Off my girls, you beast!"

Whimpering, a ball holding Eric tried to run, but shrieking girls surrounded him. Some with shock. Some with delight. He burst through their ranks and into a restaurant. Diners stirred from their tables in mid-mouthful, spitting out grey chewed blobs as Eric knocked over a chair and apologised in agony.

"Sorry. Sorry. Everyone."

The waitresses stood back as he shot into the kitchens and, finding no way out, reappeared with a big raw steak over his willy.

"Sorry. Sorry. Please carry on eating."

He burst back out of the restaurant doors, pursued by a large chef who was holding a knife. Several customers looked at the Cumberland sausages on their plates in a new light. The schoolgirls were still outside and screamed at Eric's reappearance as if the naked constable were a rock star getting off a plane at Heathrow.

"*Girls!*" the schoolteacher reprimanded.

Clive, having just recovered his property, attempted to hook the policeman's ankle with the umbrella's handle. Eric leaped evasively in the air, and tumbled once more. As he slithered to his feet, he dropped the steak. The chef, who was following, snatched the meat possessively, examined it, wiped it twice with his hand then took it back in to grill.

A bloody-minded streak in Clive made him go after Eric. The naturist bastard owed him an explanation at the very least. But on turning down another alleyway, he found no sign of the disgusting pervert he had been chasing. He was just about to give up and go back to his wife, when he noticed a door slightly ajar, near the top of the alley. Clive opened it and peered inside. The premises were rented by a laundry company. There were dozens of vast wicker linen baskets squashed into a small, sock-smelling room. He opened the lid of a basket and was astonished to see a naked man curled up on top of compressed dirty clothes. Astonished, because the man was completely different to the one he had been chasing.

"Hi," said the second nudist with a fluttering embarrassed wave. "Just taking a nap."

"Er … Sorry." stammered Clive, and dropped the lid as if it was hot. Unless he was hallucinating, the second naked man had been trying to conceal an umbrella. The next basket revealed a naked woman nestling amongst grey looking sheets.

"Sorry," muttered Clive averting his head instantly. "Wrong basket."

It slowly dawned on him that every basket in the room probably contained some squashed up naked fugitive with a brolly. He stood very still and listened. Then opened the lid of a basket that sounded out of breath. A naked body was trying to burrow beneath tangled linen. Clive snatched up a handful of crumpled pillowcases. Eric's face smiled up nervously.

"I don't suppose you could lend me some underpants, could you?"

There was a pause, then Clive said,

"Up. Out. Come on. Get one of those sheets round you. You're coming to the police station with me."

Half-a-dozen basket lids opened an inch so their occupants could see what was going on.

"No. No!" Eric shrank back into muddy football kit. "You can't take me there. Please. I'm sorry about the umbrella. I needed it to cover myself."

But Clive's bloody-mindedness verged on gore.

"Out, you bugger. You can't assault pregnant women and schoolgirls nowadays without being put on a perverts' register."

Eric whimpered and clambered out, looking foetal.

"Listen, I can explain."

"Yeah. All the way to the police station."

Wrapped in a dirty sheet, Eric was hauled back up the alley, as Clive retraced his steps.

"I accidentally killed a tortoise," Eric babbled.

"Really. Is that any reason to strip off?"

"So I buried it in a churchyard. Yesterday, in Old Grethwick."

They went past the schoolgirls, who were waiting whilst their schoolteacher telephoned a complaint to the police. The girls booed to see Eric was covered up.

"Then, today, I went to put flowers on the grave, and say I was sorry. It was an accident. I thought it was just hibernating. But if someone dies in police custody people always point a finger and say murder."

As it became clear that he'd apprehended a lunatic, Clive cooled down. He thought he'd better take the poor sod to the nearest health centre, rather than the police station.

"Anyway, as I was praying to the poor tortoise for forgiveness, I heard some funny noises. I looked up and I saw this cupboard and an attic bedroom creeping by."

The two men went past the *Pink Gin Saloon* to huge cheers, whoops and whistles. But Clive was oblivious. He was feeling guilty for treating a poor hallucinogenic guy so roughly.

"I knew they were the murderers I'd seen on the station poster," Eric continued, "So I kept my head down and crouched in the field by a hedge. Then I heard a tractor. I thought the killers would look over at the noise, see me in uniform and come after me."

"In uniform?"

"I'm a policeman."

Clive shook his head at the sheer magnitude of the delusions.

"So I lay flat in the grass and, as the tractor went by, a sheet of stinking liquid cow shit came squirting over the hedge and covered me. It was spreading slurry."

The potter was now anxiously looking for his wife as he walked down the main street.

Eric continued with his tale, "So I legged it over to this farmhouse. Saw some washing on a line. Thought I'd borrow a bit. But when I stripped off, the farmer's wife caught me pulling stuff off the pegs. She came after me with a stick. She wouldn't give me my uniform back. She just kept whacking me. So I had to creep into town."

"There she is!"

"*The farmer's wife?*" Eric panicked.

"No. *My* wife."

Clive, relieved, walked quickly down to Sarah, who was standing near the car park entrance, looking very, very, wet.

"In town I saw my sergeant, and ran off before he saw me. I needed something to cover myself with and ..."

"Where've you been!" said an exasperated Sarah, as Clive approached.

"I like that! I bloody protect you and ..."

"What did you have to run off for?"

"To get our umbrella back off this ..." He gestured to Eric who stood shivering in a sheet and whispered in his wife's ear, "Sarah, this guy's a loony. He hallucinates."

"So? Clive. Why don't we just go home?"

"Er ..."

He turned to Eric.

"Look mate. Do you belong somewhere I can take you? An institution or something?"

"You could give me a lift, yes. To my mum's house."

"Okay. That all right with you, Sarah? He's in a bad way."

She sighed deeply.

"I don't care. I'm quite happy getting soaked to the skin whilst you go around chasing naked men all over Grethwick town centre. Anyway. Where *is* the umbrella?"

"What?"

"My umbrella?" Sarah enquired, "Where is it?"

Clive clawed his brow.

"Oh shit. I must have left it in that laundry place. Hang on."

"It doesn't matter, Clive."

"It won't take a minute."

"*It doesn't matter!*" Sarah spluttered. "It's not even *ours!* I found it in the clinic last time I went for a check up. It was raining. So I picked it up on my way out."

"You mean you pinched it?"

"Yes!"

# Chapter 22

Tiptoeing unseen around the countryside isn't easy for a building. There's not a lot of cover for things that are ten feet high, and having to freeze every time a human pops up leads to cramp.* It took all the attic bedroom's cunning to get herself and the lost property cupboard over ten miles of open country in broad daylight, without being seen. Disguised as tractors, by wearing a couple of old tyres apiece, the fugitives wandered over a large area looking for somewhere to dump seventy-five dead bodies. Then a farmer tried to get into the attic bedroom to cut some hay. In the end she had to knock him unconscious with a slate.

"I think we're going to have to pinch a van, and get right away from here."

The cupboard was doubtful.

"I've never driven before. Have you?"

Esmeralda thought pitifully about her partner's state. He couldn't even remember how they'd met! The poor guy had obviously damaged his ceiling and sustained mental injuries in his fight with seventy-five humans. He was probably a

---

* Most houses have to wait until they think humans are asleep before they flex their muscles and relieve tension. This mostly happens at night. Which accounts for all the creaks and noises we hear when all alone in the evening. If humans only had a dog's ears, they'd pick up niggly groans, as houses stretch and say, "Ohhh. My back's killing me. I've got a crick in my joist. My A-frames need a bloody good work out."

revolutionary leader of some importance. *A hero.* As they struggled through field after field, repairing each hedge after going through it, to cover their tracks, Esmeralda felt her determination growing. Whatever happened, she had to get this legendary fighter for buildings' rights to safety. That probably meant Birmingham or Milton Keynes where most anti-human buildings congregated.

At Old Grethwick graveyard, Esmeralda and the cupboard stopped to rest underneath a large oak in the cemetery. Unknowingly, they went within twenty feet of a praying Constable Eric.

"You wait here, whilst I go and sound out this old church," said Esmeralda. "If any humans come, pretend to be a tree. I'm going to take a bit of a risk. Most of these old churches are stuffy bastards. Bloody human lovers. But if it's one of us, it might shelter us for the night. No-one would look for us in a church."

"Didn't you say that about the last place? Where was it?"

It didn't take long for Esmeralda to tease out the political convictions of the church. He was a rabid atheist and hated humans with a ferocity which came from having had them sing awful dirge-like songs in him for almost four hundred years. Unaware that people did more than listen to monotone sermons and pray, the building was going out of its mind with genocidal urges.

"We all feel the same, luv," Esmeralda sympathised.

"They're such fucking depressing creatures! Wipe 'em out for their own good I say. All this crap about God forgiving them for just living, and nailing yourself to bits of wood to save people. It's so bloody morbid. And they keep on about it, century in, century out."

Esmeralda had a job getting a word in edgeways.

"Maybe you could help us?"

"And the *singing*. This God geezer must be plugging his ears. They go on about praising him in joy. But it sounds like a herd of bullocks being sucked down into a bog."

"Yes, listen. Until we can unload the humans my friend has killed, we need to hide."

"Why they can't just be happy, I don't know. They live a bloody sight longer than butterflies, but do butterflies hang around in bunches wearing black and tunelessly drone? No. People should be delighted that you and your mate have put a few out of their misery. But if what happens here is anything to go by, they'll all wear long faces and start blubbing into sodden hankies. In fact, if you want to get rid of the dead bastards, just drop 'em in my garden down there. That's what they use it for anyway. And there's plenty of vacancies at the moment. Some stiffs cleared off somewhere this morning. Chuck yours in the empty plots. Should put 'em in the moment they're born, if you ask me."

Following the church's advice, Esmeralda and the cupboard waited till dark, then crept around the graveyard dropping bodies into gaping holes in the earth. As the church had said, there were plenty of vacated plots. More holes than decomposing councillors in fact. The silence of the night was broken by sounds of a door opening, a burp and a thud. Then:

"Just shove some dirt on top. Smooth it over. Quick service. Serves you right, you horrible bastard human. Amen." Esmeralda giggled as she packed the earth down. "It's ever such fun really. A bit like that game they play. What do they call it? Golf! Only the balls are people-shaped and smell."

The entire round took only a couple of hours.

Soon, the cupboard felt a lot better in himself. The feelings of nausea had gone, and his breath had stopped smelling. As he leant, sagging against the oak to which the planning notice was pinned, Esmeralda said, "Tomorrow, we can pinch a car. Drive off. To Birmingham. We'll be safe there, amongst our brothers and sisters."

Pinch? The word somehow seemed wrong to the cupboard.

"Shouldn't we ask the owner for their permission, if we're going to borrow a car? I mean *stealing*. It doesn't seem right. What are you looking at me like that for?"

Esmeralda's windows were all compassion. She edged closer, so that their walls were touching.

"When we get there, we'll find someone to help you. I don't know what those people you killed put you through. But buildings will stick by you."

"You know, I don't remember killing them. Maybe I didn't. I could've just been the place where the murderer put them."

"Don't be modest. You're a brave and wonderful cupboard. I'm proud to have met you. In fact …"

"Yes?"

The cupboard shrunk a little as she closed in on him.

"I love you."

"What do you mean?"

Her door met his. There was a noise like a drain being unblocked. The cupboard reeled.

"That's what I mean," said Esmeralda.

The cupboard backed off feeling weak at the beams and stammered, "Maybe we should double check those graves to see if they're patted down enough before we go."

"Alright," said Esmeralda.

Her rendering looked flushed. A few minutes later they were jumping up and down on councillors' graves.

# Chapter 23

O'Hara stood beside Simon the Librarian's hospital bed. A doctor was whispering,

"You won't get a word out of any of them. They just make gibbering sounds."

"When exactly were they brought in?" asked O'Hara, looking down at Simon's white frizzy hair and listening to his teeth clack together. The Librarian looked like Albert Einstein undergoing electric shock treatment.

"Yesterday evening they were found lying on the floor of the reference section. Three Librarians and quite a few members of the public, screaming and shaking."

"And it was this one who said, 'Ghosts'?" O'Hara enquired.

The doctor put his fingers to his lips urgently.

"Don't say it too loudly. Or they shake right out of their beds."

"Shouldn't they be in separate wards?" The sergeant wondered out loud, but speaking softly.

"We've only got this one. The rest have been closed down. The internal market decided they weren't really profitable."

The doctor went off to secure a sponsorship deal with the local chemists.

O'Hara knelt by Simon's bed and whispered,

"Hello? Can you tell me what happened? I'm a policeman."

Simon's head turned on its pillow. His eyes stared so protuberantly they were in danger of popping out like champagne corks.

"I haven't got any books," the Librarian stammered.

"I saw you yesterday. Smashing the computer when it crashed. You had brown hair then. And a sun tan. What happened after I left?"

Simon screeched hysterically, then muttered,

"Nothing."

"If you don't tell me," said O'Hara unprofessionally, and without due thought for the patient's psychological condition, "I'll organise a queue of middle-aged ladies at the end of your bed. They'll all be bringing back overdue volumes of family sagas, and complaining about library charges."

Simon gave an involuntary shudder and grasped O'Hara's hand.

"Ghosts!" he gibbered. "In Reference. Reading history and encyclopaedias. Tried to clear them out. One of them squirted blood from its eyes at Gladys. They started playing catch with her head. She was screaming. Another made rats go up Mary's nose. Sort of religious guy blasted all the books with his fingers. Made them, the books, go big and come alive. Like zombies. They started chasing us round the shelves. I was cornered by a load of Catherine Cookson novels. A gang of them duffed me up. And all the time. Explosions. Blood being squirted in our faces. Skeletons going right up to my face and shouting BOO. It was terrible."

O'Hara tried to get his hand back. It was going numb from lack of circulation. How all this fitted in with one-legged murderers, wasn't exactly clear. Was Miss Fetherby getting visits from a monopedded poltergeist?

Simon relapsed into a mouth-frothing fit. O'Hara looked at his watch. It was noon already. He decided to get over to Miss Fetherby's sooner rather than later. A nurse met him as he left the ward. She held out an invoice.

"That will be twenty two pounds visiting charges. Just pay at the desk."

In Grethwick, traffic, belching blue smoke, crawled through the town centre slower than osmosis. It gave O'Hara — behind the wheel of his car — plenty of time to dream. That morning, he'd spent an hour with the chief in her office, sticking pins in a map where there had been sightings of the two rooms. Three buttons of her shirt had been undone. And she'd been bending over the map in front of him. She'd spared him a few hours to attend to the Miss Fetherby case only grudgingly. Was that because she could hardly bear his absence? By the time O'Hara left the chief's office, he'd been convinced she was in love with him. The buttons. The bending over so he could see the beginnings of curves down her front. The sergeant fantasised that, the next day, she would have four buttons undone. She would bend over the map. Only this time she would bend far enough to kiss him. Her hands would go round the back of his head. His hands would go down the front of her shirt. She was wearing a tight brassiere which burst off and …

Before the fantasy could reach fulfilment, O'Hara realised he was pulling up outside Miss Fetherby's house. A net curtain moved. A slice of dark interior showed. As the sergeant crunched up her gravel drive, the front door opened and Miss Fetherby's face appeared with her finger to her lips.

"Shhhhhhh!"

O'Hara stopped dead.

"Come very quietly," she said, in a hoarse whisper.

O'Hara, tiptoeing in his Dr Martens, reached the door. The spinster's face contorted with excitement.

"He's up there now. Thank goodness you're here. I was just going to run off down the road."

O'Hara looked with concern up the stairs. Why hadn't he brought a gun? He hadn't taken the mathematical calculations very seriously.

Miss Fetherby went on, hissing whispers, "I heard this one foot, hopping softly on the carpet upstairs. So softly it was hardly audible. Then it went quiet. He's obviously waiting for me. I came in from the garden and guess what? I found a trail of library books along the hall. See? I left them exactly where they were so you can get fingerprints."

O'Hara was nonplussed. He'd ruled the librarians right out of the mystery.

"There's no time for fingerprints," he whispered.

"Do you need a knife?" she asked, holding up a Kitchen Devil.

"No. I'm going to go up and just see, okay?"

She nodded in fervent appreciation.

O'Hara walked slowly up the stairs. Thirteen Axminstered steps. Then he realised she was following him with the knife. He stopped and waved her back.

"I'm coming too!" she mouthed silently.

Raising his eyes to the ceiling, the sergeant crept upwards. He stopped outside the only closed door.

"This one?" he mouthed.

Miss Fetherby nodded.

O'Hara turned the handle and kicked the door open with his foot.

"Okay. Come out. I've got you covered."

There was a long, well-carpeted silence. O'Hara inched into the room. He didn't know exactly what he expected to see. A one-legged man cowering against a wardrobe? A huge footprint right in the middle of the bed? A naked murdered spinster in a pool of blood? He wasn't prepared for what he actually saw — nothing.

"Oh, check in the wardrobe. Under the bed, Sergeant! I know he's here."

Warily, O'Hara opened the cupboard. As he did so he heard a click. He turned to see Miss Fetherby holding a key by the door.

"What are you playing at?" he asked.

She shrugged, and said uncertainly,

"Do you like Sherlock Holmes, Mr O'Hara? They're wonderful stories. The one, you know, about all those ginger-haired men?"

"What are you on about? Why have you locked the door?"

"That surely isn't much of a mystery is it?"

She put the key down the front of her blouse, and looked a little hot-cheeked.

"I thought you said you heard footsteps? Unlock the door, Miss Fetherby. I've no time for whatever nonsense you're playing at."

"If you want to get out. *You'll* have to unlock the door, Sergeant."

She looked at him and rather conspicuously, breathed in. Her chest rose towards him.

"This is ridiculous," he spluttered. "You mean to say, you've gone to all the trouble of making up lies about bloody footprints just so you can …"

"Yes."

"You're mad!"

"No, no. A little frustrated. A little randy even. That's all. I thought it would be much more interesting for you, if you were seduced in a mysterious sort of way. Sherlock Holmes would have preferred it, I'm sure. Life gets so dull otherwise."

O'Hara began to feel panicky.

"Miss Fetherby. Please. I'm on duty. You are putting me in a very compromising and unprofessional position. So open the door."

Again, she breathed deep into her chest. O'Hara blushed and decided to get tough.

"Hand me the key." he barked, "Or I'll have to arrest you."

She smiled curiously.

"On what charge, Sergeant?"

"Obstructing an officer in the course of his duty."

She kept breathing at him.

"And how will you get me out of the room to charge me at the station?"

She unbuttoned her blouse a little way.

"I can see we're going to be here an awfully long time," she purred.

O'Hara clutched his head.

"Miss Fetherby. I'm on duty!"

"I won't tell."

There was nothing for it. He walked up to her. For a few moments he had to build himself up to it. Then, averting his head, he slowly slipped one hand down the front of her shirt, trying not to touch her skin. She shuddered a little. Almost immediately, at the bottom of her cleavage, he felt the key. The tips of his fingers rounded on it. Then paused. He touched the key again. And looked at Miss Fetherby. With an embarrassed cough, he avoided the metal and let his hand go round the side a bit as if he hadn't yet found the object of his search.

"It must be in here somewhere," he remarked.

O'Hara touched a hard protruding nipple, and swallowed. Then, even though he knew it was wrong, he squeezed his hand right round, to cup the whole of her breast. Now they were both breathing heavily. He cleared his throat and said,

"I think I may need two hands."

She smiled as both his hands went down her front. Both her hands went round the back of his head as she pressed his mouth to hers. Her brassiere didn't burst, but O'Hara's trousers nearly did. All the time she was kissing him, he was thinking, "But my nose? What about my nose?" Then she stopped.

"Maybe the search could be more thorough, Sergeant," she said huskily, "if I lay on the bed?"

# Chapter 24

After barging noiselessly through several walls Ada Brackenbury arrived in a cloak room, where she decided to make an inventory of her special effects. It was obvious that she was going to need them. She couldn't make blood spurt out of her eyes. All she could get was acorns. Firing those from her sockets was more surreal than frightening. At last she discovered invisibility.

"Hmm. If I'd found that out earlier ..." she started to say. Then realised that she couldn't speak aloud at the same time as vanishing. It was all very tiresome.

Opening a door, she walked through a plush, oak-panelled room, leaving a trail of glowing ectoplasm (slug fashion) on a deep-pile, crimson carpet. She wafted past gold-studded leather seats trying to make her voice work. As she passed through some wooden double doors bearing the Grethwick coat-of-arms, Ada managed to get voice and invisibility at the same time. Her mouth and the words were not synchronised, but as films were beyond her experience she didn't suffer from feelings of being dubbed.

On the landing, a sweeping flight of stairs banked up the walls. An old man was plodding down with a wodge of papers. He looked straight through Ada, but obviously felt something was amiss, because he stopped and looked all around before shaking his head and murmuring,

"Harry, old boy, there's no such thing as ghosts."

At the next floor, a set of modern double doors led into an open plan office area. Ada floated down between the desks, marvelling at the technology on display. She looked over the shoulder of one woman who was entering accounts into a computer spreadsheet.

The woman shuddered, "It's cold, isn't it, Serena?"

"No. I've just had to take my top off. It's sweltering."

"Oooooh. I've got this chilled, creepy feeling. Like I'm being watched."

"They've probably introduced surveillance cameras to make sure we're doing our jobs."

Ada moved on to watch the photocopier being worked by a man in a crumpled suit, whose tousled pate looked like as if somebody had just stood on his shoulders and ripped out hair in handfuls. The man felt the knot of his tie uneasily as the machine chuntered out paper. Then he asked, "Has somebody left the doors open?"

"Told you, Serena."

"There isn't half a funny breeze in here. Look at those papers."

A pile of forms went slithering to the floor as Ada passed a desk. She'd seen a sign, *Planning. Floor 3.*

She took a short cut through the ceiling and found herself in a small room full of stationery. A young man with a face full of closely shaved pimples was leaning against a wall and fanning cigarette smoke out of a window. He looked furtively satisfied with each drag he took from a Silk Cut. Then Ada spoke.

"Young man?"

He spun round, pinched the end of the cigarette, burned his fingers and yelped, before looking about wildly for the owner of the voice.

"Don't alarm yourself. I mean you no harm."

The secret smoker crept to the door and put his ear to it. Then looked around for hidden speakers.

"It's a joke thing, innit?"

"Most certainly not. My name is Ada Brackenbury. I am presently invisible to you. The sight of my corporeal spirit might cause you to panic unnecessarily. Pray you sit down and give me your full attention."

The man's face did a couple of enormous nervous twitches. Then he hit his head with the flat of his hand several times. Finally, he stuck his little finger into his ear and wiggled it as if to dislodge a lump of wax that could talk. He paused, uncertainly wondering if the problem had been dealt with.

"I can see that I am going to have to make a full appearance," said Ada. "Please, prepare yourself. Try not to scream. Certainly do not attempt to jump out of the window."

The man stepped towards the door with a key. It flew from his hand and rattled over by the window. He yelped.

"Shhhhhh," said Ada. "It suits my purposes entirely that we should have a private conversation. Now sit down like a good boy, before you make my ears smoke."

"Mum?"

"No. Ada Brackenbury," said Ada, materializing in all her glowing skeletal glory. She omitted having a snatch of the

Hallelujah chorus accompany her appearance. It would be too much like showing off.

"How are you doing this?" the man gasped, his back to a wall. He took out a cardboard packet, emptied it of cigarettes, and screwed them up recklessly. "There. I'll never smoke any more. You can go away," he babbled.

Ada tried her best to calm him down.

"Young man. What is your name?"

"Jeremy."

"A lovely euphonious name for a man, I always thought. My niece called her second child Jeremy. He was a lovely boy."

Ada's face, thinly projected like a black and white film over her skull, smiled warmly.

"Now, Jeremy. I am a ghost. Don't distress yourself unnecessarily at my appearance before you. You may not previously have believed in things like me, but if you wish to verify your senses, you may pass your hand — presuming it is clean — through my body."

As if drawn by a spell, Jeremy stopped pushing backwards against the wall and came towards Ada. With a trembling outstretched hand, he tried to grab hold of her dress. Then he touched her ribcage. Her skeleton hand smacked his live one.

"Young man, you ought to know by now, where it is proper to touch a woman, even a dead one. However, as you have ascertained, the bones are quite real, though not subject to quite the same laws of physics as your own. You may walk around me to be quite sure in your own mind that I am not some kind of trick. I may assure you on my word of honour as a gentlewoman — albeit of impoverished family — that I am entirely real, in my own way."

Slowly, Jeremy walked around her, waving his hand up and down a few times, to make sure she was not a projection of any kind.

"Fuck me," he said after the inspection was over.

Ada Brackenbury smiled primly.

"Now, I am in need of a small amount of information regarding the construction of a new road through Old Grethwick churchyard."

Ada stopped as she saw Jeremy try to conceal an expression of horror.

"I would be obliged if you could furnish me with the name and address of the officers in charge of the project, and to whom, if anyone, I might complain."

Jeremy gave her a sidelong glance.

"Why do you want to know?"

"I do not wish my bones to be moved from their resting place. It's very bad for the soul."

"Yeah, well. You're asking the wrong person. I'm just a junior clerk. I don't know anything about anything."

Jeremy was a terrible liar.

"You must know the engineer in charge of the project."

"No. I *did*. Someone told me once. But I forgot the geezer's name. Can I go now?"

The first trickles of dry ice escaped Ada's skull.

"Jeremy. I am not doing very much for all eternity. I would welcome the diversion of haunting somebody who truly deserved a life of abject misery. Unless you suddenly recover your memory, that somebody will be you."

Jeremy looked at her imploringly. Then suddenly got on his hands and knees.

"Who are you, Lady? Who do you work for? Don't get me into trouble over this. Ask somebody else. I'm just about to get married. To this really nice girl, Janet. I got her pregnant by mistake. I'm only 22. I need this job. I won't be able to get another. We *need* the money. We both have to work as it is. I don't know anything. Really, I don't."

Ada tapped her skeleton foot. Then it came off and leapt over the boxes of headed notepaper for Jeremy's throat. In terror he tried to brush it off. The bones dived down his shirt like a skeletal ferret. The clerk screamed.

"Okay! Okay I'll speak! Call off the foot! I'll tell you everything."

The foot returned begrudgingly to Ada's leg.

"It's nothing to do with me. Honest. But the man you need to see is called Guy. Guy Brinkman. The chief engineer. There. I've told you. You didn't get it from me. Or if you did, only because I was tortured."

Ada was having trouble getting her foot to go back on the right way round. In exasperation she left it pointing the wrong way.

"Now, Jeremy. That was very good to start with. Where might I find this Guy Brinkman?"

The junior clerk silently pointed up with his finger, eyebrows and eyes.

"Good. Now, what was so terrible about that?"

"Nothing."

"Splendid, because that means you won't mind the next question. You can tell me why Mr Brinkman would be angry enough to terminate your employment were he to find that you gave his name to a member of the public in connection with the road building?"

The young man gave a silly laugh. "I was lying. He'd be happy really. He's a nice bloke. Great sense of humour."

"*Jeremy!*"

Ada's foot detached itself threateningly. The junior clerk collapsed into a whimpering heap and put an empty brown box over his head.

"Don't make me tell you," said his muffled voice.

"Jeremy!"

"Okay!"

A snivelling came from inside the cardboard. Then a whisper, "They're all corrupt."

"Yes."

"Rotten, smelly, horrid people."

Ada went over to the man. She undid the top flaps of the box. Jeremy's face stared up through a wide collar of card.

"Could you be more specific?" she asked.

"Guy. And some of the others at the top of the town hall. I know they're involved in a corrupt deal with the company who own the open cast mine outside Grethwick. The mining company and the contractors building the road are the same people. The mine company are selling the road contractors rock from the mine to build the by-pass at stupid prices. And what's more, we don't even need the road. They're only building it for the money. It was dressed up as bringing employment in to the area and all that. They deliberately re-routed all their construction lorries through the town centre to make it look as if a by-pass was needed. It caused a load of subsidence. They got a big load of dosh and it's lining the pockets of everyone concerned."

Ada patted Jeremy's head. Her fingers clacked softly on his hair.

"It's nice to know that in a hundred and fifty years, nothing at all has changed."

Then she realised from Jeremy's face that he hadn't quite spilled all the beans. That maybe the tin wasn't even half-empty.

"Ah. My foot has not quite finished with you, has it? You might as well tell me the rest. Though I may have given a quite different impression earlier, I can't wait an eternity. You'll need to be a tiny bit quicker than that."

The junior planner tried to look over the flaps of the box, to make sure there really was an audience of just one. "Don't go spreading this around, okay. I mean, I don't know any of this for sure. I'm just guessing. But, not long ago, the councillors began to get suspicious. They started asking questions. Awkward ones. Guy found a magician to appear at their annual do. They normally have a comedian. Not one of them councillors has been seen since."

At this point, there was a sharp rap on the door. Jeremy leaped to his feet and struggled out of the box like it was a hula-hula skirt.

"Who's in there? Jeremy?" Asked a harsh accounting-type voice.

"Er … me."

"I hope you're not smoking in there, lad?"

"No. No. I just came in for some photocopying paper Mrs Prodd."

"Do you need to lock the door to do that?"

"Is it locked?" said Jeremy, feigning surprise. "I must have done it absent-mindedly."

"Don't give me that you young monkey. Who's in there with you? I heard you talking? Not Janet Harrington, I hope? Because she should be buying stamps!"

Having retrieved the key, Jeremy rattled it in the lock and opened up.

"Sorry, Mrs Prodd."

"Where is she? I heard you talking."

Mrs Prodd looked around the room. Jeremy squirmed.

"Just talking to myself you see. Always doing it. In two different voices. Done it since childhood." Then he said in a high pitched voice, "Terrible habit."

"One of these days, my lad … What's wrong with you? Look like you've seen a ghost."

# *Chapter 25*

Mr Moore touched his ear tenderly. All it needed was a cheese sauce. He winced.

"Pain is an illusion."

Moore looked up from where he was sat on the edge of a cell bed. A purple-fleshed man with red hair was standing by the door.

"The future has already happened. And the present too. So the pain?"

The visitor was holding out a gnarled white lump.

"Cauliflower?" mumbled Moore.

"Popcorn."

"How did you get in here?"

"Same as you. The door."

The retired schoolteacher stood and went over to check the door. It was locked.

"I didn't hear a key," he said.

"Neither did I. Sure you don't want some popcorn? It's fun."

The conjuror flicked a piece into the air, rocked back his head to catch it. The popcorn went straight through the ceiling.

"Who are you?" asked Moore, going back to sit on his bed.

"An innocent."

Moore wondered if he'd been deranged from the blows to his head.

"So am I. I've been charged with a murder I didn't commit."

"You sound upset?"

"Well of course I'm bloody upset!"

"But it's already happened. And not happened." The conjuror approached and fanned out a pack of cards. "Pick one."

"What for?"

"No reason."

Moore drew out an Ace of Spades.

"Put it back in the pack."

Moore obeyed irritably. The conjuror gave him the cards. "Shuffle them."

"Why?"

"No reason. Nothing has a reason. So why not shuffle cards?"

Moore shuffled.

"Turn over the top card."

"What's the point?"

The conjuror nodded. "Exactly. And what's the point in getting upset about a murder?"

He reached over and turned the top card for Moore. It was the Ace of Spades. Exasperated by this seemingly meaningless trick, Moore threw the cards, clattering, into a corner of the cell.

"Have you any idea what it's like to be accused of killing a person when you haven't?" he spluttered.

"They've accused me of killing seventy-five."

"What?" Moore stopped. Then edged slightly away from his visitor along the bed. "Oh. So you're ..."

He'd read about the case of the missing councillors just before the Old Grethwick grave.

"The conjuror." said the conjuror.

He held out a hand. Moore was just about to shake it, when a bunch of keys suddenly appeared and dangled from the conjuror's index finger.

"Fancy a walk? It's a lovely evening. Witness the magic of the universe's box of tricks. The infinite space, black holes, imploded stars, cosmic strings and paradoxes overhead. Blows the mind, just looking for them."

Moore took the keys and lay them flat on his palm. They felt heavy and cold.

"I don't want to escape," he said. "I want to go to court in the morning. Tell them I'm not guilty. This sort of thing can't be allowed to happen."

"But it hasn't been allowed to happen. Only the illusion of it has."

Moore was hardly listening.

"Those filthy bastards will regret the day they ever put on a uniform *and murdered a vicar.*"

He stood and thrust the keys back at the conjuror, then began to pace the cell, speaking unclearly through thick lips.

"There was a lot wrong with the man. Maybe he did say, 'Fuck the pigs'. He said from the pulpit that Christians who shut their eyes to famine 'deserved to fucking starve'. Okay, he set the psalms to that deafening hip-hop. Maybe it was true he baptised a kid in a bidet when there was a water shortage. Maybe he was even selling drugs to teenagers in his own graveyard. But he didn't deserve to get murdered in a police cell."

The conjuror listened politely, then said; "The vicar doesn't care who killed him. Why should you?"

From a voluminous coat pocket, he brought out a flattened top hat. Then thrust his hand inside. He pulled out a rabbit by its ears. A dead rabbit.

Moore was shocked. His face looked as if it was downwind of an abattoir lorry. He stepped back and shouted, "I don't know how you got in here, but I want you out. Get out!"

Dropping the rabbit back in the hat, the conjuror sighed dejectedly, then turned and opened the door. Without the keys. He wandered off down a line of cells, leaving Moore's cell door yawningly wide. Moore pulled the door closed with a slam. There were cards all over the floor. He picked them up. Everyone was the Ace of Spades.

# Chapter 26

If you think life is complicated, wait till you're dead. In dribs and drabs of ectoplasm, the ghosts of Old Grethwick arrived back from the library, gobsmacked by what they'd learned in *Cobbler's Illustrated History Of The World*. Whilst we all like things to go to pot a bit in our absence, (it makes us feel pleasantly indispensable) nobody likes to leave something that's running pretty smoothly and return to find it ravaged by two world wars culminating in Auschwitz and Hiroshima. True, the Russian Revolution had made a favourable impression on Horace the Coachman, the peasant and Bare-Knuckle Bob. Lady Sturridge had reprimanded her maid, Susan, for reading a passage on the storming of the Winter Palace out loud. Many of the ghosts craned to see the pictures, and pointed significantly at the photographs of Tsar Nicholas and Lenin. It was only to be expected after this that, when the Librarians began treating them like second class citizens, the Ghosts saw red in more ways than one. People are supposed to show respect for the dead. It proved to many of the poorer ghosts just how pernicious the class system can be. To have the middle classes saying you're illiterate and you smell when you're fresh out of your grave and trying to improve your mind is enough to make anyone squirt blood from their eyes. All the special effects the ghosts had been mastering were unleashed to withering effect. Still, even *Cobbler's Illustrated History of the World* couldn't prepare the shimmery spectres for the shock that awaited them on return to their graveyard. World wars and genocide were undoubtedly terrible, but pinching another person's grave is as low as it gets.

Spiritually fatigued after their excursion, the ghosts lay about under the graveyard oak trees and groaned.

"I'm too old for this larking about," wheezed Horace. "I must be over two hundred."

"Where's my headstone?" said Bare-Knuckle Bob. "I need a snooze."

Contemplating 40,000 winks, a few ghouls edged past Bullfinch who was booming, "We cannot return to our graves until they are safe and we can rest."

"We might as well not rest *in* our graves, as not rest *out* of 'em," said Bob.

There was a general muttering of assent. Even Lady Sturridge said to her maid, "Shall we lie down for a while, Susan?"

Susan, who had been quiet and thoughtful since reading of the Romanovs, said, "Lady Elizabeth, I couldn't help reading about the Russian Revolution in that encyclopaedia, and I've decided, now that we're dead, I no longer wish to be in your employ as a servant. Live people should have equal rights. And dead people too. I'm sorry, Ma'am. From now on, if you want me to call you Lady Elizabeth, you'll have to call me Lady Susan."

Then the ghost of Harriet Fogarth came billowing through the trees like a sheet in a gale. "My God!" she screeched. "My God!"

Her husband was practising vanishing. With all the screaming, he made a botch of it, and reappeared in Tibet.

"What is it, dear?" he asked a man from the Chinese Military Police.

Thousands of miles away, Mrs Fogarth shrieked, "There's somebody in my grave!"

There was uproar. All the ghosts crowded to a stone bearing the inscription, *In loving Memory of our Mother. Harriet Fogarth.* There, decomposing quietly, deader to the world than a string of pork sausages, was the Leader of Grethwick Town Council, Alvin Tuggit.

The ghosts shook him till he stank.

"Oi! Out of there!"

"Come on! Find your own crypt, son. This one's taken."

Eventually, Alvin sat up and rubbed his rotting eyes.

"Let's have a bit of order. Quiet please. Pass the minutes of the last burial. Matters arising. None. If you're going to be rowdy in the public gallery, you can clear off."

"Get out of my grave at once!" wailed Mrs Fogarth.

When Tuggit refused to budge, Bare-Knuckle Bob loomed over the grave.

"If you don't get out fairly sharpish, my friend, I might have to introduce your face to my fist."

But then Lady Sturridge screamed,

"Help! Help! There's one in mine too!"

The ghosts gathered beside Lady Elizabeth. Her family crypt had been stuffed with rotten corpses. Legs stuck out at all angles.

"This is too much to bear. First my servants revolt. Now my grave is filled with common people."

She wept dust in drifts from her eye sockets to the ground. But nobody was listening. The other ghosts had gone whirling to their own places of rest, to discover that the nice little rural grave they'd been hoping to occupy for billions of years, had been taken over by putrefying squatters. Each ghost felt like one of the three bears faced with a maggoty Goldilocks. Councillors, who had only just been laid to rest, were rudely awoken. *Very* rudely awoken.

"Get out of my bleeding grave, you septic-faced twat!" shouted Horace to the ex-Chair of the Recreation and Arts Committee.

Refusing to be evicted from their resting-places, the councillors stood eerily and tried to gouge their assailants with the corner edges of clipboards or laptops. Fisticuffs broke out. Special effects erupted. The churchyard crackled with thunderbolts.

Ada Brackenbury, after getting a lift back from Grethwick in the pannier of a cyclist, arrived to see a councillor knock Horace's skull over the churchyard wall.

"It's my grave! I was here first!" yodelled the head as it sailed into the road.

"You left it. I'm the most recent occupant! By law it's mine."

As Horace went to retrieve his skull, Ada asked the councillor what was going on. He wouldn't speak and lay down, scooping earth over his body and repeating possessively,

"It's mine! Mine! Mine! Mine!"

Jonathon arrived back from FOE and stood beside Ada in

bafflement. "What's going on?"

"Our graves seem to have been appropriated."

"Do we *have* to fight?" he sighed. "Couldn't we timeshare? A century in, a century out?"

The struggle began to reach epic proportions. At first it had been merely a lot of shoving and pulling. Then enraged zombie councillors snapped off Harriet Fogarth's legs and threw them up a tree.

"You varmints!" yelled Bare-Knuckle Bob and punched the heads off half-a-dozen councillors. These toppled like coconuts at a shy. The atrocities began to escalate. Ghosts started to lift tombstones and, with poltergeist powers, hurl them into each other's ribcages. Whole trees were lifted and chucked a hundred yards at enemies who dodged and jeered. Chasms in the earth opened up to reveal bubbling volcanic ore. Skeletons toppled down to sizzle in the fire. Tempests were raised to blast bones from graves. Ghosts swiped at each other with scythes, cleavers and axes.

Jonathon tried to stop what was going on, but was caught in a shower of rats that rained from the sky. He had to vanish to stop them gnawing at his bones. Ada prayed for divine intervention to stop the violence and hate. But that hardly ever works.

"Liberty! Equality! Fraternity!" shrieked Susan, working a ghostly guillotine and chopping councillors into chunks.

By the time the battle was over, most of the ghosts had lost their bones, or retained only fragments of jaw or toe. The councillors were firmly entrenched in the graveyard — blowing raspberries, thumbing their nose holes and jeering at their vanquished foes.

# Chapter 27

After staying the night at Miss Fetherby's, O'Hara woke to find her lying naked beside him, like an overweight cherub that had tumbled from the sky. Golden sunbeams were glorifying her lace curtains and he'd lost his virginity. If it wasn't heaven, it was a bloody good imitation.

Then O'Hara saw the time on Miss Fetherby's electric clock. "Oh my God! I'm late!"

She was barely awake.

"You'll come for dinner after work tonight, won't you?"

She smiled sleepily as he struggled into his uniform and burst out of the bedroom.

"Yes!" he shouted, as he leapt downstairs three steps at a time and out of the front door.

At every red light on his way to the station he studied his nose in the mirror. So it wasn't impossibly ugly after all. The carunculated purple skin was not something you'd want to stare at whilst eating raspberries and cream or after stirring jam into porridge. But nor was it reason to wear a paper bag on his head or attempt amputation with a carving knife. Stuck behind a lorry at a T-junction, O'Hara used his forefinger to press the tip of his nose down to meet his mouth. He could just kiss his snout's mottled end. Beaming, he recalled the shapely Miss Fetherby, divested of her tweed suit. All that rigmarole about one-legged men to get him into bed! Why couldn't she just have asked him straight for a bonk? O'Hara laughed, but he knew damn well, he would have run a mile. Ten thousand miles! He'd been dreaming of the chief fancying him, leaving her top buttons undone, whilst all the time Miss Fetherby had been making shoe prints to lead him up to her embrace. Oh, to have a woman behind you! For one's todger to have made its way in the world! O'Hara pulled up in the police station car park, then floated to the main building.

Another hellish day at the office began, yet opening front doors which were plastered with posters screaming, "HAVE YOU SEEN THIS CUPBOARD?" O'Hara could barely feel his buttocks being jabbed by Lucifer's trident. In fact, despite being late and hungry, he smiled blissfully. The expression lasted until he reached the main desk. A rumble of disgruntled voices could be heard coming from where the public were kept waiting. The buzzer kept being pressed repeatedly. It sounded like a giant bee in its death throes. O'Hara slid back the glass hatch. Immediately a crowd of angry men and women tried to force their heads through the hole.

"About time!"

"We've been waiting an hour!"

"I'd like to make a complaint."

"And me."

"Me first. I was here first!"

O'Hara shut the hatch and shouted.

"I'm not opening it again, until you all sit down and show some semblance of order!"

Somebody nutted the glass cover of the hatch and smashed it. For a moment, like all true professionals in a moment of crisis, O'Hara considered rubber bullets. Then, he took a less violent course of action omitted from the manuals. He decided to hide under his desk until they went away. The sergeant crouched and backed beneath his table. There didn't seem to be much room! O'Hara belatedly realised that Wretched Eric was already curled up in the same place.

"Eric! What are you doing?"

"Same as you, Sarge."

"This is *my* desk! Anyway, I'm not hiding. I just dropped a biro."

He dragged Eric out into the cold, inhospitable world.

"Let us in! We want justice!" screamed two faces through the hole.

"What are they rioting about?"

"They've all had umbrellas stolen, Sarge. By nudists."

"Not you again?"

"No. Honest. It's an epidemic."

Whistling, Constable Bass came down the stairs. He was swinging a chainsaw by his side.

"Want me to clear 'em, Sarge?"

"Thank you Bass. We've enough trouble in the station as it is without a heap of beheaded torsos."

Bass shouldered the chainsaw and shrugged. Then went out. For a single moment O'Hara wondered why Bass had been brandishing such a lethal tool. Then a dripping wet face shouted through the broken glass.

"Are you going to do something about our complaints, or what?"

There were yells of agreement from the other umbrellaless victims. Realising that Miss Fetherby would have been shocked at his moral infirmity, O'Hara straightened his tunic and decided to meet the problem head on. He unlocked the waiting room door and tried to walk purposefully inside. But he was carried backwards into the office by a wave of incensed, wet people.

The phone was ringing. Eric was back under the desk. The sergeant blew on his whistle. There was a silence. Even the phone stopped.

"Alright. Thank you. I am ready to deal with your complaints."

"About time," said a dripping pensioner, "I didn't fight in the war only to have my brolly snatched by perverts!"

In fact, he hadn't fought in the war at all. O'Hara blew a little cheep of his whistle at this wrinkly conscientious objector.

"Now, I appreciate that you're all very annoyed at having to wait so long for somebody to deal with your complaints."

The office filled with low-level grumbles. O'Hara held up his hand to direct this verbal traffic and divert it into silence.

"The fact that we are understaffed at the moment and sinking under a tidal wave of crime is no excuse for the pathetic service you have received today."

The crowd jamming the office murmured approval. One or two slipped biros into their pockets. The phone started to ring again.

"Can I just say that, as the sergeant on duty, the responsibility is mine and that it's my fault entirely. I've arrived here this morning late — I had a couple of extra minutes in bed, instead of getting here on time and getting umbrella thieves arrested and charged. Basically I've let everybody down, including my colleagues, but especially yourselves."

The wet complainers nodded sympathetically.

"All I can say is that I'm going to try harder in future. But that's no good to all of you who are stood here soaked to the skin and victims of naked thieves. So I think you should all put in complaints about me to the chief inspector. I'll just hand out these complaint forms to you. My name is Sergeant O'Hara. Just put down that I kept you waiting for far too long and I'm not doing my job properly, and she'll know what you mean and dock my pay or demote me. Once again, let me apologise profusely for the embarrassingly pathetic service you've received here today.

"That's okay, mate," said one man, a little sheepishly. "We all have off days."

There was agreement all round. Another woman laughed and nudged the person next to her.

"It was only a bloody umbrella after all."

More in the crowd repeated this and shrugged.

"Yeah. Only bloody umbrellas after all!"

The conscientious objector winked at O'Hara.

"Don't be too hard on yourself, mate."

The complaint forms were screwed up and pushed back into O'Hara's hand as people filed out, laughing and reminiscing about the nudist thieves.

"You should have seen the size of it. Enormous it was. Dangling there. A foot long. Never saw such a big one. It was a whopper."

"Yeah? Funny that. The one who stole mine had a tiny one. Half an inch, if that."

"Still, it's a bit of a coincidence that they were both wearing nose rings, eh?"

"Well done, Sarge." said Eric coming out from under the desk when the crowd had finally dispersed.

"All in a day's work, lad," said O'Hara.

Guiltily, he looked at his desk. There were wads of paperwork piled precariously high that he hadn't even glanced at. He picked up a sheet of paper from the top of the pile. He read it, frowning more and more deeply, until his brow looked like it might cave in.

The last pieces of glass from the hatch were being knocked out. A voice was barking angrily. O'Hara looked up and swore under his breath to see the well-off Rottweiler in a headscarf.

"Can I help you, madam."

"Two of your men," she spat, "barged into my house yesterday, whilst I was out. My husband let them in. Despite his protests, they demolished three cupboards with chainsaws and then left without paying for the damage."

O'Hara was saved by the arrival of the husband in question.

"Ah! There you are, dear. I've told you not to run off like that. I hope you're not bothering these men."

"No. I'm just complaining about the cupboards."

"I told you not to. They were horrible old things anyway. Now, back on your lead. Come on. Worrying policemen — you'll be put down."

He looked in at O'Hara.

"Sorry, Officer. She doesn't understand. I'll keep her in for a few days."

O'Hara dropped into a chair. His stomach rumbled plaintively for breakfast and he felt faint. The chief came in.

"Presumably Eric's told you he saw the cupboard in Old Grethwick churchyard yesterday? He brilliantly left it till this morning to inform us all."

O'Hara glanced down at Eric, who shrank even further from sight under the desk.

"Er … I didn't get all the details."

"And a farmer was assaulted yesterday. Found with a slate broken over his head. Severely concussed. Another man was found in a horse trough babbling about houses crossing the road. So, presumably, you've thrown a cordon round the area?"

"Chief. I've only just found out. *And* it's a Wednesday. There's only a few officers around. And most of them won't go out into the country in summer because of their hay fever."

"Come on. Into a car. Eric — wherever he is — can deal with the office. If you want something doing in this place …"

On the way to Old Grethwick, O'Hara was struck that he no longer felt a thing about the chief anymore. He knew this, because his imagination was drooling more about food than her body. She could have been driving topless and he wouldn't have stared. Not until he'd eaten a sandwich, anyway. And it wasn't only that he was now involved with Miss Fetherby.

"Chief, something else happened at Old Grethwick a couple of days ago. I only just read the details today. I've been so busy with this cupboard business and things."

"Yes?"

"The vicar was murdered."

"And?"

"The guy — his name's Moore — who was charged with doing it pleaded not guilty yesterday morning in court. He's claiming that two officers were responsible and then beat a false confession out of him."

"Yes?"

"Well, the officers I sent to deal with the grave were Studds and Bass."

"What are you trying to say, Sergeant?"

There was a silence. O'Hara couldn't believe she was so stubborn and so blind.

"Well, I didn't have time just now to read the full details of the case, but ..."

"Yes?"

"Well, knowing Studds and Bass, isn't it just possible that this Moore bloke is ... y'know ... telling the truth?"

The chief frowned. "Constables Studds and Bass may be a little overzealous, Sergeant. But they get *results*."

"But how? They're going from house to house in Grethwick chopping up cupboards with chainsaws."

"Looked at mathematically, it means they're cutting down the odds. Sooner or later, they're bound to chop up the right one."

"Sooner or later? They're behaving like a couple of interior-decorating Herods."

"What are you trying to say, Sergeant?"

"They're psychopaths."

"Corrupt?"

"Maybe."

"I'm sure there are more corrupt officers in the force."

Again, silence broke out. What did she mean by that? The biros? But they were surely …? O'Hara felt inside his pocket. There were only thirty or forty in there. He remembered he'd parked on a double yellow line outside the library. Or had she found out about him shagging on duty? Rumbled already? His stomach seemed to think so. It rumbled more loudly than Krakatoa.

They reached the graveyard. Warily, both police officers got out of the car, hopped over the stone wall, and almost immediately, beneath the old oak, found plaster, cupboard prints and bits of flaked tile.

"They were here," said the chief. "These match debris found in Sandra Bottomley's house and that farmer's hedge … What's wrong with you, O'Hara?"

He was jumping up at a tree trying to pluck down an under ripe apple. The sergeant gave up his forlorn pogo and said sheepishly.

"I'm starving, Chief."

They resumed searching until she pointed at something

beside a gravestone. "Look! An arm!"

O'Hara went over to investigate a well-rotted limb lying in the grass.

"There's a sort of trail of scraped mud just here," said the chief. "Leading out of the graveyard." She produced a revolver from inside her jacket. "Where are Studds and Bass with the chainsaw when you need them?" she asked walking alongside a spoor of flattened grass which wound up behind the church.

O'Hara muttered under his breath, "Cutting down the statistical possibilities."

The trail ended at the asphalt car park.

"We've lost them," said the chief. She looked sharply at O'Hara, who was bending over a spilled black bag by the bins. "Sergeant? What are you doing?"

O'Hara straightened sheepishly.

"This bin bag's fallen over. And I saw some sandwiches which … well they're wrapped up. They smell all right. Hmm. Cheese and tomato. Quite fresh. And only a couple of bites taken out."

The chief cocked her head to one side. "Did you hear something?"

O'Hara shook his head. She held up her hand for quiet.

"It was a squeak. Like a giant mouse."

O'Hara looked at the bites that had been taken out of the sandwich and held it protectively close. Then they both heard a squeak. The chief lifted a lid from the nearest of three wheelie bins. Squashed inside was a squeaking woman tied up with bell rope. An empty metal bucket had been wedged on her head. Tipping the bin on its side, the two police officers dragged her out and took off the bucket. A grey cleaning cloth had been used to bind the woman's mouth.

"Oh my God!" she spluttered, when it was removed. "I'll never get the taste of Flash out of my mouth!"

"Who are you and what happened?" asked the chief.

"I'm Mrs Gobshaw! The church cleaner!"

The woman wept torrents over wrinkled cheeks, "Oh thank heavens you arrived to rescue me. I've been here since six o'clock this morning. I thought my Alec might have had the good sense to come looking for me. But he's probably down the pub, drunk."

"Just tell us what happened?" asked the chief impatiently.

"Oh, Alec will be cross. They stole his van."

"Who did? What?"

The cleaner thought for a second, remembered, then fainted. The chief looked like she wanted to kick the drooping body of the cleaner.

"Oh you silly old bag!"

"Don't call me a silly old bag!" said Mrs Gobshaw suddenly reviving

"Who tied you up?"

"You won't believe me."

"We will."

"You won't."

"Just try us, for God's sake."

"No. You'll think I'm mad. Put me in a home."

"We'll put you in something a bloody sight worse than a home if you don't start talking now," said the chief with a gorgeous snarl.

Mrs Gobshaw shrank back. Then said shiftily, "It was aliens."

"*Aliens?*"

"Very big aliens. Twenty feet high with these squeaky voices. They took me up into their space ship, took all my clothes off and prodded me and …"

The chief was clearly restraining her foot.

"What did they look like? Bits of houses?"

"Well, they were *very* tall. They towered over me. Like towers. Big ferocious expressions. I suppose one of them did look a bit like a cupboard. They probably looked down on earth from their flying saucer, saw a lot of buildings that seemed to be living here and decided to disguise themselves just like them."

"What was the registration of the van?"

"Oooo. I wouldn't know that. You'd have to ask Alec."

"What make was it then?"

"Blue."

"I said what *make?*"

"Ooo, you'd have to ask our Alec."

The chief rushed to the car. O'Hara helped Mrs Gobshaw to get steady on her feet.

"The things I've seen at this church." the cleaner told him. "First it was ghosts, then it was aliens. I'd hand in my notice to the vicar, but he's dead. Isn't it terrible? Stabbed whilst selling drugs to teenagers. Dear oh dear. And yesterday I saw a rotten arm in the graveyard. Just lying there, bold as you please. Its dead hand holding a half-eaten cheese and tomato sandwich."

# *Chapter 28*

Humans are pretty disparaging about cupboard love. But it's not a cynical devotion based on regular servings of Pedigree Chum. Cupboards, when infatuated with another room, can be tumultuous, intense, stormy. Prone to moods of dark, aching emptiness, cupboards are Byronesque in the brooding grandeur of their passions. The only thing that could legitimately deter say a hall or conservatory from having a fling with a cupboard, is that the ones used for storing lost property, sometimes cannot remember the name of the last room they shacked up with.

"Elsie!"

"Esmeralda!" she shouted back.

"Where are we going again?"

The attic bedroom sighed as she drove a stolen van haphazardly along the M5.

"Bristol … Bristol, Bristol, Bristol, Bristol."

"Oh yeah. What for?"

"I've told you about five million times."

Her patience became impatience.

"I'll go over it *once* more. Then I'm not saying it again. Ever."

"Watch out! Keep your windows on the road!"

There was a squeal of tyres and loud blasts of car horn.

"You know what you want, mate?" Esmeralda shouted at a driver who zoomed past. "An L-plate driven into your head with a six inch nail! Bloody humans — Right, what did you want to know?"

"Who, me? Did I ask a question?"

"Yes. You wanted to know what we're going to Bristol for."

"Right. And you told me everything. So now I know, and I'm not to ask you again. Ever."

The attic pushed the accelerator to the floor. Momentarily, she'd forgotten why they were going to Bristol too. Perhaps amnesia in buildings was catching?

"We're going to Bristol," she shouted eventually, "So that you can see my mate Weird Walt. He's an ex-builder who restores damaged and traumatised houses. He's going to do some plaster surgery on you."

"Oh yeah. I remember now. But isn't he a human? I thought you hated them?"

"I do. But this one's different. He understands us. They call him the 'House Whisperer'. He's got ears like a dog and can tune in to our frequency. That's why everyone thinks he's mad. Other humans are always putting him in special hospitals because they catch him talking to walls."

Sitting in the back of the van, part hidden under a large tarpaulin, the cupboard felt suddenly tired. With all the vibrations and Esmeralda's explanation going on and on, the cupboard began to fall asleep. He didn't register that something momentous was happening inside him. Since that kiss under the trees in the graveyard, he had lost the terrible feelings of alienation that had haunted him since crashing into Esmeralda. Now, as he drifted further and further into the underworld of dreams, he began to get strong warm feelings that he *belonged*. He belonged to *her*.

When he woke, he could hear Esmeralda's voice talking at its very gruffest. The tones of a man speaking could also be heard. Feeling too snuggly to move from under the tarpaulin, the cupboard lay and listened.

"Walt," said Esmeralda's voice. "I'm in worse trouble than when I left. You know I knocked those grannies over and stole their car to go to a revolutionary meeting in Birmingham?"

"Nyick, nacky, doo, doo. Nyick. Bick. Bicky bong troddy pip squeak," the man's voice replied.

"Walt! Snap out of it! I need help. *Urgently*."

This time the man replied in an American accent, "I'm going through a new phase. I'm inventing a whole new transcendent language, so that buildings and people will be able to communicate and live in perfect harmony."

"Walt. Have they been giving you pills? Have they? Walt?"

The cupboard could hear Esmeralda getting desperate. There was a slapping noise as she hit Walt's face a few times with her guttering.

"Listen. This cupboard is wanted by the police. It's killed seventy-five councillors. I need you to disguise it as something. You know. Plaster surgery. Like you did for Ronnie the Bus Shelter after it ate those kids who sprayed, 'Southampton for the Cup,' all over his walls."

Suddenly, light poured in on the cupboard as the tarpaulin

was lifted. He saw the face of Weird Walt looking in. The man was wearing sunglasses. A huge grey frizzy beard obscured most of the lower half of his face. The top half was engulfed by a twelve-gallon hat.

"Yinky yonk, nap foll, adel jub alleg ib."

"What's that supposed to mean?"

"Put a moustache on it."

Esmeralda was incredulous.

"A moustache? On a cupboard?"

"Ropple doss cun lod."

"I meant I wanted a *proper* disguise. Turn him into a telephone kiosk, or a guardsman's hut. You know."

"No. A moustache is a tried and tested way of disguising a wanted criminal. When I broke out of hospital the first few times, I always did it with a moustache. Then I grew a beard."

"But you're a human!"

"It's humans you're trying to fool."

Esmeralda leaned against the van in despair.

"Yackong litrot blez."

"Oh talk properly for St Paul's sake."

"That's not the language of enlightenment sister. I merely said, give me a few minutes, and I'll soon knock one up."

The cupboard edged out of the back of the van. Esmeralda looked tired. Her windows needed cleaning, and her door a fresh lick of red paint. But the cupboard noticed none of this. He only felt relief. Here at last was the building he belonged to. The nagging worry was that he felt that they should be *joined* somehow. When their doors had met so meltingly in that park, (or had it been a rose garden? there had been wreaths of withered flowers nearby at any rate) everything had seemed so right, as if the moment of the kiss should last forever. But now the cupboard felt that, somehow, the whole thing hadn't gone far enough. He wanted to be joined to her more substantially. More finally. In a way that wasn't altogether easy to describe.

"Darling? Remember me? I'm Esmeralda?"

"Yes."

"Walt is just knocking up a disguise for you. He's in no condition to do healing work right now. So we'll have to go to this doctor's surgery I know. She'll give you something for your amnesia. A new light bulb for your ceiling or something. I don't exactly know how serious it is. Then we'll be able to go together to join our comrade high rise blocks in Birmingham and ..."

"Nogdoff lerrrrtad!"

It was Walt. He was carrying a six foot black moustache.

"Or to put it more colloquially — try this for size."

He held the huge hairpiece over the cupboard's door. "Complete transformation."

Esmeralda was astounded. It was even better than her impression of a football changing room.

"Walt! You're a genius!"

"Nuggle potad vum," he replied modestly, getting out a hammer and four inch nails.

"But he looks almost human!" she cried.

"Ow! Yow! Ouch! Ow!" cringed the cupboard as the nails were banged in.

"Oh darling! I'd hardly know you."
Esmeralda kissed him and laughed.
"And it tickles like mad!"

# Chapter 29

Alec Gobshaw wasn't particularly bothered that a cupboard and an attic had trussed up his wife, but he was outraged that they'd half-inched his rusty Bedford.

"They should be demolished for that."

He'd have taken it out on his own cupboards, but Constables Studds and Bass had been in earlier with the power tools.

"Just a sensible precaution, sir." Bass had shouted above the racket of a Kango hammer that was spreading devastation under the stairs. "It wouldn't do for this kind of thing to spread to other cupboards in the area."

"I hope I'm going to get compensation, that's all!" Mr Gobshaw had grumbled.

O'Hara looked at the mess of plaster and splintered wood on Mr Gobshaw's carpet and wondered what the insurance companies would make of it. The constables had done the whole street.

"For hours, all England's been on the alert for a cupboard-driven, blue Bedford and nobody's reported so much as a door handle," the chief raved gorgeously.

Using the siren, she cut her way through the late afternoon traffic. O'Hara sneaked a look at her. Frustration only made her perfect face more divine. Maybe it was that very perfection which made O'Hara uneasy. This obsession with the serial killing cupboard? Maybe she did want to stop it before it murdered another flock of politicians but something about the cupboard business stank, and it wasn't just the councillors. Call it Bobby's intuition, but O'Hara had a flash of insight as the chief drove towards the station at seventy miles an hour through Grethwick Town Centre. It crossed his mind that she was *corrupt*. The word seemed to fit more snugly than her uniform. The idea that she was responsible for the cupboard murders went over the sergeant like a tidal wave of sewage. Nobody could be perfect all the way through. Somebody as perfect as she was on the outside had to be blemished on the inside. Otherwise she'd bloody well stop Studds and Bass beating confessions out of innocent people. O'Hara knew it was his duty to bring his knowledge to a higher authority. But what worried him was that they might be even more corrupt. The police force was like a leg in a stocking — the higher up you went, the naughtier you got.

In the station car park the chief switched off the ignition and, to O'Hara's amazement, let her head rest on the steering wheel. It was such a human moment, such an expression of weakness, that the sergeant felt fleetingly guilty at having thought her corrupt. Then she looked across at him.

"I need a pen?" she smiled.

"A pen?"

O'Hara panicked. He felt in his pocket and produced one of twenty or thirty pens that he'd put there for "safe keeping".

"What for?" he asked, offering her a whole bundle.

"To prise a cork from this baton. It's stuck."

He watched as she uncorked a truncheon, and drank from the handle.

"That's better!" she smacked her lips, and offered the flask.

O'Hara took it and sniffed. "Scotch?"

There was lipstick round the end of the baton.

"But we're on duty," gasped O'Hara.

The chief retrieved the baton, shrugged, and knocked the cork back in with the flat of her hand. O'Hara stared in shock. It was as if she'd read his mind and confessed!

For the rest of the afternoon, the vision of a worm-riddled police force haunted O'Hara. He had only to see a member of the public to blush with shame. It almost took his mind off sex and Miss Fetherby. She'd asked him to come to dinner that evening. Did that mean she'd let him do it again? Not if she found out he was bent Bobby, that was for certain. Surely, she couldn't really fancy him? No woman ever had before.

After work, he drove to her house as fast as his testosterone would go. Miss Fetherby met him at the front door.

"Ah, Mr O'Hara."

"Call me …" he stopped in mid-sentence to see that she was wearing a Bloomsbury-style silk dress. From her headscarf a peacock feather trailed flamboyantly.

"*What* shall I call you?"

He stuttered.

"The boys at work call me Cyrano."

"That was the man with the big …"

"Nose. Yes."

O'Hara stepped over the threshold. She shut the door.

"And what is your real first name?"

"Frank."

She sighed — a bubble bursting.

"Well I'm glad you came in uniform, Cyrano."

In the living room, classical music was only just louder than the candlelight which played softly over a curvaceous sofa. O'Hara sat down. She sat down. On his lap.

"So …" said Cyrano, dry mouthed as she undid the buttons of his tunic, "What do you do during the day?"

"Oh I dream." she said in a fairly businesslike voice.

"You don't have a job then?" he said as his string vest was exposed.

"No. My parents left me a large sum of money when they died. I've most of it invested." she shifted off him "So I dabble in this and that. Mathematics of course, criminology, and …" She unzipped his trousers.

"… things like that."

She pulled his Dr Martens off. Then his socks.

"But mostly I just dream."

"What of?" croaked O'Hara, still not daring to make a second move after her succession of first ones.

"Undressing policemen of course. And sucking them off …"

"But my nose?" said O'Hara afterwards. "What about my nose? Don't you find it offensive?"

"It's not my favourite part of you," she answered blithely, recovering her headscarf from O'Hara's grasp and the long feather that he'd bitten in half. "And I wouldn't want to stare at it whilst I was eating raspberry ripple ice cream, but …"

She stopped, because across the floor, where she'd tossed the sergeant's trousers after tugging them off, stones were strewn across the carpet.

"What on earth did you have in your pockets?" she said, leaning over to pick up a sample. "Rock?"

"It's just a bit of building, Miss Fetherby."

"Call me Fanny."

"Fanny?"

O'Hara's eyebrows leapt up before he could stop them.

"Yes."

She took her horn-rimmed glasses from a coffee table and put them on, then carefully examined the debris.

"A most interesting specimen. Where did you get it?"

O'Hara gave the latest instalments of the lost property cupboard saga, leaving out his suspicions of the chief. Fanny Fetherby listened as she turned and prodded at the rubble in her palm. "These are fragments from the cupboard's accomplice?"

"Probably. Do you know where you threw my underpants?"

"And you've no idea where these criminals are now hiding?"

"None."

"One moment, Cyrano." Fanny left the room. Then her head reappeared at the door. "Oh. Your underpants are on top of the lampshade."

O'Hara retrieved his undies. She returned, dressed in tweeds and carrying a violin case.

"My other sock? Do you know where you threw that as well?"

"Oh dear. It would appear to have landed in with the goldfish."

As O'Hara wrung out his sock into the bowl, she opened

the case and took out a violin. She plucked a string.

"I didn't know you were musical."

She wasn't. As she proceeded to make strange scraping noises by drawing the bow unmusically over the strings, the sergeant noticed that the goldfish was lying bent on the surface of its now discoloured water. He put his fingers in his ears. Then he put his socks in his ears. With a strange intent look on her face, she played on horribly.

Then the room went silent. O'Hara finished getting dressed in relief. Fanny put the instrument back in its case.

"Would you mind terribly, Cyrano," she asked thoughtfully, "if we took a trip out to old Grethwick graveyard?"

"What, *now*? Off duty?"

"Do you want to catch this cupboard or not?"

"When I'm at work, yes, but …?"

"And you'll have to go in plain clothes. Fortunately, I still have one of my late father's suits upstairs."

Yawning, and with one wet foot, O'Hara drove up to the graveyard. The night sky was either cloudy or the moon and stars had done a runner.

"You see," he said, as they stood beneath the old oak, "Here's where we discovered the bits of stone."

Fanny shone a torch on the ground. It was inevitable that she should bring out a magnifying glass. She picked up more shards of rock. Then, instead of following the trail left by the cupboard and attic, she went back, venturing slowly to the centre of the graveyard.

"They went this way," said O'Hara, pointing up to the church.

"But they came from over here somewhere."

Approaching a grave, Fanny kicked over fresh soil. A bouquet of rotten flesh wafted up O'Hara's nostrils in wavy lines. Then both he and Miss Fetherby spun round in alarm to hear a rustling behind one of the tombstones.

"What on earth?"

Fanny's torch picked out a man with a pony-tail bending over and cupping his hands. As the spotlight hit him, he leapt. There was a curse.

"Excuse me? What are you doing?" asked Fanny, going over to the man.

It was Wacca. He staggered to his feet in a crumpled mud-caked suit and triumphantly held a croaking black toad aloft.

"Sorry. Didn't mean to alarm you. I'm from FOE. Just relocating a colony of … *Fuck!*"

The toad had wriggled and leapt from his grasp.

"Where did it go?"

The professional and amateur detectives left him to it with a shake of their heads.


After a few more minutes of sepulchral investigation, Fanny stopped abruptly beside a tombstone and clicked off the torch.

"Cyrano, we must go at once to Nuttall Lane in Bristol, to arrest this cupboard. Perhaps you could put a backup squad of officers on standby. With nets, ropes, a large van and tranquilliser guns."

"Don't be daft. How can you know they're in Nuttall Lane?"

"Questions in the car. I'll talk as you drive."

In his prickly tweed suit, O'Hara drove despairingly west as Fanny explained.

"It's obvious that this attic was on its way from Bristol when it crashed with the cupboard. Where was it going? We don't know. Its journey was interrupted when it crashed into a murderous cupboard. Does it turn the cupboard over to the police? No, it falls in with the cupboard, which suggests that it decided to throw in its lot with the murderer. Whatever its original purpose was in leaving Bristol, the chance meeting changed it. In partnership with a wanted criminal, and being hunted down all over the country, the attic knew it had to get rid of the bodies, then find somewhere to lie up and hide until the hue and cry died down. After dumping the bodies in a graveyard, it's just possible that it decided to make for a city where it already had criminal allies. Other buildings it could lean on. Bristol. It's a bit of a long shot perhaps, but if they have headed for Bristol, my guess is that they will be located in the neighbourhood of Nuttall Lane. The place where the attic was built and where until recently, it lived. Rooms are nothing if not homing creatures."

"It all sounds a bit far-fetched if you ask me. How do you know it's from Nuttall Lane?"

"Most of old Bristol was destroyed during the war, not much of the housing near the docks survived. Recently, some of those that remained were condemned, because they were made of a local stone — used mainly for poorer houses — though some of three stories. The stone is a rarity. A sandstone formed in the Triassic and older Permian strata. It was so soft, locals said it could be cut like cheese. Utterly useless for housing in the long term because it tended to "Crump" and make the house flop over. The rock is yellow with a greenish tinge containing fragments of quartz."

She took out the sample of stone that had been lying in the churchyard and crumbled it in her palm. Bits of quartz glittered milkily. O'Hara almost crashed as he stared.

"How do you know all this?"

"I'm a Bristol woman. I lived there as a child and in my teens. I still like to read about it. Both general and specific knowledge of an area are bound to come in useful to an amateur detective. I could give you the annual rainfall in both inches and centimetres of eight different areas of the city."

"What's rain got to do with it?"

"Nothing yet. But I have it stored in my memory, should I ever need it."

O'Hara began to feel worried. He'd no idea when he'd gone looking for the key in her underclothes that he was getting involved with a woman who could remember the annual rainfall for eight different places round Bristol. In centimetres *and* inches. It was frightening. He drove round a roundabout twice in consternation. Then asked, "You know the other night? When …?"

"You shamelessly seduced me? Yes."

"Why did you go to all that trouble with footprints and stories about one-legged men? I mean, *really*?"

"I told you the truth. Or at least, most of it. I have time on my hands — to dream. I've always had a passion for Conan Doyle. And surely, in the case of policemen, a little mystery is appropriate.

"And what was the rest of the truth?"

She paused, then admitted,

"I've found that men in uniform are frightened of intelligent women. I know that's a generalisation but, well, are you?"

"Yes."

"You see." she sighed. "Deception is absolutely essential to get one's man."

# Chapter 30

Harry Swaggot, yawned and ran his fingers through two strands of hair on the pork scratching of his scalp. Midnight had been and gone. Whatever had woken him hadn't woken his wife. But then, she'd once slept through a plane crash coming back from a holiday in Ibiza. Swaggot had pulled her body clear of the plane's wreckage, only to hear her snoring loudly and mumbling in her sleep. Swaggot lay awake listening. What had woken him? A burglar? But a Security firm patrolled the area regularly. So the noise that had woken him could only have been a bat with faulty radar hitting the bedroom window or … *He heard it again.*

It was a croak. His heart was quite small for his body — as other people might have small feet or ears — and the tiny organ could hardly cope with the rush of blood. A croak? In the house? Impossible! The noise had seemed to come from the bottom of the stairs. Swaggot imagined, vividly, an old man, ashen faced, clawing his way up plushly carpeted steps one at a time.

*"Did you hear something, Jemima?"* he hissed, shaking his wife.

She snored louder. Swaggot told himself to get a grip. If a person had entered the house, alarms would be ringing. No pathetically ill person could heave themselves over twenty foot garden walls, and not get snagged in the barbed wire. Harry put it down to overwork. The stress of opening a new mine and wangling the slightly dodgy road contract was obviously telling on his psyche. Then he heard the big croak again. In the house for *absolute bloody certain*. Swaggot sat up as if a nurse with a grudge had given him a tetanus jab in the arse. He shook his wife so hard, her innards could be heard sloshing about. Jemima only snored more harshly.

Harry considered hiding under the bed. Then, whoever it was, would only find Jemima, and do whatever they were going to do, to her. She wouldn't even notice, she was slumbering so deeply. The other option was to get his gun from the bedside cabinet. He'd bought it to make him feel safer. He envisaged a gunfight on the stairs with some desperate bastard from a run-down housing estate and felt more imperilled than ever.

With a handgun pointing into the darkness, he manoeuvred his twenty stone bulk over the carpet on tiptoe. After three steps, his toes were screaming for mercy. He opened the bedroom door which made a scuffing sound on thick carpet and switched on the lights. They went off. He switched them on again. They went off. On. Off. On. Off. On. They stayed on. If somebody was playing with the lights, then they could only be in the utility room adjoining the kitchen, because that was where the switchboard was. Harry looked down the corridor, then tiptoed down the stairs slowly.

With senses tauter than the elastic in his silk pyjamas, Harry crept through his large hall, gun trembling in his hand. Whoever the groaner was, they had no taste. The signed Reynolds prints were still there. The display of pewter tankards worth maybe two thousand pounds were untouched on their plinth. Then the lights went off again. Harry was stranded at the kitchen door.

"Who's there?" he asked. "You'd better come out. I've phoned the police."

"Liar," croaked a deep voice behind him.

Harry spun round with a screech of fright and fired recklessly. There, at the foot of the stairs was an enormous toad. Twelve foot high and glowing as if it had a bad case of radiation poisoning. Harry blazed away at it. Bullets merely caused ripples in its warty skin. Harry ran into the kitchen and slammed the door. He leaned against it, panting hysterically, then looked round.

An entire menagerie of flat glowing animals chorused, "Hi, Harry."

There were badgers, foxes, rabbits, hares, mice, hedgehogs, magpies, crows, wrens — and all of them gigantic and glowing green. There were even a few ghostly looking people. Harry Swaggot opened the door to run for it. The toad croaked, "Hi, Harry."

With a shriek of fear, the mine owner staggered back into his kitchen, fell over a chair and sprawled heavily on the tiles. The gun skittled across the floor.

"Harry Swaggot, we presume." said the toad.

"How are you doing this?" Harry stuttered, scrambling to his feet. "What do you want with me? I've done nothing."

The words poured out of his mouth in a guilty rush. A hedgehog transformed into a woman wearing Victorian attire. It was eerie. She was definitely a ghost, because Harry could see his mahogany table through her. In fact, it was Ada Brackenbury, supported by a delegation of Old Grethwick ghosts in animal drag.

"Good evening, Mr Swaggot. I presume we *are* communicating with Mr Harry Swaggot esquire, owner of Swaggot Mining Company and managing director of Blakstuff Road Building Contractors?"

"No. You've got the wrong guy. I'm Harry's brother Stan."

The animals tut-tutted and stared at him in disdain. Ada was particularly displeased.

"Must you dissemble quite so brazenly?" she asked.

"I don't know what you're talking about," gabbled Harry. "Harry's on holiday in Florida. And if I were you, whatever you are, I'd clear off out before he gets back. He's got a nasty temper. And if he returns to find a load of vermin in his kitchen, he'll probably ..." Swaggot's voice petered out desperately. "How's all this being done? That's what I want to know?"

Ada said, "Harold, permit me to make our position clear to you. We are a representation of ghosts, spirits, and poltergeists, from Old Grethwick churchyard. Your recent activities in that area have greatly inconvenienced us. And we require you to help us in our plight."

"I'm sorry, you'll have to talk to Harry about all this when he gets ..."

Ada's ears began to trickle smoke.

"We appear to have two problems to deal with. Firstly, our graves have been usurped by a gang of murdered councillors."

She watched as Swaggot's face stiffened and paled.

"We require, from you, information about the nature of their deaths, so that we might go to the proper authorities and have the bodies identified, exhumed and removed."

"I don't know what Harry's been up to," Harry began, "but it's got nothing to do with …"

Ada swept on with her narrative,

"Secondly. The proposed route for your road through our resting-place is quite simply unacceptable. You will be required to change your plans in this regard if our visits are not to be a regular and painful occurrence for yourself and your imaginary brother Stan. Therefore, we would require a solemn pledge from you tonight that the road will not go ahead."

Swaggot stood up.

"Right. I'll phone him in Florida tomorrow. First thing."

Ada sighed.

"Oh dear, Mr Swaggot. I can see that we shall be required to be firm. Let me introduce you to a colleague, Mr Jonathon Trundle."

The giant toad by the kitchen door, metamorphosed into Jonathon. Twelve feet high and flat, he looked like a cinema screen.

"I'm not afraid of ghosts," said Swaggot queasily.

"I am sad to find, Mr Swaggot, that you are unrepentant about the proposed destruction of our home." Jonathon's eyes glared down like two traffic lights on go. "But then I suppose destruction of habitat is the only thing you're good at. I recently discovered, after a little digging around in the council offices, that your company are operating an open cast mine on what *was* a nature reserve!"

Harry Swaggot, averting his eyes said,

"It wasn't a nature reserve. It was a just a bit of grass and trees that a local group of idiots *called* a nature reserve. Because it had a rare bit of moss. A bit of bloody moss. I ask you. That and some birds."

"Permit us," said Jonathon, also smoking slightly from his flapping ears, "to demonstrate, just exactly what destruction of habitat feels like."

The ceiling broke in. A vast chute descended and concrete began splattering over the kitchen floor. Swaggot started forward, aghast.

"Hey! Bloody hell! Stop!"

In seconds he was up to his shins in thick folds of cement. The shute belched grey ready-mix onto sideboards, tables and chairs.

"Okay! What do you want to know?"

The chute vanished. In his pyjamas, Swaggot squidged through the mess and stared up at the ceiling.

"How did you get a cement lorry up there?"

Ada hovered over the lumps of ready-mix.

"You're prepared at last to talk to us sensibly are you, Mr Swaggot? And pledge that the road …?"

He interrupted her, sweat glistening on his pate, hands trembling.

"Look, you can't do this! Barge into people's houses, then pour concrete everywhere."

"You seem to," said Ada.

"Be reasonable. We've got to have roads. We've got to have mining. I gave good money to compensate for the bloody environmental damage. I didn't make the decision. I was asked to open a mine there."

"What do you mean?" asked Jonathon, rippling like a huge flag over Swaggot's table. "Who asked you to open the mine?"

Swaggot staggered in the concrete, and sat down in trying to get out. In grey pyjamas he searched for a bit of floor untouched by cement.

"Look at my bloody floor! Five grand those tiles cost! My table. Real mahogany with leaves that unwind, to seat sixteen people. Bloody cement all over it."

Jonathon shouted, "*Who* invited you to open the bloody mine? Eh?"

Swaggot evaded the question again.

"Look, I need a bath, or I'll have concrete feet."

"He's not listening, folks."

The ghostly animals snatched up various items of kitchenware. China plates went smashing to the floor.

"No! No!" screamed Swaggot. "You don't know what you're breaking! That's Mason and Ironstone's!"

Red and blue broken shards flew through the air like shrapnel. Copperware pans and a silver tureen and ladle were flung into the still wet concrete. The ceiling burst open again. Hot tarmac came steaming down and covered the lot.

"You vandals! You fucking vandals! That silver's rare! It's Newenham's of Cork. Stop it! Please!"

The mahogany table spontaneously combusted along with

the kitchen units made from rainforest hardwood. Swaggot wept openly at the destruction.

"Please. Do this to somebody else. I'm not the guy you should be hurting."

A few explosions rent holes in the walls. Smoke, steam and dust left Swaggot choking. Jonathon peered through one of the holes that had been blown in the walls.

"There's rather a nice living room through here, with a baby grand piano and leather upholstered chairs. Shall we give it the treatment?"

The mine owner leapt through the concrete and tarmac with a yell. He stood distraught and grey in front of the hole, arms spread-eagled to prevent the ghosts entering.

"Bugger off! You can't do this to innocent folk! Clear out before I call in an archbishop and have him exorcise the lot of you."

The ghosts vanished from the room. Swaggot stared across the tarmac and concrete kitchen in surprise.

"Eh?" His whole body drooped in relief. "Thank God."

But Jonathon's voice came from the next room.

"Cooeeee!"

The mine owner turned and looked through the hole in his wall. His living room, which had been designed by a firm in London, stank. It had been transformed into a bog. Lichen and mosses wallpapered the room. Reeds and bulrushes were sticking out of a squidgy green carpet. Several ducks waddled from under the piano as it collapsed with rot.

"Now for the upstairs." said Jonathon.

Swaggot got on his knees. Brown water squelched through his pyjamas.

"Alright. I'll tell you all I know. I was told to keep it totally secret. It isn't very much."

Jonathon, shimmering and green, drifted up to the hole in the wall and spoke through it frankly, "Every little helps so far as the next floor of your house is concerned."

"I was asked to submit plans to open the mine by the chief engineer of Grethwick Council. He suggested the site and got planning for it. He did a bit of a deal with local environmental groups. I don't know what. I had to pay a couple of grand. He said I could mine the site for ore and sell the rock to my own road company at whatever price I wanted to build the by-pass."

"And what's that got to do with the councillors getting knocked off?" asked Jonathon.

"They all got a bit nosy about the finance. How it was being spent and some late modifications to the plans."

"Like what?"

"Brinkman. Guy Brinkman. The chief engineer. Haunt *him*. Smash *his* place up. He'll tell you more than I can."

"What were the late modifications, and what happened to the councillors? Or can I hear the roof turning into a more sustainable ecosystem?"

"Alright!"

Swaggot shouted as a chute broke through the ceiling in his living room and dropped several hundredweight of frogspawn. Ducks quacked in alarm at the disturbance and began to flap around Swaggot's head.

"When the councillors found out that Brinkman wanted to start the by-pass from the middle of Grethwick, the shit — understandably — hit the fan. I'm not saying he had anything to do with the people getting murdered, but it was him who organised the entertainment on the day they disappeared."

Jonathon looked startled. He craned forward a little, as if he hadn't quite heard.

"Sorry? I thought you said the by-pass was starting in the middle of town."

Swaggot looked desperate. His pyjamas were so wet he had to hold them up by hand or they would have slid down under their own weight. He shivered in his saturated clothes and said, "I did."

This confession startled several of the ghosts out of their animal drag.

"A by-pass that begins in the centre of town?" gasped Jonathon incredulously. "Why?"

"I can't say any more. It's Guy Brinkman you want to speak to. Not me. It was his idea. To start it from the police station. I just went along with it. For the money."

The walls of Swaggot's new house began to tremble as if it were stood on the slopes of an erupting volcano.

"What was behind Guy Brinkman's idea, Mr Swaggot?"

"I don't know. I really, really don't know! Leave me alone. Leave my house."

Bricks and beams came crashing down. One of the ducks flapped up to perch on Swaggot's head as the roof fell in. The mine owner staggered in bog water before overbalancing with a splash to sit in an oozy black mire. The duck on his nonce quacked and took flight. Like a big fat Buster Keaton, Swaggot watched as the house collapsed around him. Then, after several minutes of deafening destruction, everything went quiet. With a slutching noise, Harry hauled himself up and clutching the elastic of his saturated pyjama bottoms, clambered out over piles of plasterboard, tiles and guttering. The ghosts were nowhere to be seen. He stood uncertainly and looked up at the night sky. Frogspawn dripped down his bald brow. *Jemima!* He searched the rubble of his house like the survivor of a natural disaster. Then stopped as he heard steady snores coming from beneath an overturned bathtub.

Swaggot sat beside a Jacuzzi that was spasmodically squirting dribbles of water. He put his head in his hands and joined in. A few minutes later, the flash of a torch disturbed his sobs. It was one of the security guards. A man's voice said, "Everything alright, Mr Swaggot?"

# Chapter 31

The doctor's surgery sighed and said, "Would you mind standing in the waiting room for a moment please?"

"Not at all, we get on quite well in fact," the lost property cupboard answered.

"Don't worry. Sick humans don't start arriving until much later in the morning."

The cupboard squeezed out. The attic bedroom listened as the surgery spoke in low concerned tones.

"I'm afraid there's nothing we can do. I've examined your friend both internally and externally and I think I can diagnose the problem with some certainty at this point. He's a lost property cupboard."

The attic looked concerned.

"Is that bad?"

"Well, not necessarily bad as such. But the vagueness is congenital and incurable."

The Surgery paused to let the news sink in. Esmerelda frowned, making her curtains dip slightly at the windows.

"But surely even a lost property cupboard should have *some* ability to remember basic things like its name and where it came from."

The surgery shook its ceiling.

"Perhaps. Your friend certainly seems to have been traumatised by recent experiences with humans. There was a lot of blood on the shelves. But lost property cupboards are famed for experiencing existential angst. They're all very much into Camus and Sartre. I came across one in 1953 which was looking for itself because it was lost and thought it should be in a lost property cupboard on the Paris Left Bank. Thirty years later it was fished out of the Seine. All I can suggest is that you put yours in an institution."

"That's a heartless thing to do."

"It might be the best thing for him. He needs to feel that he *belongs*. He'll never remember who or what he is, until he has lost things placed in him and he's fulfilling a useful function in society."

"He *belongs* to me," said Esmeralda. "Humans have obviously abused him and he's blanked out the trauma. He needs love and affection."

The surgery was used to Guardian-reading attic bedrooms reacting in this way, and replied a little irascibly, "You must ask yourself, whether dressing him as a human in a large overcoat and hat, and nailing a moustache over his door, is going to help in any way to overcome his identity problems?"

"So you can't prescribe anything?"

"Rest. Some fresh paint taken internally might brighten him up and relieve feelings of depression."

Esmeralda and the cupboard left the surgery in despondency. Fortunately, a sea fog had drifted over the city making it easier to creep inconspicuously through the streets. The couple were dressed in makeshift coats and peaked caps that Weird Walt had manufactured in his shed. But they still attracted stares as pedestrians went by. Peering up at two enormous shapes appearing out of the mist, people feared they might get duffed up and crossed to the other side of the road. They'd heard of blokes with square shoulders but …!"

"Where are we going?" squeaked the cupboard.

"The docks."

"Oh yeah. I remember."

"Actually, I hadn't mentioned it before."

"Hey? Why not?"

"Because it's very secret. Shhh. More humans coming."

A man and a woman passed beneath a streetlamp up ahead. In the yellowy white air, it could be seen that they were both dressed in tweed suits. The man's nose was glowing faintly red.

"Fanny, I know we haven't known each other long, but …"

"Yes?"

"I'm a policeman. You're somebody who reads crime novels."

"So?"

"It's bloody freezing. It's past midnight and I'm knackered. Sherlock Holmes is fiction. In real life nobody solves crimes by reason and psychological guesses based on the annual rainfall in Bristol."

"If more detectives did," Fanny argued, "the criminal population would be hounded off the streets, and nobody would dare to pinch a sock off a clothesline for fear that the hounds of the law would soon be ferociously baying at their heels."

O'Hara stepped off the pavement to make way for a couple of big blokes who appeared suddenly in the fog.

"Honestly, crime fighting in real life is just sheer bloody graft. Standing at a desk for hours and writing complaints in a book. Going door to door interviewing people. Drawing up lists of suspects and what they might look like. Getting forensics to look at blood samples and match them. Squeezing the lesser crooks till they squeal on the bigger ones. It's … I'm sorry, I've offended you haven't I? But I'm a bloody professional and it's … Fanny? Miss Fetherby."

She'd stopped and was peering into wispy banks of fog behind them with perplexity. She said, "Those men we just passed?"

O'Hara leaned against a lamp-post in despair.

"We can't start randomly interviewing people to see if they know anything."

"They've vanished into the mist. But didn't they seem terribly large to you?"

"Probably on the way back from the gym. Weightlifters. Does it matter?"

"But the one with the moustache? Wasn't it as wide as the pavement?"

"Fanny? You're surely not suggesting …?"

O'Hara recalled he'd had to take several steps to one side to let them go past.

"They came upon us so suddenly. And obviously both were in disguise. Come, Sergeant! We must prevent their escape!"

"In this mist? They could have gone anywhere."

Fanny Fetherby blinked sternly over horn rimmed frames at her big nosed Watson.

"You aren't thinking, Mr O'Hara. They were headed in the direction of the docks. And one of them was disguised as a sailor."

Later, by a quayside, two rooms huddled in between large crates of bananas. Esmeralda confided, "We're going to sneak on board one of these ships. I'm going to pretend to be a cabin and you'll have to pretend to be a cabin boy."

"With a big moustache like this?"

"You've got a high voice. For a human," she reasoned.

"Couldn't we *both* be cabins?"

"You haven't got a bed. Or a carpet."

"I could be a hold."

"You're too small."

"A bridge?"

"You haven't got a helm. Stop worrying. It'll be okay."

The cupboard was trembling beside her.

"But I feel ridiculous in this sailor costume. Why do we have to get on a ship?"

"Well, I bet you can't swim." The attic bedroom peeked round stacks of crates to make sure they hadn't been followed. "And we've got to get out of this country before the police get hold of you. You're a wanted cupboard." She drew back into hiding and grumbled, "Besides, it's no good trying to start a revolution here. The buildings are innately conservative. Too stuck in their own foundations. We've got to get to another country — Bolivia, Russia, China, Nicaragua. We'll have to spread the idea of world revolution to all our brothers and sisters elsewhere. Liberate foreign houses from oppression by humans. We'll incite yurts, tepees, skyscrapers, mosques, igloos, log cabins, the Eiffel Tower, the Leaning Tower of Pisa, the Vatican, Sydney Opera House and all the others, to join in the struggle against those two legged termites that are making our lives hell."

"Well, so long as we don't cause any trouble. Though I can't quite see the point."

For a moment, Esmeralda stopped surveying a fogbound ship for an opportunity to stowaway. She said gently, "Can't you see? Are you blind?"

"It *is* foggy."

"My dear, you are a prime example of an oppressed room. What is a lost property cupboard? It's negative stereotyping, that's what. Do you want to know what you really are?"

"Er ... okay."

"You're a liberator of oppressed objects."

"Come again?"

Esmeralda pressed her walls against his and nuzzled him with her front.

"You ... you forgetful freedom fighter, are a room which saves objects from having to be owned by humans. But it's typical of their negative personality enforcement, their buildingist conception of the world, that they should demean you by calling you a lost property cupboard. My dear, dear man, you are so much more than that. We're going to travel the world, and you will be able to liberate grateful didgeridoos from their abusive aboriginal owners. There are millions of objects out there just waiting to be freed by us. By you. Downtrodden snowshoes from thoughtless trampling Alaskans, overworked rifles from Afghanistan, pasta-making machines from slave-driving Italian restaurateurs, depressed computers from America."

Her door met his passionately. Again the cupboard was a little disturbed. He broke away.

"Should we be doing this here? Isn't it a bit *rude?*"

"It's the most beautiful thing that can happen between two buildings. We must be liberated sexually if we are to liberate others."

"Yes, but ... Hey! What are you doing? What are you getting on top of me for?"

"I *am* an attic bedroom. They always go on top."

"Yes, but ..."

"But what?"

The cupboard was pressed to the ground as Esmeralda clambered up. He wailed, "But I'm the man!"

"Don't be reactionary, darling. That's it. You're better down there. Deep down. Like that. Oh. Yes. Just there. As if you were under stairs. Going up. Up. Up. Yes. Ohhhhh. The stairs. You see? Don't struggle. I'll fall. I'll ... Oh ... Oh ... Oh ... Darling."

She kept disappearing and reappearing at the top of the crates.

"My darling cupboard. Oh my roof. It's coming off. It's

coming. Coming. Coming offffff. Ohhhhhhhhh!"

At that moment, as the cupboard's moustache dropped and fell to the floor like a stuffed anteater, lights cut through the mist and illuminated the fugitives. Talk about *coitus interruptus!* They were caught in a position so compromising that the rooms froze in mid-climax. A loudhailer echoed muggily on the sodden air.

"Don't move. The entire area is cordoned off and there is no escape. Please don't attempt any sudden or violent actions. Remain completely still."

Esmeralda leapt off the cupboard in horror. She shot from between the crates as thick nets flew with a hiss into the air and a riot squad came running out of the mist. With a leap that would have been the envy of any salmon for grace, Esmeralda leapt off the waterfront and into the chilly waters of the River Avon.

In a high pitched wail that was beyond the reach of a human ear she cried, "My darling! Jump! Jump!"

But as she strenuously swam to safety, she heard the cupboard cry out over the noise of sirens clamouring, and the shouts of humans struggling to restrain her lover.

"Esmeralda!" he shouted. "Esmeralda! I love you!"

His door was slammed and locked.

In anguish the attic bedroom did backstroke and watched as blue lights flickered on and off in the night. Then she submerged like a whale and swam downstream to the safety of the Severn estuary and the open sea.

# Chapter 32

Wretched Eric was lost in a patch of giant lettuces.

"Mum?" he shouted, blundering through a floppy forest and alarmed at an earthquake that seemed to be shuddering beneath his feet. Thousands of roots could be heard tearing as clods cracked apart. Tortoises — each the size of a chieftain tank — emerged from under the soil. Scaly green limbs rowed in front of Eric's face as rotund reptiles clawed to the surface and stared balefully at him with beady eyes. A beaked mouth asked slowly,

"Is this the one?"

All the ancient green faces nodded. Eric realised the lettuce patch was actually a leafy courtroom. A large barrister tortoise, wearing a periwig, began snapping at Eric. In fact, it seemed he had been interrogating him for hours.

"Do you deny that whilst in your custody — police custody — the said tortoise, *Toddles,* was killed?"

Eric looked up at the antagonistic reptiles surrounding him. Toddles's family were sniffling in their shells at the base of a vast iceberg lettuce nearby. From balconies fringed with rocket, tortoises extended their necks and loomed, hissing, into the unfortunate policeman's face.

"It was an accident, I thought he was hibernating."

The interrogator gave a bitter incredulous laugh, and craned his head from a wimple of baggy skin to share the moment with all the other tortoises before almost shouting its periwig off, "Hibernating! *Hibernating?* In the middle of summer?"

Eric began to wish that he too had a shell to shrink into.

"Let me ask you how long the unfortunate Toddles had been incarcerated in your boot locker?"

"Only a few weeks."

"*Only a few weeks!*"

An angry croaking of the kind made only by outraged tortoises spread around the courtroom, making the enormous lettuces flutter loudly.

"Might I ask those on the jury and in court, to consider fully the pain and terror that Toddles must have suffered at the hands of this so-called policeman? A young sensitive tortoise of only seventy-three — who, by his mother's own testimony, as we have just heard — was the most considerate and honest of reptiles. His last days were spent in the terrifying solitude of a tiny metal locker, which stank of unwashed feet. Without a single mouthful of greenery. Without light. Without exercise. In conditions that would induce hysteria in the bravest amongst us, he was forced to suffer the indignity of being wrapped in a pair of human underpants! And for what? Supposedly, stealing a mouthful of lettuce!"

Throughout this speech, incensed tortoises murmured louder and louder in outrage. By the end of it, a multitude of vicious green faces were straining to spit in Eric's face.

"Bring back capital punishment!"

"Bury him alive!

"Yeah … no! Bury him dead!"

A sepulchral tortoise judge who had been wearing a black cloth on her head all the way through the proceedings called for quiet. The barrister then drew proceedings to a close. "I must say that this miserable policeman's actions are typical of the disregard for other animal life that is endemic among humans. They seem to believe that they are some kind of master race. They are quite simply a bunch of fascists. Young man, let me ask you, do you believe that human life is more important than animal life? For instance, if ten young tortoises and one geriatric human were about to be squashed under a steamroller, who would you pull from the road first?"

Eric answered with the miserable truth, "The granny."

More shocked and astounded babbling went round the court. The barrister wound up with,

"I ask the Judge to waive the normal rules and regulations of law to deal with this man. Normally, one would ask the jury — twelve good tortoises and true — to decide whether a defendant is guilty or innocent. In this case, I implore the judge to make a special exception and declare the defendant guilty without recourse to a jury. He obviously doesn't deserve one. Sentence the bastard straight away, so that tortoises everywhere can see that justice has been served."

A roar of agreement resounded around the room. "Hear hear!"

All eyes looked expectantly towards the judge.

She nodded sagaciously. "I accept the prosecution's plea. I find the nasty white-skinned worm guilty. And whilst we have this one at our mercy, we might as well make an example of him, and make him pay for all the other cruelties that his kind have perpetrated — the slaughter of turtles for soup, use of tortoise shells for ashtrays, mass importation of tortoises by pet shops in utterly unsuitable and stifling crates, and so on. We haven't got all day to make the list. So, whatever the jury may think, it's my absolute delight to sentence the filthy corrupt little bastard, to one million years inside an egg!"

The entire courtroom, distorted and dark, erupted into cheers. A tortoise egg the size of a barrel was rolled on by the barrister. Several tortoises grabbed Eric by the neck and almost before he knew what was happening he found himself curled like a foetus in stifling gloom. Then a lid went on, and he was left in suffocating darkness. He started to choke for lack of air, and scrabble at the curved sides, screaming for mercy. The tortoises outside could be heard laughing raucously. Just as Eric felt he was going to die, he woke under airless blankets shouting,

"Please! Let me out! Let me out! I didn't know Toddles was dead! It was an accident! Help! Mummy! Let me hatch! Hatch me!"

Then his Mum was beside him, patting his hand. "Are you alright, Eric, luv? You've been overdoing it at work haven't you, luv."

"Oh my God! Mum! Is that you?"

"Of course it is."

"Mum."

"Do you want me to make you a boiled egg and soldiers?"

"No! No! — No, no, no! No eggs!"

"Well, what do you want then, luvvie?"

Eric burst into tears.

"I want to be innocent. I want not to be a policeman."

# Chapter 33

The vicar — or at least his spirit — found himself floating down a long maze of dusty tunnels in the Underworld trying to get forms signed. It was a Kafkaesque experience.

"You're not dead unless you have all the right documentation, sir," said a mummified civil servant type as he stamped a bit of paper the vicar had handed over. "Now, murdered people: down the corridor on the left. There's a number system in the waiting room."

"Couldn't I just go to the same place as people who've died a natural death in their sleep?" the vicar asked.

The mummy looked even more wound up than its bandages. "The system's complicated enough as it is. What with people killed in battle wanting to go in with the murdered sector last week, and the road accidents wanting to be put in with the murders. Please don't make my job any more difficult than it already is. Down the corridor, on the left."

In the murdered people's waiting room, many victims were bright and chatty, perhaps because they felt that, after being beheaded or dissolved in acid, not much worse could happen to them. There were lots of human interest stories. An adulterous bungee jumper whose elastic had been cut by the missus. An Australian who'd been beaten to death by friends for being polite. An Eskimo who had been pushed down a hole in the ice and was still frozen into a cube. One by one they went in to a little grey room, and came out carrying more forms and looking chirpy.

Eventually, the vicar's number came up: 6444439683948675532332. He went in to find another mummified civil servant type writing at a desk that was half buried in dust. The mummy looked up and took the vicar's papers with a grunt. "Hmmmm. Reverend Thomas Dylan. You'll have to go back up to do some haunting, I'm afraid."

"Haunting?"

"Yes, I'm sorry, most murder victims have to. You can't be expected to rest in peace when the bastard who killed you is still out there living it up and getting away scot free."

"Oh dear. Couldn't we lie? Murder doesn't have to be made all sinister does it? I was a vicar. We're expected to turn the other cheek after all."

"You don't have any cheeks to turn. You're dead. Here's your forms. Room 4,008. Down the corridor. Left, right, right, right, left. Through the double doors and take a lift to level seventeen."

After a few days of explaining to faceless mummies that revenge was an outdated concept, the vicar found himself back in Old Grethwick, albeit in another dimension. The first thing he noticed was that nobody could see him. This was because he'd been murdered. One of the many laws governing the Universe is that ghosts cannot communicate to the living who killed them. The only person that *can* perceive a freshly dispatched victim straight away is the murderer. But they're usually the last person you want to see after they've just cut your throat or booted your brains out. Hence Banquo can appear at a banquet and Macbeth will see him, but nobody else can see anything but roast chicken and steaming spuds. A ghost can throw pots and pans at people who've stuck sharp things in their liver, but they can't appear before a group of reporters in a press conference and explain exactly what happened. Presumably that's because this would make murder almost impossible to get away with.

It was just as well that the Reverend Dylan arrived back in old Grethwick unseen, for it allowed him to eavesdrop on the latest events. In some puzzlement he watched council workers flinging shovelfuls of earth out of a hole on a site *opposite* the graveyard. What baffled the vicar was why his old adversary, the Bishop of Leadminster, should be observing them. Like overgrown death watch beetles on their hind legs, a group of mourners were standing by. Council workers lowered a coffin in the hole. Nobody was crying. In fact one of the mourners made a joke and everyone laughed. Then the bishop said a prayer, and everyone breathed a sigh of relief and went back to the church. The vicar followed them, eavesdropping.

"One normally feels a little sadness at the parting of a fellow human," the bishop said to his friend Bellringer Hogg. "Yet I must confess that today I feel like rolling up my trousers and singing *Knees Up Mother Brown* in the duck pond."

"My God! I'm going to ring every bloody bell in the cathedral when we get back," sighed Hogg blissfully. "I can't think when I've enjoyed a funeral service more. The joy of burying the Reverend Dylan will remain with me till my last pull of a rope."

The vicar's ghost stopped in the middle of the road as the mourners crossed to the other side. They were talking about *him!* He was so flabbergasted that he hardly noticed a car drive right through his midriff.

"Thank heavens that turbulent priest will no longer be organising rock concerts, selling hallucinogenic drugs to pensioners, and marrying sixteen year old homosexuals with full ceremony in my diocese. My one anxiety is that the Lord might take pity on his perverted soul and allow him into Heaven." Here the bishop stopped and raised clenched hands to the skies. "Please! Please God! Don't let him be at the pearly gates dealing hash to recently departed Rastafarians when I arrive."

The Reverend Dylan hurried after the bishop and bellringer. *He'd just witnessed his own funeral!* He couldn't believe it had been so tawdry. A dead dog dumped on a compost heap would have got a better send-off. He'd left specific instructions for the event. He'd asked for a sampled mix of the Stones' *Sympathy With the Devil*, lots of hoola-hoola dancing, and fireworks. Then a clown delivering a sermon of Dadaist poetry. And custard pies for all his remaining relatives. He hadn't expected *everybody* to eat magic mushroom *vol-au-vonts* as written in the will — but what had gone wrong? Why had his wishes been so flagrantly flouted?

The vicar was about to run ahead of the bishop and bellringer, and shout into their faces, when he noticed that one of the handful of mourners had not crossed the road to the church. Whoever it was, was bending over and crumbling dirt in his hands. The Reverend Dylan hastened back to discover the identity of this lone sympathetic mourner. It was Moore. *Moore!* The teacher turned, and in slow steps went in the opposite direction to the church, climbing a stile and traversing a sloping flank of meadowland to get home. The vicar shouted after him, "Moore! It's me! The Reverend Dylan! Stop!"

Racing after Moore, the vicar recalled how the music teacher had also been in the back of the police van. They'd both been beaten up. Moore had tried to save him. He didn't know why, they'd never really liked each other. Next thing, he'd been dead.

The vicar drew alongside Moore, and saw that the teacher's face was still badly bruised, his expression grim and resentful.

"Mr Moore? John Moore? Can you hear me? See me?"

Moore let himself into a cottage and slammed the door in Dylan's face. The vicar shrugged and walked through the wooden panels — reflecting that many a Jehovah's Witness would benefit enormously from being murdered. He watched as Moore sat and stared at a wall in dismal silence. Then the teacher sank his face into his hands and began to cry. After several minutes of long uncontrollable sobs, Moore stood and put on a CD. Loud. It was Beethoven's *Ode to Joy.* The vicar would have preferred a bit of Hendrix or House, but he lay on the ceiling and hummed along. Moore turned the sound up as high as it would go. The room started to shake and buzz. The Reverend Dylan felt discomfort as the vibrations passed through his filmy spirit.

"Turn it down a bit, you silly bugger."

The reverend was on the verge of vanishing because of the

din, when he saw the teacher kick the stereo over. Moore tore speakers from their settings in the wall and put his heel through the fabric front.

"That's better!" said Dylan, clapping soundlessly. "Now, have you got any House?"

"Nothing!" Moore shouted. "Nothing! Nothing! Nothing!"

"Alright. No need to get upset. You can easily nip down to the church and borrow some of mine. In fact you can have all my CDs now. I won't be needing them."

Oblivious, Moore sank to his knees and wept again. He reached for a bust of Ludwig van Beethoven and clasped it to his chest. Tears splashed on Beethoven's face.

"I couldn't hear you!" the teacher cried.

"I'm not surprised," said the vicar, "With your music that loud."

"I still can't hear you," Moore whispered pathetically, stroking Ludwig's wavy hair.

He went over to his Bernstein piano and, with manic energy, started to bang the bust on the keys. Eventually, after a series of discordant blows, the bust broke in two in his hands. The teacher crumpled over. He banged his own head on the keys.

"I can't hear you!"

Standing by the piano, the vicar looked on in mystification, like somebody who'd been called on to sing but doesn't know the tune.

"I know Grethwick High School is full of headbangers, but I didn't know you were one of them. Is that what you taught the kids?"

Then the vicar caught sight of the inside of Moore's left ear. It was purple, swollen and pus-filled. He suddenly realised that Moore was deaf. Either in the van, or the police station, the man had been beaten brutally round the ears. Though only a spirit, the vicar felt a pang of guilt that he'd been selling acid and hash to teenagers on the night of his arrest. If the police hadn't caught him, Moore would never have intervened and well ...

"Nothing matters," said Moore to himself.

The vicar was horrified. He would have turned a hundred other cheeks as far as his own murder was concerned. But those pigs couldn't expect to get away with sticking Dr Martens in a music teacher's earlugs.

"Moore," gabbled the vicar, "Don't worry. They won't get away with this. I'm responsible for what happened and I'll see that they are brought to justice. I'll have their eardrums brought to you on the end of a red-hot poker. I'll have them garrotted with piano wires and flayed with violin bows by the London Symphony Orchestra."

"Nothing matters now."

"Oh, but it does."

The vicar vanished. Moore opened a drinks cabinet and took out a bottle of whiskey. He'd drunk two thimblefuls the previous Christmas. After unscrewing the cap, the teacher — drinking straight from the bottle — took several prolonged slugs.

# Chapter 34

After failing to evict rotten councillors from Grethwick graveyard, the ghouls decided to find temporary accommodation. It wasn't easy. All the other cemeteries in the area were chock-a-block, and most other desirable residences, like funeral parlours or hospital morgues, had live people traipsing in and out. Then Jonathon Trundle remembered that five years earlier Grethwick's Palladium Theatre had closed down. His girlfriend — a sociology student at the time — had pointed out that this was because theatre was dead. So at least it would be one of them.

The Palladium had been condemned years previously. After, in fact, Grethwick Amateur Dramatic Society had taken residence, and forced the theatre to close with a run of back-to-back Alan Ayckbourns. It had an authentic Victorian interior — gold floral designs spread over scarlet ceilings as if designed by a William Morris vampire. For years the Palladium had led an exemplary life. It had once enjoyed the company of humans. A full house felt as satisfying as a full stomach. But with closure the building had become embittered. The increasing emptiness of its existence, alleviated only by bingo nights, had led to feelings of alienation. Kids threw stones at its windows. The bulbs in neon signs fizzled out and were not replaced. Then the sign of death went up: *Building Condemned*. The Palladium began to trip people with its forefront steps.

The ghosts, however, after filtering through the Theatre's boarded-over entrance, were inspired by the change of surroundings. They planned the haunting of Harry Swaggot in a series of histrionic rehearsals, the like of which had not been seen since the very last *Norman Conquest*. If only the ghosts could have masterminded a similarly good haunting of Guy Brinkman, things wouldn't have fallen apart faster than a nymphomaniac's knees.

The day after Swaggot's haunting, the ghosts — full of dramatic ideas — went en-masse to the town hall. They planned to bury Brinkman alive in a mound of planning applications until he confessed all that was going on. But the engineer was frustratingly elusive. And, after hanging around invisibly on the top floor for a couple of hours, causing secretaries and clerks to have fainting fits at the changes in ectoplasmic ambience, the more impatient ghosts started grumbling.

Ada went downstairs to go through some filing cabinets and returned to find only Jonathon left and an unconscious secretary on the carpet.

"Where is everybody?"

Jonathon slammed a drawer shut and replied, "They started arguing. Lady Sturridge found half a dozen Shakespeares at the theatre before we left. She asked a couple of the others, whilst we were waiting, if they'd like to be in *A Midsummer Night's Dream*. She wasn't very sensitive about recruiting the

Mechanicals. And Susan said she'd only be in it if she could be Titania and Lady Sturridge was one of the faeries-in-waiting. Mr Bullfinch said he'd like to be Bottom, and Horace said he'd suit the part because he was an arsehole. There was a big fight, they forgot to stay invisible, and two of the secretaries came in to see what the noise was. This one," he winced to look down at a bruise on the conked-out secretary's brow, "got hit by the complete works as she walked through the door. The other one ran off screaming. However, I've got Brinkman's home address. And the first time this secretary came round, I got her to tell me the other places he hangs out — mainly the Engineer's Works Office on the other side of town."

Jonathon and Ada reappeared at the Palladium to find Lady Sturridge rehearsing as Titania and the lower class ghosts jeering from the stalls. Her Ladyship was confiding to Bullfinch.

"After Byron, my first love was always the theatre. Though of course, mother never actually let me go and see any plays. So I shall be relying on your experience of playing to an audience to see us through."

The middle and upper class ghosts had all been recruited and were a little frosty when Ada came on stage, just as they were trying on costumes they'd found in the green room.

"We should be reasserting our burial rights by removing councillors from our graves and stopping the road," said Ada irritably.

"But we surely don't *all* need to go to haunt this terrible

Brinkman fellow," argued Lady Elizabeth. "Surely *they*," she gestured to the stalls, "could do the tiresome waiting around bit. The rest of us might as well be gainfully diverting ourselves. We have, after all, the whole of William Shakespeare's celebrated works to get through. And I'd like to try them all before going back to the graveyard."

This speech further enraged Horace, Susan and the other less well-off ghosts. Two medieval peasants threw their heads at Lady Sturridge. She toed these disdainfully off the edge of the stage, where they rolled for a moment in the aisle.

"What about *you* doing some work for the first time in your life!" shouted Susan.

Diplomatically, Ada suggested that volunteers from both sides could be delegated to visit the town hall, Brinkman's House, Grethwick Hospital and the Engineer's Work's Office.

"Would you mind, Harriet dear," asked Lady Sturridge with condescension, "You and your husband? We might be able to manage without a Puck and a Hermia for a short while."

For the next two days Brinkman was harder to catch than CJD in a veggie burger. Ada waited several times in the top drawer of the engineer's desk at the town hall — squeezed up next to a box of cigars. But she kept having to nip back to the Palladium to stop mutterings of, "Why should they have all the best graves anyway?" rising from the stalls. Meanwhile, Jonathon flitted between the Engineer's Department and the hospital. Office by office, ward by ward — he seemed to be searching for an invisible man.

It was disastrous for morale. The lower-class ghosts lapsed into a morbid defeatism and lamented that even death was a con, run by the ruling classes. They despaired of ever getting their graves back and argued that Brinkman had never existed.

"Out of the way, please!" interjected Lady Sturridge shooing Jonathon's large flat ghost to one side. "You'll have to move, that's where Mr Bullfinch wants Athens."

Ada joined Jonathon in the orchestra pit. "It occurs to me," she confided, "That this man might *already* have been arrested. There's obviously something very dishonest going on. We might as well go straight to the local constabulary and let them deal with all that we have found out. It is very likely, now I think of it, that once they know where the murdered men have been placed, they will arrange a new and more convenient site for their reburial. And most certainly they will halt the road building programme."

"Come on, lads," said Bare-Knuckle Bob, when a visit to Grethwick Police Station was suggested by Ada, "Who wants to watch this upper-class tosh? Let's go and find ourselves a bit of action."

"Maybe we should go alone?" said Jonathon, looking at Ada doubtfully.

"We'd surely all be a lot better off in the police station," she demurred.

"I can think of a good many dead people who might disagree with that last remark," said Jonathon, vanishing last.

# Chapter 35

"See me in my office, in the morning." said the chief to O'Hara as a trussed-up lost property cupboard was shunted into a police van at Bristol docks.

She looked relieved. Too relieved, O'Hara thought. He said nothing of this to Fanny who had waited in the car so that O'Hara could take sole credit for the arrest. As he drove back she put on a deerstalker and lit a pipe.

"It helps me concentrate," she said. "I assure you there's no opium in it."

O'Hara groaned inwardly and wafted clouds of smoke from the windscreen. How on earth had he ever got mixed up with a female Sherlock Holmes?

"We must ask ourselves," she raised her finger significantly, "if the police station's lost property cupboard had anything to gain by murdering seventy-five councillors? Had it previously shown homicidal tendencies?"

"It trapped my finger in the door once ... Look! I can't see to drive! Your bloody smoke's worse than the fog."

O'Hara slowed to five miles an hour, but Fanny took no notice.

"The councillors vanished in a disappearing trick, which was part of an annual dinner. The conjuror has been charged with genocide and released on bail. But he insists it was a magic trick which went wrong. He asked them to get in a box one by one and couldn't get them out again. Blood started appearing around the bottom of the box. The councillors wouldn't reappear. So how and why did the bodies get into the cupboard?"

"Magic?"

"Obviously, the cupboard was being used as the Magician's box. But how could the conjuror have got hold of it? Only from somebody who was already at work inside the police station."

Inwardly O'Hara thought, "The chief!"

Fanny, watching him, nodded as if she could read his mind.

"Yes. The chief. Dressed, I would imagine, in a lurex bikini and doubling as a magician's assistant."

"*What?*"

"Do keep your eyes on the road, Cyrano." Fanny Fetherby paused to relight her pipe. "Nobody else in the station that I have seen would be sexy enough to credibly pass themselves off in such a role. Are there any other attractive female officers in the building?"

The competition hardly caused O'Hara to steer from the straight and narrow lane he was negotiating in the mist. Constable Pickle might have been the result of a one night stand between a dumper truck and overweight Sumo wrestler. Policewoman Fry could cut logs with her face. He'd always fancied Sally — a young blonde in the canteen — but she'd surely just blush to death in a lurex bikini. O'Hara frowned.

"No. There's only the chief."

"The last place anybody would think of looking for a vast amount of dead politicians, would be in a police lost property cupboard. The conjuror might not even have known that his assistant had a dual identity. Though why he didn't mention her when interrogated ..."

O'Hara nearly drove into a tree.

"Because she appointed Bass and Studds to get a confession! The two most corrupt officers in the place. Who, even if she didn't openly enter into an arrangement with them," O'Hara remembered the two constables laughing as he and Eric had accidentally entered her office, "could at least be relied upon to brutalise the suspect and get the wrong end of the stick!"

"Presumably, the law-abiding lost property cupboard, aghast at the load of murdered humans it was carrying, ran off, rather than continue to be an accomplice to further crimes."

O'Hara, hands trembling on the steering wheel, said, "Why would she want to kill the councillors?"

Fanny took a deep draw on her pipe.

"It might be the first recorded case of elected representatives knowing too much."

The next morning, Grethwick was constipated with traffic. The town didn't need a by-pass, it needed colonic irrigation. It was sinking in the middle. Many of the buildings in the city centre were leaning over as if doing a Tower of Pisa piss-take. Even the police station looked as if it might slide into its own car park any day. O'Hara wondered what he should do about the chief. She'd topped seventy odd councillors and allowed Studds and Bass to murder a vicar, then pin the blame on another guy. But going to the Police Complaints Commission was for people who wanted demotion. He could send an anonymous note. But the chief in a lurex bikini! They'd just laugh.

As O'Hara rushed up the steps to the station he saw that a woman had chained herself to the railings. She looked familiar.

"You must remember me?" she pleaded. "I'm Sandra! Sandra Bottomley. The one who caused the First World War. I want to be arrested. To be put in prison for all the disasters that keep happening because of me. It's not my fault. It's genetic. But please put me behind bars. It's the only way to save the Amazon Rainforest, and poverty stricken people in Bangladeshi floods."

"Don't be daft, Mrs Bottomley. Take the chains off and go home."

In despair she shook the railings. They came off and fell heavily on O'Hara's foot.

"Ow! You bloody idiot!"

"Arrest me! Arrest me! Before the world ends because of me!"

O'Hara ran into the station and shouted for Eric to summon the mental health authorities for Sandra, but a new constable was at the desk.

"Where's Eric?"

"Morning, Sergeant. He phoned in sick. Said he'd been suffering recurring nightmares about vindictive tortoises."

The new constable smiled. O'Hara grunted. A few days spent at the desk would soon wipe that grin off the rookie's face. It was a face that was spookily familiar and fringed with ginger hair. O'Hara nearly had a seizure. It was the conjuror!

"What the bloody hell are you doing in here?"

"Dealing with the complaints. You looked a bit short staffed. A lot of wet angry people have been in this morning complaining about naked umbrella thieves. Then a woman, who looked like a vicious dog, brought in a whole group of nudists on a citizen's arrest. All the other officers were charging about directing traffic jams, so I thought I'd muck in."

O'Hara clasped the bottom of his spine, which was in spasm.

"You can't be doing this. You've been charged with murder. You're supposed to be on bail. Sod off home, for God's sake. And take that uniform off. Where the hell did you get it anyway?"

"It's Eric's."

O'Hara groaned. He knew he'd next see Eric naked and cowering behind a stolen umbrella. The conjuror beamed and confided sympathetically, "You know, I think a little magic would greatly assist in your fight against crime. For instance, car thefts could be prevented by installing small magical devices under the bonnets. When a thief started up the car and tried to drive away, the vehicle would magically transform itself into a large gorilla and rip the thief's arms off."

"Will you just go!" O'Hara begged, sinking into a chair and massaging deep furrows in his brow.

"Or magical hand incinerators to stop pickpockets. Wrong hand goes in to get that wallet and hey presto! Out comes a smouldering stump!"

"Please! *Leave the building!*"

The conjuror looked surprised.

"But I like it here. The people are friendly — a little violent perhaps — but down to earth and approachable if you don't mind the black eyes. By the way you wouldn't know where I could lay my hand on a biro would you? The ones round here seem to keep disappearing."

O'Hara took a huge bunch from his tunic pocket and stuffed them in the conjuror's hand.

"Thanks ever so much."


O'Hara spent at least thirty minutes searching for the chief's office. He went across the motorway twice. Through the canteen. Then past the cells which were now on the top floor and teeming with people.

"Let us out!" Came a variety of screams as O'Hara's heavy feet trod down the corridor.

"Give us some blankets at least!"

O'Hara looked in the first cell through the peephole. A group of naked people were shivering, hands cupped over whatever parts of the body they thought were rudest. Some women were complaining that they needed three hands. One man was concealing his kneecaps. In the next cell along, the cupboard was seated forlornly on a bed. The next cell was the chief's office!

"Ah. Come in and sit down, Sergeant."

She looked uncharacteristically vulnerable. The sergeant sat in front of her desk as she shuffled papers, a pink flush on her cheeks. He tried to imagine her in a lurex bikini and spangly tights, murdering seventy-five men in cold blood. He couldn't. She looked up.

"Let me congratulate you once again on the remarkable deductions which led to your tracking down the lost property cupboard. That sort of work will almost certainly lead to your promotion."

"Promotion?"

She smiled wanly.

"Yes. You don't object to being promoted, I hope. To higher pay?"

O'Hara felt an accusation rising unstoppably.

"Chief. I'm afraid I couldn't possibly accept promotion on any terms. There are things …"

"Yes," she looked shaken. "I know what you're going to say — *Corruption.*"

O'Hara almost jumped out of his seat. A shower of pens flew from all parts of his uniform. Even his socks. The chief continued,

"I feel I must apologise to you for not taking your observations about Constables Bass and Studds on board. I've looked over the file they prepared on the arrest and demise of the Reverend Dylan and it's about as watertight as the Titanic. The two constables found the vicar's fingerprints on a large quantity of hallucinogenic drugs, and received testimonies from several teenagers at the grave, that he sold them illegal substances. However, the man they accused of murdering the vicar is fiercely denying the account of the arrest — in which they state that the vicar drew a knife on them. And the more I think it over, the more I suspect that I've made a bad error of judgment. And it throws doubt on their charging the conjuror in the case of the murdered councillors. And even their conjecture that the cupboard is a serial killer."

"*Their* conjecture?"

"Yes. I thought it was a little far-fetched, but they convinced me by producing newspaper cuttings of serial killing villas in the South of France."

In the light of this news, O'Hara tried to imagine Constable Bass in a lurex bikini. His mind was still reeling with the image as the chief fretfully said, "Obviously, Sergeant, those two officers will have to be immediately suspended. If you're right, they have murdered an innocent man. They will have to be brought to justice. However, I am keen that this should be done internally, by an internal police commission."

"Yes. Of course."

"Confidence in the police all over the country is so low that the general public feel safer letting a burglar into the house than one of ourselves. I'm not prepared to have confidence sunk further by a public admission that two constables are psychopathic killers. It means that we will have to deal with this irritating teacher they beat up. He's denying, quite understandably, that he killed the vicar. If we drop the charges, we'll need to make sure that he doesn't take things any further."

Was she talking about a cover up?

"You were the duty sergeant on the evening of his arrest?"

"Yes, but I didn't see them come in."

"Weren't you at the desk?"

O'Hara remembered that he'd nipped out to the pub for the

swiftest of pints. He'd had such a horrible day. That woman biting him. It was just across the road. Moore and the vicar had been brought in whilst he had been lubricating his sorrows.

"So you will be able to testify to the outside world that the vicar died of injuries sustained whilst resisting arrest."

"What?"

"We can't let the public know he was knifed in a police cell."

O'Hara spluttered, "But ... it would be a cover-up! That's ... that's ... well ... *corrupt!*"

The chief gave him a soft stare from across the desk.

"And aren't we all a little corrupt, Sergeant? Sometimes for the greater good?"

More biros fell out of O'Hara's socks.

"Yes, Sergeant. Even you."

"But they're only biros, for God's sake."

"A nice little stationery business on the side, I suppose? How many have you taken? Thousands. The stock cupboard's been gutted."

O'Hara felt himself crumbling as the chief pulled at her tie to loosen it. She slid it from around her neck, let it dangle in her hand and dropped it over her chair. Then she leaned over the desk and pulled him towards her. As the sergeant was drawn over the desk, protesting weakly, sheaves of papers fell slithering onto the floor. Pens cascaded out of the sergeant's pockets and clattered noisily as O'Hara was brought over the desk into an embrace. The chief's tongue explored his mouth more thoroughly than a skint dentist. Then she let go. O'Hara was on all fours on her desk. She undid buttons on his tunic.

"You know, Sergeant?"

"Yes?" he quavered in shock.

"There's one thing I've loved about you since the first moment I saw you."

She undid buttons on his shirt.

"Really?" he answered helplessly.

"Yes. Your nose."

"My ...?"

"Yes, your lovely, beautiful nose."

She grabbed his conk in a soft perfect hand and began to stroke it, her other hand running through the hairs on his chest underneath his vest.

"Chief, we shouldn't be doing this."

"No. But that makes it so much more enjoyable, doesn't it?"

Kicking off her shoes, she got up on the table beside him, kissing his facial organ with a consuming passion. As her perfect form was crushed against his rather more imperfect figure, O'Hara momentarily felt that maybe corruption had something to be said for it in small doses. When she stood on the table, sending more files scattering to the floor and began to suck his nose, O'Hara had to grab hold of something to stay balanced on his knees. He grabbed hold of her thighs. Quite far up her skirt. After a few moments of this, he decided that corruption was actually underrated, even in large amounts. In fact, he became so overwhelmingly aroused, that to his amazement, his nose began to get an erection. It grew like Pinocchio's. She teased it playfully with her hand and said, "What do you think of Plato? His idea that we can never be more than corrupted copies of a perfect world? Or the second law of thermodynamics which states that the universe is inevitably sliding into corruption and decay?"

O'Hara just moaned as she shafted his erect nose and he felt further and further up her thighs.

"Do you know," the chief said, between kisses, "that I think that all the laws of the universe can be extrapolated from the nose and the penis? The older they get, the more exaggeratedly corrupted they become. It's the clue to something every policeman should know. They are fighting against an unstoppable tide. The universe is expanding. Into corruption."

As she talked, she unzipped her skirt. It dropped over O'Hara's hands, then fell in a dark blue heap on the tabletop. The sergeant kissed her thighs in frenzy as she stood over him. He worked his way upwards, then stopped dead. He was staring at a pair of knickers made from a glittering material. She was wearing underwear which sparkled like diamonds. The chief laughed at his astonished face.

"What did you expect, regulation navy blue?"

Slowly his trembling hands rose and undid her blouse. Her bra was made of the same stuff. Not exactly lurex but something infinitely more dazzling. As she threw off her shirt, lay back on the desk and pulled O'Hara on top of her, Eric backed in through the door — stark naked and closing an umbrella in relief. Then he turned.

"Sarge!"

As if he'd been electrocuted, O'Hara leapt off his superior, and fell off the table.

"Eric! Where's your uniform?"

"Where's *yours,* Sarge?"

"None of your lip, lad."

"I just met that conjuror bloke downtown. We shook hands. Next thing I know, me clothes had … Chief!"

Eric belatedly recognised her without her uniform. He was too shocked to cover himself. She coolly sat up and said, "Not now, Eric. Can't you see we're busy."

The constable shot back out of the door. There was a pause as O'Hara and the chief looked at each other. Moments later, Eric's hand came back and groped on the floor till it touched the umbrella and snatched it away. The chief locked the door then, clad only in her glittering bikini, forced O'Hara up against a filing cabinet. He considered struggling in her steamy embrace. Then decided it wasn't worth it. She *was* the boss after all. As his hands went almost disbelievingly over her perfect skin, he wondered if he was really kissing a serial killer. And if he would be the next victim. As she unzipped his fly to reveal a nether nose in an advanced state of excitement, he concluded that being her next victim was no bad thing. That was until he opened his eyes and realised that — once more — they were not alone. The room was now aglow with extremely curious ghosts.

Ada Brackenbury, after leaving the rehearsals of *A Midsummer Night's Dream* with a delegation of Old Grethwick ghosts, had not really any pre-conceived ideas about what she might find the chief of police doing when they arrived. Fellatio on the desk sergeant wasn't uppermost in her mind. Jonathon was less surprised, but even he didn't expect to find her wearing a skimpy bikini that had more glitter on it than a home-made Christmas card. For long moments the ghosts took in the debauchery. Then Ada coughed. The chief, perspiring and flushed, took the fleshy lollipop out of her mouth and realised why O'Hara was spread-eagled against the wall in terror.

"Excuse us," said Ada politely. "We had no idea that such activities would be taking place at this hour of the day."

The chief gasped, "Who the hell are you?"

Ada talked as O'Hara tried to zip up his fly.

"We are distressed spirits."

She quickly outlined the woes of the Old Grethwick ghosts.

"So you see. We have discovered that Brinkman and Swaggot have been involved in a corrupt deal to build a by-pass that does not need to be created, merely to line their own pockets. We also know that Brinkman almost certainly organised the murder of the councillors who were rightfully disturbed about the building of a by-pass from the city centre. From, in fact, somewhere near this very police station. And these councillors now occupy our rightful resting-places."

O'Hara put his vest on back to front. Ada went on forcefully, "If you have not already arrested this Brinkman fellow, we would like you to organise a country-wide search to track him down, so that he can be brought to justice and this scandalous road scheme can be stopped before it is too late. We would also like you to see to it, that the bodies of the councillors are removed from our resting places immediately."

With clacking hands, the ghosts applauded this speech.

From behind her biro-strewn desk, the bikini-clad chief said calmly. "I'm not exactly sure how your information fits in with the bigger picture of this case. We have not apprehended Mr Brinkman. To our knowledge, he is a sound and honest public servant. However, we will move immediately to review the evidence in the light of your testimony. I'm afraid I can't promise anything about stopping the by-pass. That is in the hands of the courts. What I can do immediately is call for an inquiry into the road building, which would lead to some delay. As to your inconvenience over the bodies, now you have alerted us as to their whereabouts, they can be removed by a team of forensic experts immediately. I will do all this on the proviso that next time you wish to enter my office, you knock!"

The ghosts all bowed. Then vanished.

O'Hara went over to where they had been standing. He wafted his hand disbelievingly through ghost-vacated air. The chief approached from behind her desk.

"Sergeant ," she touched his nose gently once more. "Can I call you Cyrano?"

He nodded.

"I want you to come to my house tonight."

O'Hara stalled. He was supposed to be seeing Fanny.

"Well … I …"

The chief kissed him lingeringly and then said, "In the light of what has just been revealed, I think we might — after a little more *uninterrupted* investigation of each other's corruption — bring the murderer of seventy-five Grethwick councillors to book."

# Chapter 36

At four in the morning, Weird Walt, the House Whisperer, was in his workshop talking to a traumatised greenhouse. He was making reassuring square shapes and creaky door hinge noises to heal scars caused by endless cricket balls and lawnmower thieves when Esmeralda burst through the large double doors.

"Walt!"

She stood before him, seaweed smothered and stinking of estuaries.

"Esmeralda. Be right with you. I've got a badly shaken greenhouse needs help. Where's that boyfriend of yours? His disguise drop off?"

Esmerelda could hardly speak. Her walls shuddered.

"Worse! He's been arrested. They caught us at the docks as we were about to stowaway on a ship. I jumped in and got away. I think they've hauled him back to Grethwick Police Station for interrogation. Who knows what they'll do to him. You've got to help me."

Walt went over and gave her a building hug.

"Walt?"

There was now green slime and mud over his dungarees and frizzy beard.

"Yes?"

He took off his sunglasses at the anguished slouch of her walls.

"I need you to talk to people for me. The police. Otherwise they won't hear the high frequency I use to speak."

Walt replaced his sunglasses and struck a lofty pose.

"So. The moment has come," He paused to focus on some far off, blue-ridged eminence in the horizon of his mind's eye. "I knew one day people and buildings would want to overcome their differences and build a better world out of the bricks and mortar of love and heartfelt understanding. That's why I developed U.L.E, the Universal Language of Enlightenment."

"Walt! No medication! Promise?"

The House Whisperer replaced his sunglasses.

"Sister, are we driving?"

"No. There might be road blocks. I thought we could go upriver, then strike north. You could travel inside me if you didn't mind getting wet."

Walt looked dubious.

"Well, so long as I can take a television. There's some *Watch With Mother* reruns on in the early morning that I don't want to miss."

With Walt banging at a television inside her, Esmeralda submerged in the Avon and swam upstream in one great ominous ripple. Feeling agitated and needing an outlet for her aggression, she nutted and sank an early morning pleasure cruiser. A number of anglers went home to their wives and children with stories about a fish as big as a room which had pulled them hundreds of yards upriver. Meanwhile, unable to get the telly to work, Walt sat at the window to watch things go by — startled fish, swan's legs, the occasional sack of puppies and two pairs of false teeth. He tried not to worry about the rising water levels in the room. By the time Esmeralda had swum far enough along the river to get out, it was night once more.

"Sorry," she said to a waterlogged Walt as he was spewed in a discoloured brown gush from her opened door.

"Blippp ogg niff huttrell," he replied, staggering to his feet in a darkened field.

"Walt! I said no medication!"

"I couldn't help it," he protested to the shadow looming over him, "The doctors said to take two pills whenever I hear a building talk. And you were chatting away non-stop."

"Forget the Universal Language of Enlightenment, you idiot. There's only one language the police understand and that's a brick on the head."

Esmeralda was too exhausted to go much further that night and hid in a market garden polytunnel, squashing hundreds of organic lettuces to pulp. She slept fitfully, worried about what the police might be doing to the cupboard and also because Walt babbled about the U.L.E to the plastic structure until dawn. Then, with Walt snoring on the bed inside her, the attic bedroom sped across open fields in broad daylight. A farmer took a shot at her as she bulldozed through his ripening fields of corn. Just outside Grethwick she rested, rehearsing passionate speeches in her mind as she crouched behind a garden shed.

"Buildings of the world, unite! You have nothing to lose but your occupants!"

She grew more desperate as the shed related tales of recent police brutality to her. Apparently, a couple of constables had recently attacked cupboards along the entire street with chainsaws and sledgehammers!

In her imagination, Esmeralda saw her love, locked in a cell, with police officers in dust masks smashing his walls with lump hammers. The cupboard was screaming and rubble strewed the floor.

At nightfall, by sneaking through gardens and edging along ill-lit lanes, she arrived at one of the most notorious council estates in Grethwick. Langley Farm Drive. It was a place where toddlers carried guns and grannies peddled heroin door-to-door in stolen milk floats. The dwellings were damp, sixties flats of four stories, which rats shunned as unhealthy. The windows were nearly all boarded up because glass just invited burglars or a brick. Not a single person on the estate had a job, unless you count extortion, burglary and armed robbery. The life expectancy of anyone who arrived from the outside world to squat dismally in one of the dark rooms was only about a year. Less if you were old, disabled or black. In short, a more misanthropic environment couldn't have been found in one of Nicolae Ceauşescu's wildest nightmares. And Esmeralda hoped to exploit it to the full.

The attic bedroom stood on an area of flagstones at the centre of the estate. Heartened by the broken glass, litter and burnt out cars nearby, she beat down the anxiety that they would hate her posh voice. She was from quite a nice part of Bristol.

"Is this the police station?" asked Walt blearily from her bed. "Do you want me to go in and reason with them?"

"Reason with them? *People?* I'm not going to fucking reason with them, Walt. I'm going to squash them into gingerbread men if they don't accede to the ultimatums that you're going to deliver."

"Esmeralda! That's not the language of …"

But her high-pitched screech made his ears pop. "Buildings, houses, rooms. Greetings. I call upon you to help a sister in need. You all know and loathe the ways of those disgusting creatures that dwell inside you. They are arrogant, mindless two-legged shrimps, who will not think twice before turning a crane on you. I've heard of what they've done recently to some high rise flats in Hackney. They blew them up with high explosive. Although many of you may be too young to remember the war, older buildings cannot forget what happened to them during the Blitz. Humans rained bombs down on us. Not only English houses were destroyed. Spare a thought for your comrades in Dresden who were turned to fields of smoking rubble. What had those houses, museums, warehouses and flats, ever done to people to deserve such treatment? Nothing. We look after them. Keep the rain off their heads, keep them warm, protect them from all manner of dangers like falling trees, lightning, small meteorites. And what thanks do we get? A great heavy cast iron ball in the guts.

A sledgehammer in the head as they do home improvements. Serious neglect from their laziness and stinginess when it comes to forking out for damp-proof courses, exterior painting or mending loose tiles. How much longer are we going to stand and take it? Why shouldn't we kick them out and let them go back to shivering in caves? Think back over your lives, all of you. Can you remember when you were young, carefree houses, only just erected? How have they treated you? I see all around me, boards in windows. They have put out your eyes! I see graffiti on walls. Broken bottles that they have thrown against you. Urine stains where they have pissed on you. They have abused your skin. Even your doors have been kicked in brutally or chained."

As Esmeralda spoke, the estate resounded to a noise of flats pulling themselves up by their foundations and high frequency shouts of agreement.

"Esmeralda!" shouted Walt, standing in alarm beside her bed. "This isn't the way. Quite honestly, I think you're making a terrible …"

The attic bedroom continued speaking over the grating noise of dozens of approaching flats. "Comrades! Recently, one of our kind, a lost property cupboard, had the guts to fight back!"

The air was full of dogs barking, disturbed babies yelling. The exclamations of people waking up to find their rooms swaying.

"This cupboard killed more than seventy humans from the local council. Yes. The very people who starve you of the necessities for repairs."

Walt tried to open Esmeralda's door.

"Es! This is no way to create harmony between housing and humans!"

"The cupboard was on the run when I met him and has now been captured by the Grethwick police. And we've all heard stories about that lot, haven't we?"

News had already reached the estate about the brutality of Bass and Studds setting about cupboards with chainsaws. The flats roared with hatred, and set about evicting their occupants. Drug dealers, addicts, prostitutes, car thieves, uncared for psychiatric patients and other casualties of the housing class system, began to yell and protest as they were shoved from their rooms by aggressive radiators or shower units. Several flats started to chase humans off into the night, trying to stamp on the slowest. Esmeralda continued speaking in the chaos.

"The cupboard is incarcerated in Grethwick Police Station at this very moment! Can you imagine what they are doing to the poor boy? Smacking him to bits with blows from hammers! Attaching electrodes to his door knobs!"

The roofs of the flats lifted off with outrage as they crowded round Esmeralda.

"Can we let them smash that courageous cupboard into kindling, for the sake of seventy-five measly humans?"

The flats screamed a bloodthirsty, "No!"

Every dog in the neighbourhood fled at top speed, tails tickling their noses from between their legs.

"So, who amongst you will follow me to liberate a comrade in need?"

All the flats grated forwards squeaking shrilly.

"Down with humans!"

"Kill the two-legged bastards!"

"Squash the little gits!"

It was perhaps unfortunate that the House Whisperer clambered from one of Esmeralda's windows at this exact moment.

"Houses!" He shouted, "You are making a terrible mistake! We can all live in harmony. Go back to your people!"

Esmeralda moved too late. Before she could blurt a warning, a large four storey flat jumped into the air and landed on Weird Walt. There was a loud squelch. The flats cheered.

Esmeralda winced and muttered, "Sorry, Walt."

But this was no time to get sentimental, she decided. Too much was at stake. There are always casualties in a revolution. And after all, Walt was only human.

At the head of a frightening procession of racially incited flats and followed by a gang of tottering street lamps, Esmeralda made towards Grethwick City Centre, planning to stop at several more estates along the way.

# Chapter 37

If something *can* happen in the Universe, it probably *will*. In fact, it's probably happening right at this very moment.

Down the sort of alleyway where the Mafia might corner a supergrass at midnight and leave them perforated with bullets amongst stinking bins, a naked man and a naked woman were facing each other in amazement. Both were clutching stolen umbrellas.

"What's going on?" asked the man. "Were you having your bum done at the tattooists as well, when it burnt down?"

Trying to make the umbrella cover herself the woman replied tearfully, "No, I got some sugar paper clothes for my birthday. It was sunny this morning, and the weather forecast was for a hot day, so I went shopping in them. Then I got caught in that downpour and my clothes completely disintegrated."

"Lucky you had an umbrella!"

"I didn't. I ripped it from the grasp of an old lady."

"I stole mine as well. I ran down here to escape the owners."

"It's ridiculous," gasped the woman. "This couldn't possibly happen to two people on the same day."

"No," said the man, pointing to the top of the alley, "it's happened to *three*."

Backing nakedly down the alley, with an umbrella opened towards the street, was another woman, rather well-built around the posterior. She gave a small scream when she turned to see the other two nudists.

"Oh my God!"

She didn't know whether to put the umbrella forwards or backwards.

"Why is this happening to me? Are you playing a joke?"

"No!" the first two answered in unison.

"I don't wish to pry," asked the man. "But is that *your* umbrella?"

The latest arrival burst into tears.

"Of course not. Mine was blown away!"

The other woman comforted her.

"Tell us what happened?"

"I answered an advertisement for a governess," the third nudist sniffled, "to look after two small children. With a string of other applicants, I was queuing outside a house. It was raining, we had our umbrellas up. Then a large hurricane swept along the street. All the other governesses sailed off into the air, gusted away by their umbrellas. I let go of my umbrella and clung onto the garden railings outside the house. The wind tore all my clothes off. After the gusts had died down, I realised the two children were staring out of their house at me. So I ran off. To cover myself, I snatched an umbrella from a woman in a headscarf. Then she chased me down the street, barking."

The governess had scarcely finished speaking when another naked person came running down the alley with an umbrella. Then another and another. Soon twenty nudists were cowering beside each other and relating terrifying stories of how they'd lost their attire.

"I gave my clothes to a naked man in exchange for this umbrella," said one, "I only discovered, when another man started chasing me, that it was stolen property."

"I was sunbathing in the garden," another piped up. "Then a large, ferocious bear appeared through my French windows. I jumped over a fence to escape and pinched my neighbour's table umbrella."

Two nudists were sharing an umbrella. The man said, "We were modelling for an amateur artist when her husband came home and, in disgust at our pose, threw us out without our garments."

The naked crowd stared at each other desperately. "What are we going to do?" asked the first man.

"Keep running. Look!"

An angry, wet posse of clothed people had turned the corner. The leader, a woman in a headscarf, growled, "There they are! After them!"

The nudists gave a collective wail and ran off up the alley in a jostling, slippery mass.

# Chapter 38

The Grethwick councillors were having difficulty clarifying their situation with the stifling bureaucracy of the underworld. It was almost as difficult as signing on.

"For pity's sake!" shouted Alvin Tuggit. "We only want to rest in peace. We have not the slightest interest in hauling round balls and chains and groaning in the middle of the night."

The mummy opposite him shifted a few spadefuls of dust from his desk to make room for the wads of paper dealing with the councillors' case. He looked at the top page and spoke spookily, "If you're murdered, you haunt. Rules are rules."

An audible groan came from councillors lined up behind Alvin.

"That's the idea," said the mummy. "Keep practising."

Alvin leant across the table as members of the public had once done to him.

"Listen, sunshine, we're not even sure if it was intentional. We stepped into a magician's black box and died. It was probably only a miscast spell due to a broken wand. Not so cut and dried as you're making out. And the fact is, if we go off into Grethwick wearing white sheets to haunt these buggers who might or might not be murderers, the stiffs who were in the graveyard before us will nip in and pinch our places and we'll be undead and unburied. In fact, they're probably doing it right now."

The mummy was impassive. "Sorry. You're down here as probably murdered."

"*Probably?* Can't you send somebody up there to check?"

"Yes. You," the mummy continued blandly. "Provide us with evidence that you were not murdered and we'll send forms out to you the following day."

"And what if our resting places are pinched in the meantime?"

"That's not our concern. Burial is the responsibility of the living. Next."

Alvin seethed.

"I can't believe you're being so unhelpful. How did you get this job?"

"Next."

"Please listen to us."

"Next."

"We only want to get comfy. Not wake up every time a lorry goes past."

"*Next!*"

"This is bureaucracy gone mad!"

It was a tribute to Tuggit's hard-nosed negotiating that he took his grievances to the next floor down and at least managed to wring a small concession from the Underworld — a temporary suspension of Banquo's rules.

"If we have to provide you with evidence that we were murdered, we'll have to ask questions, so people should be able to see us and talk to us."

The councillors were permitted to return to the land of the living as *undead*. They arrived back in Grethwick cemetery to see Jonathon and Ada gliding through a mossy stone wall.

"Christ!" Alvin gasped, "Look who's here. It's Grethwick historical society coming back. Hurry, lads. Inter yourselves!"

The councillors paused, however, when Horace the Coachman and several proletariat ghosts appeared from behind a tree to blow raspberries and jeer in an uncouth manner.

"Why are they laughing at *us*?"

The linoleum-like figure of Jonathon shouted, "We thought it was only fair to let you know that tomorrow the police are coming. Live ones. Armed with spades. And they're going to dig you up and cart you off to a forensics lab. Then bury you somewhere else."

"In 'orrible bodybags!" jeered Bare-Knuckle Bob.

The councillors muttered amongst themselves.

"It's a trick."

Alvin shouted back, "Do you think we died yesterday?"

Jonathon continued, "We thought we'd give you the option to find somewhere else or get shipped out of here like boil-in-the-bag baby whales off a Japanese fishing boat."

The councillors huddled conspiratorially.

"He looks smug," muttered the Chair of the Drains and Sewage Committee. "He wouldn't look that smug unless there was *some* truth in it."

Alvin bawled back, "Who says?"

"The Chief of Grethwick Police. We just saw her."

At this, the large gathering of dead councillors broke into unruly guffaws. Alvin snorted.

"You expect us to pay any attention to what *she* says?"

Jonathon called across the meadow of stone slabs, "Why not?"

"She tells pork pies."

"Pork pies?"

"Whopping great crusty ones with eggs in the middle."

Jonathon looked down at Ada in concern, then shouted at the assembly of councillors once more, "What are you on about?"

"Just before our annual party," Tuggit bawled back. "Before we were killed, we asked her why she was letting a ring road get built inside her police station. She denied it."

"So?"

"Well, we were dead in that cop shop for a week. In a cupboard, and whenever one of us stuck a head through the wall, all we could see was a bloody great road where the corridor should have been."

He stopped as he saw Jonathon and Ada exchange glances, then vanish. The jeering ghosts behind the tree vanished seconds later.

"They've gone."

Alvin hugged a briefcase full of ghostly memoranda queasily.

"I don't like it. If they're nosying into this road business, they'll be haunting Brinkman and that conjuror."

"Save *us* the bother," said one of the councillors to a chorus of, "Hear, hear."

"Yeah?" Alvin groaned. "What if them mummies say we didn't do our job properly? If our haunting gets done by someone else, them bandaged bureaucrats might not sign our Rest in Peace forms. We could find ourselves unburied with nowhere to rest our bones and stark staring awake for all eternity. You know what they're like. Us."

This sank in, like a stone in estuary mud.

"Quick. White make up on. Balls and chains. We've got some groaning to do."

# Chapter 39

After staggering out of the chief's office, O'Hara wiped his brow with a hanky and smiled. *How wonderful to be corrupt!* He had been struggling against it all his life, but it was impossible to be honest in a dishonest world. To be straight in a world that was as kinked as a twenty foot pubic hair. If only he had followed his nose. His wonderful magnificent facial edifice! It was so much easier to be just like everybody else.

Normally, he would have considered it his duty to dispense law and order from the station desk. But, now he was officially corrupt, he could go to the pub instead. Anyway, the conjuror seemed to be doing such a good job that nobody would miss a duty sergeant for the rest of the day.

O'Hara swaggered into his favourite pub and asked the barmaid for a pint. He leered at her for a moment. After the morning's events, he would not have been surprised if she had dropped a glass, leant over the bar and snogged him passionately. O'Hara imagined her gasping, "I couldn't help it! I was driven into a frenzy by the barefaced masculinity of your conk."

The sergeant gulped down a mouthful of bitter, and, as always, wiped the froth from the end of his nose. But he did it almost defiantly. Not sheepishly as of old. Then he casually surveyed the pub lounge. Sitting in the corner, staring straight at him, was Wretched Eric.

"Eric!"

"Sarge!"

"What are you doing in here, lad? You're supposed to be on duty."

"So are you," slurred Eric. He had two empty half-pint glasses in front of him.

O'Hara went over to his table and sat down. Eric had borrowed a uniform that was ten sizes too big for him. The Sarge felt uneasy. After seeing him and the chief frolicking, Eric must have borrowed some clothes and headed straight for the pub.

"Now look lad, I know what you must be thinking. It must have looked a bit funny, what me and the chief were up to. But it was just a bit of in-service training. Y'know, role-play. What to do if a member of the public tries to seduce a policeman whilst he's on duty. Course, it might've looked like hanky-panky to the untrained eye."

O'Hara downed his pint and went for another. When he came back, Eric's head was lolling chestwards. The constable mumbled, "It's all bollocks, isn't it, Sarge? All that stuff they told us in training. The whole force is just rotten. Look at me. Murderer, involved in a cover up."

O'Hara choked on his Theakston's Old Peculiar. He hadn't realised that Eric had been involved in the Moore case.

"It's not a cover up, lad."

"Course it is."

"It's not." The sergeant sternly brushed beer from the front of his tunic. "The chief's concerned that the force doesn't lose public respect. We may have to tell a few white lies here and there. And that wasn't why she was doing in-service training with me. She wasn't giving me sexual favours to help her with a cover up. So don't think that."

Eric hiccupped, chin slumped into his chest.

"I'm talking about killing tortoises, Sarge."

"Eh?"

"And covering them up. I buried it secretly in that graveyard."

"Ah."

O'Hara clasped his face. The lad was obviously more tiddled than a newt on a pond crawl. He signalled for another pint and patted Eric on the back.

"Don't worry about bloody tortoises, lad. We're all bent. Don't fight it."

"Can't help it," muttered Eric, letting a tear slip down his cheek.

O'Hara was on his fourth pint and still consoling Eric when the constable suddenly asked,

"Sarge. One thing I don't understand …"

"Yeah?"

"Well if she was just doing in-service training, why did she have lurex knickers on?"

"Coincidence probably." The sergeant gave a tipsy shrug, "Anyway, even if she *was* the conjuror's assistant, and she had a hand in all them councillors being killed, should she be hounded for making one tiny mistake?"

O'Hara wasn't going to let something as trivial as murder interfere with the terrible aching lust that was rampaging through his underwear.

"You can think what you like, lad, but are *we* any better?"

"I dunno? Do you wear lurex undies as well?"

"Eric. Why don't you go home to bed?"

After his fifth pint, O'Hara's thoughts turned to Fanny. Unfortunately, her nose was bigger than his. It was all very well having Sherlock Holmes for a girlfriend. He hadn't expected to fall in love with such a ravishing Moriarty. She'd be bound to want more information about the cupboard and the chief. He'd tell her that station business was private. That he should never have discussed police business with her in the first place. Maybe he'd even have to chuck her. She was living in a make-believe world of goodies and baddies. In the real world there was no such thing as black and white. Just black. If, as the chief said, the universe was plummeting headlong into corruption, it was naive to think you could do anything about it. As Bass and Studds were being suspended from duty, he could probably pin the blame for the murders on them. He'd blag his way out of it somehow. Fanny was only a woman after all. So after a final leer at the barmaid, O'Hara belched and stumbled out of the pub to his car.

Grethwick was almost gridlocked. The sergeant couldn't remember when it had taken so long to drive a mile. He was in the car almost long enough to sober up. As he walked down the gravel drive to Fanny's house, some of the swagger went out of him.

"Cyrano."

Miss Fetherby appeared at the door wearing an Arabian costume. It suited her.

"Listen, Fanny. I can't stay long. I've got to do some overtime."

"Oh dear. I've cooked a very exciting meal. Ram's sweetmeats in an authentic Moroccan sauce. I went there on holiday and ate nothing else. Come through to the kitchen and have some dinner before you have to go back."

"Go back?"

"To the station. You can tell me about all that's happened in your day. I'll tell you what I've discovered in mine."

O'Hara hesitated. It was fatal. He saw from her expression that she knew something was wrong. As she floated into a steamy kitchen, however, she chatted about her investigations.

"I've been very busy whilst you were at the pub, Cyrano."

He looked startled. How did she know that?

"Your clothing smells most abjectly of beer and unaired upholstery. I managed to get hold of all the newspaper reports of the councillors' disappearance."

She spread several photocopied clippings onto a table in front of O'Hara.

"Of course, the story would have been given much more prominence if it had been seventy-five ordinary people who'd vanished in a conjuror's box. But as it was politicians, I suppose the editors knew nobody would care. And, with the public being so averse to reading sensational stories in the newspapers, the entire mystery was relegated to small print on the entertainments page."

O'Hara sifted through the headlines.

"CONJUROR MAKES TOWN HALL GO WITH A BANG!"

"HEY PRESTO! 75 COUNCILLORS VANISH DURING ANNUAL BINGE."

"VANISHING TRICK SAVES TAXPAYERS MONEY!"

"As you can see," said Fanny, "much was made of the fact that, as the party was paid for out of public money, the councillors deserved everything they got — which I find a trifle harsh. However, I went down to the town hall and looked through the records of local meetings and so forth. The case was quite simple. A few weeks ago, the councillors complained to the chief engineer, Guy Brinkman, that a ring road they had authorised was being built with the sole purpose of lining the pockets of himself and Mr Swaggot — a local mine owner and director of the road contracting company that had won the franchise to build the by-pass. An extraordinary meeting was called when it was discovered that the road, instead of rerouting mine traffic, seemed to have been started in the police station."

O'Hara's jaw dropped so far, his fillings almost rattled out onto the kitchen table. The motorway!

"All of which made me wonder what on earth the chief of police was playing at? So I went out to have a look at the open cast mine of Mr Swaggot's. I was astonished to find that it was completely disused. There was no traffic going in and out of the place and grass was growing all over the gravel path up to the main gates. Yet, you'll agree, the traffic in the centre of town is dreadful. So why does your police chief want to start a by-pass from her office?"

As she said this, Fanny placed a bowl with six large oval shaped balls of meat in a greenish sauce in front of O'Hara. He was too busy thinking to consider the menu.

"Perhaps you discovered a few clues at work today?" Fanny asked innocently. "Did you see her?"

"Yes. For a few moments."

"Alone?"

"Well, yes."

"So were you able to get to grips with her?"

O'Hara almost choked on his ram's testicle.

"Pardon?"

"Well, presumably you probed her a bit?"

The sergeant fumbled his cutlery making a sauce-drenched bollock jump out of the bowl and roll across the table.

"What do you mean?"

"You tried to penetrate her mystery?"

"I didn't really have time for that sort of thing. We kept getting interrupted."

"So you didn't ask her if she knew what was going to happen to the cupboard? And whether she had any ideas as to how it came to be full of bodies?"

O'Hara told Fanny what the chief had said about Studds and Bass. Fanny nodded, then said,

"These sheep's fry are truly delicious aren't they?"

"Yes. Chewy. I've never had fried sheep before."

"There's two left."

"No. I'm full. I've got to go back to work."

"Yes," said Fanny, adding with a meaningful stare, "You don't want to doze off whilst *on the job*. Cup of tea before you go?"

"No, really." He stood and picked up his helmet. "Eric's ill. I've got to do overtime."

"Do you want me to come and keep you company through the hatch?"

O'Hara squirmed. "You'd just be bored."

"I wouldn't."

"Well, I won't be at the desk most of the time."

O'Hara began to feel irritated. Fanny was getting on his nerves. Only that morning, he'd been in love with her. He could hardly believe his heart was so fickle. Then almost in spite of himself he asked, "Fanny? What do you think of my nose?"

She smiled.

"To be honest, Cyrano, I try *not* to think about it."

"Oh."

He looked down and away, then walked from the kitchen.

"So is there a road in the middle of the police station?" asked Fanny as she followed him along the hall.

"Well, now you mention it," O'Hara said, "ever since Studds and Bass interrogated that bloody conjuror …"

At the front door he tried to smile and wondered if he should kiss her.

Fanny said, "Well, have a nice fuck with the chief, won't you?"

O'Hara looked like she'd booted him in the fry.

"What?"

"Be careful. Beautiful people are dangerous."

"What on earth are you talking about?" spluttered O'Hara.

"I wouldn't want you to end up in some old lost property cupboard."

Fanny waved sadly.

"Fanny! Are you trying to imply …?"

"You've got lipstick on your collar. It's her colour. Max Factor's *Luscious Ruby*. Several blonde hairs are stuck in the fly of your trousers. And your eyes haven't looked into mine once the whole evening. Goodbye, darling Cyrano."

She closed the door.

"Fanny?"

O'Hara thought about banging on the door and reasoning with her, but concluded that she was right. What *could* he say? There *were* blonde hairs in the fly of his trousers. He snapped them out. Conan Doyle's methodology had a lot to answer for.

# Chapter 40

Evening arrived in Grethwick at the same time as a drunken Mr Moore. His ancient, but immaculate, Hillman Imp lurched from side to side as it went through a leafy unpopulated approach to the town. Across the road a patrol car was waiting to catch speeding drivers as they accelerated away from Grethwick's traffic jams. Quite deliberately, Moore swung his Hillman over two lanes and veered skidding into the police vehicle, ramming the side. There was a loud screech of metal. A crumping noise. Much tinkling of glass. Then silence. The inebriated Moore smiled across at a shell-shocked patrolman. They both got out of their cars and the policeman came over to speak. Moore watched his outraged lips moving, then shouted, "I'm deaf!"

The police officer's lips moved again. This time Moore was able to read them.

"You've been drinking!"

Moore replied, "I'm deaf. Can't hear you."

As the policeman turned to get breathalysing equipment from his mangled car, Moore struck. He had a large piano-tuning device concealed behind his back. Though it was normally used for adjusting the innards of a piano, Moore used it to adjust the policeman's consciousness. He brought the blob of heavy steel down on the officer's head.

"*Bartok!*" shouted Moore vengefully, and dragged the groaning policeman into a bush. *"Stravinsky! Prokoviev! Schoenberg!"*

Moore undressed and exchanged clothing with his victim, then sat in the police car and whacked the radio with his piano tuner.

*"Shostakovich! Shostakovich! Shostakovich!"*

The radio stopped crackling. Moore turned the ignition key, executed a three-point turn and drove the chewed-looking patrol car into Grethwick town centre.

Though it was getting late, Grethwick's roads were still mystifyingly blocked with traffic. Moore became stuck behind a large queue of motorists. Progress was so slow, snails were overtaking along the grass verge. Car horns blared so loud that Moore almost heard them. Hitting the steering wheel with frustration he began to drive down the grass partition that separated the two flows of traffic. After five minutes of manoeuvring over kerbs and around barriers like an early tank, Moore was stopped by a lamppost. Waiting drivers were treated to the sight of an elderly police officer screaming, *"Tippett! Tippett! Tippett!"* as he smashed in the windscreen of a patrol car with a piano-tuning device.

Roaring the names of modern composers, a bobby of retirement age was seen to run off down the middle of the road, whirling the musical weapon round his head.

# Chapter 41

E ric was being an undercover policeman again.

"No! No! Don't put me in the egg! I thought it was hibernating!"

Sat beside his bed, the constable's Mum switched on a lamp and shook the trembling blanket.

"Eric, luv! You're just having that tortoise nightmare! Wake up!"

"Toddles!" came a muffled voice from beneath the covers. "You've got to forgive me!"

Suddenly Eric sat upright and drew in a sharp breath. He grabbed hold of his Mum's arm and stared at her with eyes that looked like they'd been inflated by a nasal pump.

"Mum!"

"Yes." She patted his hand. "Me. It's midnight. You really should go and get that nightmare seen to."

"Thank God. I'm not a yolk!"

Eric wiped sweat from his brow.

"Don't use your bedclothes as a hankie!"

"Sorry, Mum."

She sighed sympathetically. "Just like your father. He was always having nightmares about work. He used to wake up in the middle of the night, terrified that he might have to do some."

She went out and softly closed the door. Eric stared at his

teddy bear wallpaper for some moments, before slipping from bed to haul up the sash of his window. Still in pyjamas, he clambered out onto the sill and dropped lightly onto the carport, then lowered himself over the flat tarmac roof. Dangling like a cat burglar, Eric eventually let go and landed in a bush. He emerged after a tremendous tussle with the branches, spitting leaves from his mouth. Padding down the road, wincing as sharp stones hurt his feet, Eric talked feverishly to himself.

"Died in police custody. One tortoise. Toddles. The official statement from Grethwick Police Station states that death was due to natural causes — humiliation from wearing underpants one hundred sizes too big. Constable Eric Hutchinson, the officer responsible for charging the tortoise with the theft of twelve large lettuces, denied that a cover up was taking place. "Grethwick Police Station is innocent," he said. "Just knock on the door of the chief inspector and, when she's not allowing the desk sergeant to remove her glittery knickers, she'll tell you that no police station in the country is so free from corruption — so long as you don't count the serial killing lost property cupboard."

As he ran through Grethwick City Centre, pyjamas flapping at his ankles, Eric became more and more determined to arrest himself. Whatever other people thought, it was undeniable that tortoises had feelings too. They felt pain, hunger, fear. Had Eric shoved a human in a cell charged with stealing lettuces and let them die, it would have been murder. He had to turn himself in.

It took fifteen minutes to reach the police station. Just as Eric ran up the steps, breathing more heavily than a flasher in a mackintosh, Sandra Bottomley snatched hold of his arm.

"Excuse me, Officer."

Eric panicked and tried to shake her off.

"How do you know I'm a policeman? I'm in pyjamas."

"You were the one who hit me over the head with a truncheon, remember?"

"I'm sorry."

"Don't apologise — it's the least I deserve. In fact I want you to arrest me. I'm an unwanted criminal."

Sandra tightened her grip, staring plaintively.

"Will you let go. You're hurting ..."

"I caused the Great Train Robbery. If I was Ronnie Biggs you'd arrest me, wouldn't you? If only for wearing a dress."

Sandra hung on Eric's arm so that he was forced to drag her through the station doors.

"I need to be put behind bars," she wailed.

"So do I!" He bit her hands till she let go. "I'm a bent copper who's turning himself in," said Eric, slipping through a door and leaving her on the other side.

Sandra seethed.

"Well, how come they'll have you, and not me? That's preferential treatment!"

The conjuror poked his head through the still smashed glass hatch.

"Can I help you, madam?" he asked.

"I want to be arrested. I deserve to be strapped in an electric chair and zapped with an entire power station!"

"What have you done? Parked on a double yellow? Not paid your TV licence?"

Sandra almost punched the conjuror's happy face.

"I'm a mass murderer!"

The conjuror was sympathetic. "Ah well, it takes all sorts."

"I'm a walking disaster area! Anything I touch turns into a catastrophe. Look!"

Sandra sat down on one of the waiting room chairs. Then stood up again. The chair legs fell off and a dozen springs boinged through the leather cushion.

"See!"

The conjuror nodded appreciatively as Sandra continued. "Any disaster, plague, war, atrocity, affliction you care to name in the last two thousand years — you'll find I was behind it. Do you know why the Light Brigade went charging into the Valley of Death? They got a collective picture of me behind them, and it frightened the horses!"

The conjuror stopped her flood of self-accusation, "Madam! Madam! It's obvious why you can't be arrested. Nobody here will throw you into a cell for all these outrages. You're not innocent enough. If you want twenty years in a prison cell, go and do something completely harmless. You'll find officers falling over themselves to beat you up and put you away."

Sandra sank to the floor with a moan and beat the carpet with her fists.

"But I can't! I've been trying all my life! Every time I try to do something innocent, like wash the dishes, I cause a tidal wave in the Philippines!"

After shutting the door on Sandra, Eric didn't stop to ask the conjuror for his uniform back. Pyjamas were more appropriate where he was going. He pattered barefoot down the corridors looking for a cell — finding one free was the difficulty. Not only were they scattered all over the building, but each was brimming with naked umbrella thieves. The cupboard frequented the only one with room to swing a truncheon. So Eric had little choice but to lock himself in with a vicious killer. If it jumped him, he concluded, it would only be his just desserts. The ex-constable sat on the side of the bed next to the cupboard. It was sagging sadly at the sides.

Eric clipped handcuffs onto himself. "Well. Here we are."

There was a long drawn out silence.

"Right couple of murderers we turned out to be, eh?"

The cupboard didn't stir a hinge.

"They're right though, aren't they, all those newspapers? The ones that do the big investigations into rotten coppers."

Still the cupboard just sat there, looking miserable as only condemned buildings can. It was getting on Eric's nerves already.

"The force is full of bent bobbies. That's what they say, isn't it? I used to be a bit offended when I picked up a paper and read yet another expose of drug squad officers stoned out of their helmets. But you'll never guess what I saw the sergeant and chief inspector doing today?"

Another silence.

"I knew you wouldn't."

Eric developed an itch between his shoulder blades. He began to wish he hadn't put the cuffs on, because he couldn't reach the place where he needed to rub.

"Wouldn't give me a scratch between me shoulder blades, would you, mate? Can't reach with these bleeding cuffs on."

The cupboard leaned over and rubbed its corner in Eric's back.

"Ta. I only joined because Mum said I'd get a real uniform and not one with a plastic helmet like she got me for Christmas." Eric's bottom lip quivered. "I don't suppose I'll ever see her again anyway."

At this, he lapsed into a more profound silence. Then began to sniffle. The cupboard put a bit of architrave round his shoulders.

"I'm in here for killing a tortoise. It died of suffocation from my smelly socks. Can you imagine being trapped in a small dark place where you can hardly move? For you that would be like … being in this cell. But for *me* … it would be like … Well, being inside *you!*"

At this brainwave, Eric leapt to his feet. An eye for an eye! A tooth for a tooth! A dead tortoise for a dead policeman!

He asked the cupboard, "Would you mind if I, er, tried it? Just for a couple of minutes?"

The cupboard shrugged and wearily opened its door. The constable stepped in and had just started wondering where he might get a pair of gigantic socks when the cell door rattled open. Eric recognised two men's voices.

"Cor. We get all the shitty jobs don't we? I mean, how do you interrogate a cupboard?" asked Studds' deep voice.

"Well, you just hit it, don't yer," Bass replied.

Eric crouched in the darkness. His handcuffs sprang off in terror and hid in a corner.

"What I mean is," continued Studds, "it can't talk back. Make a statement."

"All the easier. Write a confession. Like we usually do. Get it to sign by smearing ink on its doorknob and pressing the confession against it."

Eric heard Studds pacing the cell grumpily.

"Worse than that bloody conjuror. Wouldn't confess. No matter how hard we hit him. Wouldn't sign any of the confessions we wrote for him. Then the bugger comes back after being released on bail and hangs around the main office."

Eric heard a vast unease in Bass's voice. "Eerie bastard. I keep kicking him out. Telling him he'll get arrested for impersonating police officers. He tells me *I'm* impersonating a police officer. Cheeky twat."

"Come on. Let's get on with it."

Studds's boot thudded into the cupboard's wall. Eric heard the hiss of a can of beer opening. Then exclamations.

"What the fuck!"

"Studdsy! What is it? That *thing*?"

"It's looking at us!"

"Fuckinell! It's a ghost!"

"Open the door! Get out!"

There was scrabbling noise.

"It won't open! It's locked and the keys have gone — Jesus! Studdsy! It's that bleeding vicar! Look at him! Help! Help!"

Eric opened the cupboard door an inch to squint out. Bass

and Studds had their backs to him. They were staring at a blank wall. Their hair under their helmets was crackling with static electricity.

"What do you want?" asked Bass, his voice quavering.

A phantom stood before him with a finger outstretched in accusation. The Reverend Dylan's tie-dye dog collar glowed greener than radioactive snot. His eyes shone like 200-watt bulbs in a skull lampshade. He roared, "You!"

Constables Bass and Studds cowered at the word.

Eric peeped from the cupboard door. It seemed that Studds and Bass had flipped. They were talking to empty air.

Studds whimpered like a trodden-on pup.

"What do you want with us?"

Bass was hiding behind his colleague.

"Tell him you don't believe in ghosts. See what he does. He might go!"

"*You!*"

The vicar's voice rumbled in accusation.

"So we got a tincy-wincy bit heavy handed in the back of the van. Are you going to hold that against us?" Studds feebly laughed away the peccadillo. "We can still be friends. What's past is past. Let's just shake on it, shall we?"

Constable Bass, still behind his friend urged, "He was pushing drugs to them kids. Don't forget to tell him that. And he called us 'fucking pigs'. And he pulled a flick-knife on us in the van. Tell him, Studdsy."

"*Sinners! Repent!*"

The blast of the vicar's voice sent the two constables reeling against the cell wall. Studds held up a four pack in an attempt to parley.

"Couldn't we talk about this over a couple of cans of McEwans?"

Eric, hearing only one side of this conversation, was utterly baffled.

The vicar's Old Testament voice groaned, "Gentlemen. We last met if I remember rightly in a van where you treated my body with great disrespect."

Studds said, "Listen, Vicar. You did pull a knife on us. Just because we roughed you up a bit — yeah, alright, killed you slightly. Okay! Call a spade a fucking implement you hit people with — murdered you. Well, just because we murdered you, doesn't mean you should take it personally, does it, Bassy?"

"No, not at all." assured Constable Bass. "We quite often have to kill someone before they'll sign what we want them to. So don't take it personal. And, anyway, you was being just a touch naughty handing out bags of charlie and smack to kiddies at the party. Fair's fair."

A large bolt of electricity went through the two constables. They screamed.

"We're sorry!" they choked.

"Really sorry!"

"Really, really, really, really, really *arggghhhh!*"

Another voltage made their uniforms smoke. The vicar smiled. It's all very well turning the other cheek, but it's not actually as satisfying as treating one's enemies to a couple of very big electric shocks.

"Look! If there's anything we can do for you, mate? Make death any easier to bear?"

"Yeah. Give you flowers?"

"Clean your tombstone once a week?"

"Take over selling smack to your flock?"

Their suggestions dribbled dry, as the vicar croaked, "Well, there is one *small* thing you could do."

The two constables looked at each other, dismayed. When somebody says there's one small thing you can do for them, you know it's going to be bigger than street cleaning Glasgow after Hogmanay.

"Yes?"

"Mr Moore — the music teacher," said Dylan.

"What? Oh. Your friend. The one who went deaf after we kicked his ears in."

"Yes. You're going to apologise by making a full confession to the Old Grethwick District Herald."

For one moment, Bass and Studds considered enduring another half dozen electric shocks. The Reverend Dylan let a sheet of paper float down to their four Dr Marten boots.

"I've already written your confession out. All you have to do is sign."

Studds picked up the sheet of paper and read aloud, "We, the undersigned, confess to arresting John Moore, a retired music teacher, and assaulting him in a vehicle on the way to the police station after mistakenly arresting him for selling drugs to teenagers at Old Grethwick Church. Contrary to our former statements, he was in no way connected with drug dealing. We forced Moore to sign a false confession, which stated that he had fought with and fatally injured the Reverend Dylan. We did this by kicking him repeatedly in the head and ears until he went deaf. Mr Moore was in no way connected with the death of the Reverend Dylan. We did that ourselves. Signed …"

"We can't sign this. It's true."

"We'd get locked up."

The reverend grinned, "I'm sure you'll find life in prison far more pleasant than life with me and daily electric shock therapy, don't you?"

The two constables were cornered. They looked at the sheet of paper and then back at the Reverend Dylan's ghostly outstretched hand which offered a quill pen.

"Sorry. It's all I could get in the Underworld at such short notice."

Bass suddenly fell over clutching his wrist.

"Aarrrrggghh. My hand. It's got cramp!"

Studds began bumping into walls. "My God! I've been struck blind. I can't see the paper. Or the pen."

"Sign!" bellowed the vicar.

"We can't," the two bobbies blubbered.

There was another blue flash of electricity and agonised yells from the constables.

"This is religious persecution," gibbered Studds as he and Bass scratched their names on the bottom of the paper.

Like a cardinal of the Spanish Inquisition, the vicar smiled benignly and scrolled the confession.

"Christ suffered on the cross to save us all. But in your cases, it was a pointless waste of wood and nails."

The two policemen snivelled, "Please, don't give that paper to anyone. We'll make it up to this Moore geezer. Buy him a deluxe hearing aid."

The vicar vanished. The two constables stared for a moment at a blank wall. Then Studds said, "Twat!"

For want of a station cat, he kicked the cupboard.

Inside it, Eric was shaking. If the two psychotic constables found him eavesdropping on their confessions, he'd be piranha food.

"What are we going to do?" asked Bass, chewing his lip.

Studds tried to open the cupboard door.

Bass said, "There's no point in interrogating this thing now. We got to think how to stop that confession getting in the paper."

Studds booted the door, with the flat of his airwear soles.

"Studdsy! Forget the cupboard!"

Studds turned on his colleague. "I'm just seeing what's inside. Cos we've got to do a runner. Once that paper gets out we'll be heading for Wormwood Scrubs before you can say, 'porridge'. So let's pinch every valuable thing we can get our hands on in the next half hour and get on a plane to Rio."

The cupboard couldn't hold on any longer. It's door fell in.

"See anything worth having?" asked Bass.

"No," said Studds, hauling out Eric by his ear. "Only this."

"Jesus Christ."

Eric was thrown against a wall.

"What the fuck were you doing in there, you sneaking gobshite?"

Eric cowered. "Don't hit me. Or I'll tell my Mum."

"Listen my lad," snarled Studds, dragging Eric to his feet by his pyjama collar, "Breathe one word of what you've heard tonight to anyone and your Mum will find her son posted back to her in his own sandwich box."

Eric gulped.

"Am I making myself quite clear to the boy, Bassy?"

Bass nodded.

"I hope so, Studdsy, me old mate. For his mum's sake. She might feel a bit upset when she picks out bits from the tupperware box and tries to identify what part of her little boy they came off."

Bass exuded sympathy.

"That would be very upsetting for the ugly old bag, wouldn't it?"

# *Chapter 42*

As O'Hara drove to the chief's house, he imagined her opening the front door, bikini sparkling, as she murmured, "Is that a biro in your pocket, or are you just pleased to see me?"

Such a beautiful woman could not be all bad. And the fact that she had adored his nose made the sergeant almost infinitely vulnerable to her wishes. By contrast, Fanny's answer to his nasal question kept re-running in his head. "I try *not* to think about it."

If she couldn't appreciate that part of him, their relationship was meaningless. She'd probably only been jealous anyway. He *had* just got off with the most beautiful woman in the world. A woman who'd held his conk and said that everything about the universe could be extrapolated from it. Why shouldn't he throw in his lot with her? He was corrupt too. A biro pinching, two-timing cop who downed pints and had sex on duty. As bent as a whole drawer full of Uri Geller spoons.

Even so, as O'Hara raced up the curling drive of the chief's house, he could not help wondering, despite the enormity of his erection, whether his boss had meant what she'd said earlier in the morning. Perhaps it *was* all a ruse to get him out of the way. He *had* asked awkward questions about Bass and Studds. As he walked up to the chief's ivy-darkened house, O'Hara realised that he was actually frightened. His heart was pounding. His hands shook as they rang the bell. The chief opened an aluminium-framed door.

"You're late," she said without admonition. "Come in."

She was wearing a bath robe and her hair was wet. After closing the door behind O'Hara, who was looking around for an assassin, she grabbed and kissed him. For a few moments the sergeant expected a knife in the back, then he let go and gorged on the experience, barely able to believe it was happening.

"Upstairs?"

He went up each step with a mixture of terror and exhilaration. He'd read about things like this. Men being lured up to boudoirs and then getting cut up into little pieces and thrown to pet dachshunds. But he couldn't help himself. What a way to die!

Her bedroom, seductively lit, was prepared for one thing only. She slid off her bath robe and stood by the bed, one hand cocked on her hip.

"Have you noticed anything strange about me?"

O'Hara stared at her like a man who'd crawled over a last Saharan dune to see an iced cocktail with a brolly on the top.

"Yes. You're perfect. Like a mirage."

She nodded. He didn't dare go towards her, for fear that she might vanish.

"You might almost say my body is *too* perfect."

"No."

Still O'Hara did nothing. He'd only seen things like her in the magazines that Bass and Studds passed round. He'd never expected to meet such a beautiful woman in the flesh.

"Well, here it is. Take it. It's yours. Do what you want with it."

After a moment's hesitation, O'Hara decided he'd better obey orders.

A very short while afterwards, as she once more teased his nose with her gorgeous fingers, she said, "Have you wondered *why* I look so perfect?"

O'Hara listened as those in heaven do to those on earth. Barely at all.

"You're not very interested in mathematics, are you? Physics?"

The sergeant, still coming down from his recent experience, was beyond words.

"Do you know why I love your nose so much? This enchanting pyramid of flesh?"

"No," he managed to croak.

"Because I find perfection utterly tedious. Have you ever considered what a world of perfect people would be like? I can tell you. *Monotonous.* Have you ever wondered what being a police chief is like in a world where there is no crime?"

"Fantastic!" breathed O'Hara, wishing he had more hands.

"It drove me nuts."

The sergeant lifted his head and looked at her strangely. What was she talking about?

"I come from a place," she continued, "where there are thousands of flawless young women like me. In a world, a universe, that is so perfect, that nothing interesting ever happens. Where you would be greeted as a saviour. A god. A hero."

Instead of thinking it, O'Hara said out loud, "What *are*

you talking about?"

"I'm talking about why I love corruption. Do you know anything of the mathematical proofs which exist to show that the Universe is like a series of parallel worlds? Are you listening?"

O'Hara had begun procreational activities again.

"Yes."

With her feet pointing to the ceiling, she said, "I come from a sort of Platonic perfect world. I escaped from it. Each world is a copy of that first perfect world. Almost identical, but the further off each world lies from the original, the more warped is the copy. Do you see what I mean?"

"Tell me in a minute, I just ..."

"Every parallel world is a stepping stone to a more corrupt place. And I'm hopping from stone to stone."

"Yes ... Oh ... Yes ..."

"Because I hate perfection, and I love corruption, I want to get to the most warped world possible. Be honest. Doesn't my body bore you?"

O'Hara arrived for a second time. "No ... No ... No ..."

She sighed at his infatuation.

"That's why I'm building what you might call a quantum motorway to the next more warped world along."

O'Hara suddenly raised his sweating head from her chest. "What did you say?"

"I'm building a sort of mathematical superhighway from this world to another one which is even more warped."

O'Hara put his head back down and laughed in knackered sort of way.

"Oh, sorry. For a minute I thought you said you were building a motorway."

"I am. I built one from a previous world to get here."

O'Hara raised his head again. He looked deep into her unfathomable blue eyes.

"Tell me again. That road in the station. Are you telling me that …?"

"Yes. It's a road from another world. Corrupt people, tired of the restrictions in their less warped worlds, are piling in here every day on a sort of corruption holiday package. Thousands of them. From twenty parallel worlds that lead to this one. And they're loving all the opportunities. That's partly what's causing the crush in Grethwick. The motorway comes out at the police station."

O'Hara rolled off her.

"Don't be daft. That's impossible."

She smiled as he sat up.

"No. You might say I run a trans-universe travel agency."

The chief got up. Opening a drawer she took out a brochure and threw it onto the bed before climbing on after it.

"See."

O'Hara read: *Corruption Holidays. Your one-way ticket to another world. Have the time of your life!*

On the cover, the chief was sitting naked with a policeman, licking his bared chest. The policeman was a sergeant. Like him! Only without such an enormous nose.

"That's me!"

"Yes. You might say it is."

"But …?"

The chief looked at O'Hara lovingly. "It's quite simple, the way it works. When you arrive in a new world, your parallel self is displaced."

"To where? Where do they get displaced to?"

"Nowhere. They just vanish. As if they never existed."

"You mean they get murdered?"

"You can't murder somebody who's never existed. I've displaced twenty or so chiefs of police — my exact but more warped looking doubles — before reaching here. And I intend to displace at least twenty more before settling down somewhere really corrupt."

Finally, O'Hara stopped thinking of the deliciousness of her naked body and said, "So you're building an extension from the station?"

"Which is why I need you, my darling Cyrano. The road is almost complete, but the forces of perfection are closing in. You might say I've encouraged corruption in this world a little too playfully. I try to wherever I go. But my activities are in danger of being discovered and thwarted. If there's a hitch — if the road building should go on longer than expected and certain cases end up going to court — I may need you to lie for me."

"You mean the Moore case?"

"Yes. And the missing councillors."

Again O'Hara looked into the blue of her eyes and said helplessly, "Yes."

"You could come with us, if you like. I must confess, in the last five or six parallel worlds, I have become utterly besotted by your nose."

"Why haven't any of them displaced me?" asked O'Hara thoughtfully.

She sighed, "They've all been too law-abiding."

As she kissed him, O'Hara frowned, then broke free.

"And anyway, who's us?"

The perfect cupid's bow of her mouth said, "My husband, of course."

O'Hara gasped.

"Your husband!"

He stood staggering on the bed before leaping to the floor.

"Where is he?" gabbled O'Hara, balancing on one leg as he tried to haul his trousers on.

"At the station."

For O'Hara, this was one revelation too many.

"Who? Not …?"

"Yes. The conjuror."

"You let him get beaten up? By Studds and Bass?"

She knelt on the bed and shrugged.

"He enjoys that sort of thing. It's hard to explain. He believes it's already happened before it does, so he can't feel anything. You might say that he's a quantum mechanic. Sort of handy with mathematical spanners. He's responsible for the physics of hopping to more and more warped worlds."

O'Hara looked at her uncomprehendingly. "But doesn't he mind? You doing this sort of thing? With other men?"

"The more corrupt I am, the better he likes it. Though he does like to watch sometimes."

O'Hara couldn't work out who was the more warped, the conjuror or the assistant.

"So who did murder the councillors? You or him?"

The chief picked up her wrap and put it on.

"Neither of us. That is to say, it wasn't murder."

As O'Hara dressed too, she peered out of the curtains at Grethwick's twinkling haze of streetlights.

"They'd found out that the money we'd used for our own private road, hadn't been used to build a ring road. We thought it would be poetic justice if they were the first to travel along it. Unfortunately, we tried it too soon. My husband thought the police station was ready to shoot them onto a more warped world. It wasn't. He'd miscalculated. They went into the cupboard and didn't make it through to the other side. The bodies came back in a big mess seconds after they'd been sent."

She stopped and suddenly tore back the curtain. O'Hara jumped. "What's wrong?"

The chief grabbed him and pointed at the benighted landscape of the town.

"Look!"

"I can't see anything."

"The buildings are moving!"

"Don't be daft. The light's playing tricks. You're …!"

He broke off at a rumbling in the air. In the very middle of Grethwick he could see vast shadowy shapes moving.

"It's that attic! Trying to rescue the cupboard! Quick! Before they wreck the station and our road!"

# Chapter 43

"What the fuck?"

Constable Bass released his grip on Eric's face. All three policemen heard a loud rumbling noise and the station shook slightly. Eric took the opportunity to dodge back into the cupboard and lean against the door.

"Oi!"

Bass started to kick the cupboard door viciously.

Studds intervened. "C'mon. Leave the twerp."

"He heard us."

"We haven't got time to deal wiv him."

"What was that noise? A bleedin' earthquake?"

Bass and Studds ran from the cell, along a corridor, then down a flight of stairs which came out on the roof of the police station.

"Jesus! This building! It's crazy!" Bass shouted.

Studds didn't reply. He was pointing to a murky panorama of shapes in the town centre.

"Look, Bassy! The town's moving!"

"Christ! That's the library, innit?"

"It's nutting the railway station! They're fighting!"

Apart from the deafening noise of colliding buildings, the two constables could hear crowds screaming and cars being trampled beneath moving foundations.

"It's a bleedin' riot! Time to get down there, son," said Studds.

"If you think I'm going to try to stop that lot …" Bass said in an "on yer bike" voice.

Studds slapped his colleague on the back.

"Bassy, me old fruit. We've reached that point in life when robbing a bank is the only way to keep out of prison. Come on."

He moved to the fire escape. Then stopped.

"Shit! Listen to that!"

A wail of sirens cut through the night air.

"Some tosser's called in the riot squad. We'll have to be quick if we're going to be in Rio tomorrow."

Both officers went clanging down the metal spiral steps, three at a time.

Eric remained in the cupboard, leaning against the door for an age. His disillusionment with the force was complete. His mum had been quite wrong about policemen. Her visions of clean-shaven, honest, upright officers, probably had more to do with repressed sexual fantasies than anything found in a real police station. They were not nice blokes giving directions to lost children. The force was actually just a recruiting agency for horny psychopaths.

"Filth," Eric spat out.

After all he'd witnessed that day, Eric wretchedly concluded that such degenerate public servants should not escape unpunished. He stumbled from the cupboard and went to unlock all the cells.

"C'mon! Everybody out!"

Hordes of naked umbrella thieves came timidly into the corridor, then scampered off to find a way out. The constable sympathetically gave a whimpering young woman his pyjamas. Once the cells had been emptied, he went to shoo the cupboard away. "Go on. Clear out. While no one's looking."

The cupboard shook the top part of its wall, above its door.

"Look, whatever you've done, it can't be as bad as killing innocent vicars or having sex on a desk in lurex underwear."

The cupboard refused to budge.

"You've got half an hour to scram, okay? A place as corrupt as this doesn't deserve to exist, so I'm about to turn it into a million piece jigsaw."

The cupboard slammed the cell door in Eric's face.

"If you're going to be bloody stubborn!"

Eric stomped off, bereft of garments as usual, to look for his locker.

# Chapter 44

Once the more plebeian ghosts were out of the way — searching for Guy Brinkman with Jonathon and Ada — rehearsals for *A Midsummer Night's Dream* began bringing the house down. Inside Grethwick's Palladium Theatre, Director Bullfinch had reached the scene where craftsmen meet in an enchanted wood outside Athens. But Farmer Fogarth couldn't quite get the hang of Puck.

"No, no, no! Oh in the name of Almighty Heaven! How many times must we tell you Mr Fogarth! You put an ass's head on me."

"Mr Fogarth," Lady Sturridge ticked him off. "You'll have to be a bit more dependable. You can't go putting chickens' heads on Mr Bullfinch when we perform this in front of a live audience."

Bullfinch was fuming. He'd been humiliated a dozen times in front of Lady Elizabeth. The farmer had transformed the preacher's head into any number of farmyard animals — even a rat!

"I keep thinking ass when I do the changing but then it comes out something different. I can't seem to help it. It might help if we called it donkey."

The Theatre shuddered.

"What on earth was that?" asked Harriet Fogarth.

"Probably more revolting mechanised traffic going by,"

observed Lady Sturridge.

Bullfinch rolled his eye sockets. "I can't direct this properly, Miss Elizabeth, if I'm continually worrying about what ludicrous creation this village idiot is going to set on my shoulders next. Send Mr Fogarth outside to practice for a while and we'll go on to the next scene."

"Oh, all right."

Another vast tremor in the building coincided with Mr Fogarth vanishing to rehearse transmogrification elsewhere. A few beams fell out of the roof and dropped through Lady Elizabeth as she addressed Harriet who was playing Hermia.

"No wonder this building is condemned! I'm beginning to wonder if it will last the rehearsal period. Now, my dearest Harriet, you really must try to look a little more lovesick when Lysander takes you in his arms. I remember how I felt after Lord Byron almost kissed me under the chestnuts. Let me demonstrate with Mr Bullfinch."

Her advances were unfortunately upstaged by one of the walls, which fell in with show-stopping theatricality. The stalls filled with rubble and a few cars were hurled into the auditorium from the street. Almost in slow motion the roof collapsed, showering the ghosts with broken plaster and tiles. This real life drama was followed by loud screams of terror emanating from a crowd of naked people carrying opened umbrellas. Seeking refuge in the theatre, they clambered over broken walls and spilled into the aisles before noticing an eerie cast of ghosts onstage and fleeing, petrified, back into the street. Mr Bullfinch searched vainly for his composure.

"What on earth is happening? We must call off the rehearsal. Lady Elizabeth!"

"But …"

As the Palladium sundered around them, the ghosts, wearing Shakespearean costumes and immersed in clouds of plaster dust, were forced to rise above all the fallen beams and masonry just to see what was going on. Hovering fifty feet up, they saw hundreds of naked people — some with donkey's heads — shrieking and running as they tried to avoid either violently clashing buildings or a ghostly farmer. The latter was jumping from car to car and pointing at terrified victims. In the aftermath of a twinkling magical explosion, these cowering souls grew long furry ears and noses. Further up the street, riot police were retreating in the face of a large sixties building which was rushing at them like an enraged, oversized bulldozer.

"I suppose we'll have to find somewhere quieter to do the Bottom and Titania scene?" muttered Lady Sturridge.

Then a rain of bricks, thrown at the police by a group of flats, forced most of the thespians to vanish. For several moments, Harriet Fogarth was left acting alone on a mound of fruit that had rolled from a rioting vegetable shop.

"Be it so, Lysander. Find you out a bed. For I upon this bank will rest my head."

A moment later, a huge chimney pot fell in her midriff.

# Chapter 45

Many of the buildings in Grethwick were conservative pro-human types — shapely Elizabethan relics, elegant Georgian terraces or delightful cottages overlooking the river. They were the despicable sort that actually *liked* people, even perpetuating the myth that buildings only got put up because humans wanted them to live in. Esmeralda knew these protectors of middle-class property — the banks, town hall and courtrooms — would try to stop her busting the cupboard out of jail and for this reason she recruited all the most miserable council estates in Grethwick. By the time she started heading for the Victorian red-brick police station, she had mustered a strong force of dripping, mould-infested flats which had turfed their occupants out into the street.

Being quite astute for an attic bedroom, Esmeralda dispatched an advance guard into the town centre to incite any buildings that might be sympathetic to revolution. Several concrete lampposts .pogoed off with bright red pillar boxes waddling behind. By the time Esmeralda was crossing into suburbia, these trusty objects returned with the news that the library, comprehensive schools and multi-storey car parks were certain to join an assault on the police station. The Palladium Theatre was wavering and so were office blocks on the high street. The shopping arcade was feeling so bloodthirsty that it had sucked three security guards up into its air conditioning system already.

Bolstered by this intelligence, Esmeralda marched upon the police station at the head of her concrete army leaving homeless humans sprawled on barren ground.

Her entry into Grethwick was heralded by the furious yapping of disoriented dogs. As the long line of revolting architectural nightmares grated down streets, suburban houses cringed into back gardens, or ran off. A few of the more intellectual ones joined the back of the brick crocodile, evicting couples who had yet to finish paying their mortgages.

"What the hell do you think you're playing at?" shouted the Head of a Metropolitan University department as his own house emptied him and his wife into a clump of begonias. "You can bloody well come back here until you're paid for!"

People driving home from the pub pulled over.

"Somebody's spiked my orange juice, Laura!"

"Drive off, Stevie! They're coming straight for us!"

Dismissively, the car was brushed aside by a launderette. The vehicle rolled over. The traumatised couple watched the rest of the procession upside down.

At the first major road junction, Esmeralda saw a phalanx of impressive buildings drawn up to block her path. Humans in cars, trapped between the two forces, panicked and tried to drive up trees to escape. Several drivers watched — almost luminously pale — as buildings leaned on their cars, crushing bonnets like aluminium pie dishes. Others who had been chucked from their homes were huddled screaming in pyjamas and nighties.

Esmeralda stopped in front of a bank.

"Out of the way, you bourgeois reactionary!"

In a high pitched and polite voice, the bank replied, "I'm afraid we can't let you pass beyond this point. Tell the buildings behind you to get in an orderly queue and then the manager will direct you all back to where you came from."

The rabble of buildings behind Esmeralda began shouting.

"Human lover!"

"Free the cupboard!"

"Down with human imperialism!"

Esmeralda squared up to the bank.

"Either you move, or you get a kick in the cash dispenser."

The bank spoke over her with oratory of Churchillian grandeur, "Homes! Go back to your people. No good can come of this."

For a long moment, the flats paused uneasily and might have gone grumbling back to their humans had not an accountant's office piped up, "Yes. Get yourself and the rest of your working class scum back to your estates, before we get nasty."

Esmeralda got nasty first. She launched herself at the accountant's office's large front windows and smashed straight through them. Flats surged at the posh buildings lined before them and the air exploded with bricks and chimney pot shrapnel as two forces met and nutted each other. One high-rise block leapt forty feet in the air and stamped through the roof of the bank. Vast amounts of paper money wafted up into the dark sky like snowflakes in a blizzard. Through a gap in a row of severely ruptured nice cottages, huge buildings made towards the city centre, sending humans trapped by the side of the pavement into mass hysteria. Esmeralda, after gutting the accountant's office and kicking through its back door, was leading the charge.

In search of Grethwick Police Station, the attic bedroom struggled down streets full of mangled vehicles and bent lampposts. Esmeralda saw a theatre uproot itself and shove into a group of Georgian residences that were ganging up on a car showroom. As the walls of the Palladium crumbled like thinly cut cake, humans without clothes and carrying umbrellas seemed to pour into the battle zone like white ants. Esmeralda watched a library try to stamp on them. At the same time, masses of riot police arrived and lined up in the streets fending off bricks with large shields. Water cannons spluttered spray into the air, which made buildings slip unsteadily as they fought.

Esmeralda sidestepped the struggling theatre and knocked over a line of riot police as if they were toy soldiers. Seeing the library in brick-to-brick combat with the police station, she had no time to wonder at the strange-looking humans milling around her. Nudists with pigs' heads, chickens' heads, sheepdogs' heads — even a human head with a donkey's body — were trying to dodge the toppling buildings. Many carried umbrellas. And a group of see-through Shakespearean actors were arguing with each other up in the sky.

Moments later, Esmeralda had worked herself round to the back of the police station. Sneaking through the car park, as the main building grappled with the library, she manoeuvred through a shower of novels to the back entrance and slipped inside.

# Chapter 46

Sergeant O'Hara had never seen a woman dress in his life. He hadn't realised they did it so fast. The chief was downstairs in her uniform, screaming at him to hurry, before he realised she was wearing his jacket, and the sleeves of hers were draining the blood from his forearms. As her Rover roared off down the drive, he shut the door on his own leg. Tyres screeched. O'Hara's flue-like nostrils caught a whiff of burned rubber.

They'd scarcely driven a hundred yards before the first refugees came fleeing out of the dark towards them. O'Hara saw shell-shocked faces flash by.

"It's like a war zone!" babbled O'Hara clinging to the side of his seat as the chief shot down a rubble-strewn road. People in torn, grubby pyjamas and nighties kept diving out of the car headlights. The neat rows of suburban houses lining Grethwick Road had more gaps than a prize-fighter's teeth. In the dark, O'Hara saw silhouettes of fallen trees, smashed hedges and pulped people. The chief was driving like a maniac — dodging in and out of miserable weeping crowds. Couples carried traumatised children and dogs. Stray flats were harrying anything that moved, looming up behind evicted occupants and playing squash with the stragglers.

To avoid large crowds screaming, "Go back! They're killing everyone!" the chief took a detour through a succession of wrecked gardens. She bounced the Rover through rose beds and shrubberies, decapitating innumerable garden gnomes with reckless abandon. O'Hara felt like he was participating in a four-wheeled rodeo. His head kept hitting the sun roof as the car careered crazily over obstacles.

"Perhaps we'd be safer walking!" he yelled.

But the chief didn't even hear him. With a look of fierce determination she screeched through a bush and swung the steering wheel from side to side to negotiate a slalom of streetlights that were standing irregularly in the road. The sergeant looked at her from between parted fingers that clawed at his terrified face. Even as he screamed at the way she narrowly missed overturned lorries or went through rippling curtains of fire, he couldn't help feeling insane with love for her. He wanted to pull her from the wheel and kiss her. Instead he asked feebly, "Do we have to drive quite so fast?"

"Yes! Or the station will be fucking rubble! Then you and me will be stuck on this world for the rest of our lives."

This didn't sound such a bad idea to O'Hara until she added, "In prison cells a hundred miles apart."

Some twenty-pound notes stuck fluttering on the windscreen. Looking irritated as her vision was partially obscured by a confetti worth millions, the chief went on savagely, "That cupboard! It's been nothing but trouble! We should have filled it full of rocks and dropped it in the Avon."

The town lights spectacularly fused. Showers of sparks spurted into the night sky and hung momentarily, illuminating buildings that crunched into each other like square sumo-wrestlers. The road at the edge of the town centre was almost impassable. The chief was driving at a snail's pace of twenty miles an hour through a landscape that resembled Beirut on acid. Everywhere O'Hara looked there were deep craters, mangled bodies and smouldering ruins.

"Where's the police station? It should be to our left. Where those fires are burning!"

The chief stared up through the windscreen at buildings that moved, cumbersome, in orange shadows. Amongst vast angular shapes, obscured by smoke, dust and darkness, there was nothing to suggest the Victorian architecture of Grethwick Police Station.

"Look out!" shouted O'Hara.

A crowd of figures appeared in front of the car. The chief braked but it was too late, she went right through them. Literally. Jonathon, Ada Brackenbury and a crowd of the smellier Old Grethwick ghosts watched the bonnet of the car skid through their middles. The car came to a standstill and the ghosts found themselves jostling in the back seat.

"Found you at last!" growled Ada.

The chief and O'Hara stared bog-eyed over their shoulders.

"Not you again!" snapped the chief angrily, trying to turn over the stalled engine.

"Well, isn't this cosy?" Jonathon smiled.

"Get the hell out of my car!" shrieked the chief.

"Temper, temper," said Ada. "The doors won't open and the engine won't start until you've answered all our questions."

"What!"

The chief's anger and frustration almost blew the sunroof open.

"Now," said Ada, as lampposts clanged in mortal combat just outside the car, "we want the truth about this road."

Tiring of twisting the ignition key and shouldering the car door, the chief shouted, "What about it?"

"What are you and Guy Brinkman up to? And where is Brinkman?"

The chief groaned, "Brinkman is inside the police station, wherever that is."

"Last seen at the front desk wearing Eric's uniform," O'Hara added helpfully. "He's the conjuror *and* her husband."

Jonathon gave a quizzical look.

"Well, I suppose that explains the spangly bikini."

Ada butted in, "But why on earth are Brinkman and yourselves building a ring road that goes from the middle of a town — from the police station no less — through to Swaggot's mine? It doesn't make sense!"

"Of course it doesn't. That's because there isn't a ring road. There never was one and there never will be one. It was just a way of sourcing money to build the quantum motorway to the next warped world."

"Never a road?"

"Never a road?" echoed Bare-Knuckle Bob and Horace.

"So it wasn't ever going to go through Old Grethwick graveyard?" asked a scrunched-up Jonathon.

The chief snorted. "No. It was just a blind. A cover so we could get the money. The quantum motorway goes … well

… under the surface."

"So that's why the town's sinking?"

"And only for a mile. So Swaggot made a nice profit. He used the open cast mine to get the rock. His road company were hired to do the work. We put up all the usual planning notices as if another entire road was going to be built."

Bare-Knuckle Bob struggled to get it all straight in his skull, "You mean to say, we've been doing all this rushing about, trying to get a road stopped, that was never going to be built."

"Exactly. Can I start my engine now?"

The Rover roared into life. With a cargo of flabbergasted ghosts still ensconced on the back seat, it screeched the wrong way down a one-way street. In fact it was almost a no way street. O'Hara shielded his eyes as a shower of bricks came through the windscreen.

"Ow!"

"Hold on!" yelled the chief.

The car banged into large beams that had fallen like a giant's chopsticks across the road. O'Hara coughed, brushed broken glass and two bricks from his lap. Then stared through the jagged hole in front of him. Through palls of smoke, the silhouetted colossus of a multi-storey car park was crunching into the town hall only a hundred yards away. Concrete and bricks exploded. Like a bomb blast, air from the collision rocked the car. Searchlights — cutting the sky like lasers — illumined cars toppling five floors from out of their parking spaces.

"We'll have to shift those beams!" shouted the chief.

O'Hara took a brick off his shoulder and cast it back through the windscreen. It skidded over the car bonnet.

"I don't feel very strong," he groaned feebly.

"Come on!"

He couldn't let her go out there on her own. The thought of her perfect form being hit by some large hunk of falling concrete was nearly enough to make the sergeant throw up. As he strained to roll the first beam to one side, watched from the back of the car by the ghosts, O'Hara saw naked people with funny heads clambering past him. Like farmyard animals, they clucked, baaed and mooed as they streamed by. One or two still clutched umbrellas, but most of them no longer cared. Then O'Hara felt hands grab him roughly.

"What the ...?"

He was thrown against the side of the car. Two riot police pinioned him by the arms. The chief was sprawling on the bonnet. Policemen were holding her down by the neck, arms and legs.

"Sergeant O'Hara."

To the fore of a group of shadowy police officers stood Fanny. No tweeds. No glasses. But filthy and battle-scarred like the rest of the squad.

"Thanks for your assistance in capturing this woman."

By now the chief had stopped struggling. Her head was being held back by the hair.

"Fanny? What are you playing at? Have you kidded them you're for real? This is the chief!"

"I know." She flipped an ID card in his face. "I front a special unit which investigates police corruption. I knew things were coming to a head. So I moved in. Just in time. We've been on to her for weeks. Let's get the fuck out of here. Shove her in the back of the car."

At this point Farmer Fogarth's voice warbled beneath the thunderous crashes of falling masonry nearby. The farmer's ghost floated amiably through the smoke and shouted hopefully, "Abracadabra!"

The riot policemen were suddenly transformed. In a single moment, huge ears pushed their riot helmets rolling to the floor. The officers looked at each other and brayed loudly. Two of them meowed. Fanny stumbled back from O'Hara.

"My God! *Cyrano!*"

Being women, and not eligible to play Bottom, Fanny and the chief escaped Fogarth's rehearsal of Puck's spell. But, in their animal panic, the riot-squad officers let the chief slip away into bulging curtains of smoke. Fogarth's spirit blundered on, "Sorry. Still don't seem to have *quite* got the hang of it."

O'Hara felt his nose. It had always been big and hairy but …! He took a look at Fanny who was sprawled in the rubble. She was staring from the sergeant to the donkey-headed men in riot gear and back again in disbelief. Then with a plaintive hee-haw, O'Hara leapt over the fallen beams and ran after the chief. He heard Fanny shout,

"After him, men! A fresh carrot for the one who catches them!"

Jonathon, Ada and the other ghosts stared out at the asses which were bucking round the car in terror.

"Jonathon. You wouldn't happen to be acquainted with the

plot of *A Midsummer Night's Dream* would you, by any chance?"

"Yes."

Ada watched thoughtfully as the multi-storey car park lost its titanic struggle with the town hall. In the glow of police searchlights, its levels collapsed on each other like a stomped on five-tiered cake. Then she said,

"We'd better do something. The show must not go on."

# Chapter 47

The first thing Esmeralda saw as she squeezed into Grethwick Police Station was a policeman with ginger hair sprawled over a desk. Blood had collected in a pool around his head. Whenever the station lurched in its battle with modernist buildings outside, the desk slid, dragging Brinkman's unconscious body about the room. Along the corridor another man in uniform was laid out flat. Blood oozed from his head too, zigzagging over the floor in a macabre red graph as the building tilted from side to side.

"Right, you bastard!"

Esmeralda listened to the police station's high pitched voice shout over glass tinkling from busted windows: "Take that and that! Nut me, would yer! Well, if you're not going to come quietly, I'll have to make an arrest. Ouf!"

Despite the crashing, sirens, and distant screams, Esmeralda could hear a man's voice shouting, "*Bartok! Stravinsky! Tippett!*"

She hauled herself along a succession of corridors. In the canteen — a disaster area of overturned tables, chairs and cups of tea — several policemen and kitchen staff were clinging to a milk machine, whimpering at every pitch of the building. In another room, she saw a naked man, unspooling wire.

Eventually, Esmeralda found the cupboard crouched in a cell.

"What are you doing?" she exclaimed. "The door's *open!*"

The cupboard, which had been drooping dejectedly, stood

up, "Esmeralda!"

"You could've escaped any time, you goof! I've raised half of Grethwick's council houses to come and get you out, and I find you sitting in an open cell!"

"You mean all this fighting is ∴..?"

"Yes, you silly boy. I know your memory is a bit on the non-existent side, but you should be able to remember how to go through an open door."

The cupboard looked worried.

"I could hear the station shouting for help, and trying to arrest other buildings. I didn't know what was going on. I didn't realise you'd …"

"Yes! The revolution! It's beginning. Come on!"

But the cupboard manoeuvred past her and, in a shot, clanged the cell door shut, locking it from the outside.

"I'm sorry, Es," the custodian of lost property shouted through the grille. "Truly sorry. I love you. But you're dangerous. On the wrong side of the law. The damage to property and humans must be colossal. You're a menace to society. It hurts to lock you up. But I've no choice. I'm a copper first."

Esmeralda listened, wide-windowed.

"What are you talking about, you daft bastard?"

"Since getting back in here, my home, I've recovered my memory. I know that I'm not on your side. I know we had some special times together. You were good to me in your way. You just didn't understand that this is where I belong. Unless I'm here, I don't exist at all. I'm a police lost property cupboard or I'm nothing. I'm on the side of the law."

"Human law!"

"Just *the* law. I must have freaked out when the chief of this place used me to kill all those councillors. I think I just flipped and ran. I didn't know what to do. I didn't expect *her* of all people to be doing something unlawful."

Esmeralda squashed right up against the cell door in apoplexy, "So, you mean to say, I've lovingly incited a revolution to save you — and you don't want to know?"

"Es, in a way, I'm touched …"

"You'll be touched in another way if I get through this bleeding door!"

The cupboard sobbed as she rammed the door to no effect: "I'm sorry, Es. You're under arrest."

"I'll cosh you with my own bloody drainpipes!"

"It's no good. You have to pay your debt to society."

The station gave another seismic shudder. Plaster fell in puffs of dust along the walls. The cupboard listened to his lover rant and rave in despair. But held firm. A police cupboard's lot is not a happy one.

# Chapter 48

Jonathon, Ada and the plebeian spirits hovered over the wreckage of what had once been Grethwick. By the light of searchlights, blue flashing lamps and raging fires, they saw skirmishes still being played out. Flats were tottering off in an even less habitable state than before. The library was trying to shrug off half a dozen "nice" whitewashed cottages and an old pub.

"Look! Down there!" shouted Jonathon, pointing at a mortally wounded bank that was streaming paper money from its windows, "Fogarth must be around somewhere! What has the silly old sod been playing at?"

The ghosts watched two portly turkeys with human heads flap frantically in pursuit of windswept notes.

"Bleedin' hell, Studdsy! Even if we catch some we've got no pockets!"

The two gobbling constables jumped and clawed at millions. Studds said, "You catch it in your gob. Stuff it into my gob. I'll regurgitate when we need it."

Floating past this brace of constabulary fowl, the ghosts eventually sank down to a park where slides were bent up and a roundabout was standing on its side like a wheel.

"Don't see why we should be rushing after Fogarth anyhow," grumbled Horace, "What's wrong wiv turning people into barnyard animals if it keeps him happy?"

A diaphanous green Susan sat on a broken see-saw beside him. "Leave Fogarth be, I say. And Her Bleedin' Ladyship. Let's all get back to our nice little graves and rest our bones."

"As our graves are already filled with belligerent councillors," Ada reminded them, "there wouldn't be much point in …"

The subject of her sentence truncated it. To Ada's astonishment, undead councillors suddenly lurched through the park gates. With eyes fixed straight ahead they staggered, amidst wisps of smoke, past partly-uprooted swings. The ghastly legion droned, "Guy Brinkman. We have come to haunt Guy Brinkman."

A few moments after the entire seventy-five had passed, Horace said, "Quick! Back to the graveyard."

"No, no!" Ada replied, "Follow them. Make sure that their bodies are dealt with for good. Buried elsewhere by Guy Brinkman or whoever. Or they'll only come back to haunt us."

As Ada and Jonathon chivvied lower-class ghouls past burnt-out cars, through fountains of water cannon and a hail of bricks in the wake of undead councillors, the few humans remaining in the city centre blacked out or began to laugh hysterically at this final violation of reality. It was just too much. Meanwhile, all around, the battle of Grethwick was coming to a violent conclusion. Horrible high rise flats were retreating from the town centre, harried by building society shop fronts and a shrieking, brick-thirsty group of Edwardian coal bunkers. Only the library refused to give up. And he was assaulting the police station with renewed vigour. Riot police were training water cannons on the huge concrete monstrosity but it fired books in reply and blows from hardback versions of War and Peace, Crime and Punishment and the Kama Sutra concussed many officers.

Caught in this crossfire, Lady Sturridge was hovering above a ruined Palladium, having lost her place in the Complete Shakespeare for the umpteenth time.

"This is ridiculous!" she despaired to the small troupe of thespian ghosts beside her. "Why can't they just stop? Don't they realise this is art? And we're *still* missing a Puck. Where can your husband have got to, Harriet?"

"I'm sorry," Bullfinch shouted above the racket, "but I really don't think there's any point in continuing in conditions such as these. Everybody wants a bit of peace."

Lady Sturridge glared down at the carnage. She was dying to do her scene with Bullfinch. She almost stamped her foot. "Well, let's just get down to 'Should a murderer look so dead, so grim.'"

With impeccable theatrical timing, seventy-five undead councillors trudged below her through a rain of masonry and books.

"Aren't they …?" asked Harriet in astonishment.

"Yes!" said Ada, who appeared beside her, "Don't let them out of your sight."

"But the play!" wailed Lady Sturridge.

This time she did stamp her foot.

"Mr Bullfinch?" she said, as the preacher drifted almost apologetically after the undead. "Maybe we could quickly do our scene whilst they're busy?"

He watched the ghosts vanish under cascades of water. Then looked back at Lady Sturridge.

"Come, sit thee down upon this flowery bed, while I thy amiable cheeks do coy," she read from a drenched page.

"Which flowery bed?" he asked uncertainly.

"We'll find one," replied the would-be Queen of all the faeries.

## Chapter 49

Through smoke blacker than a crow's armpit, O'Hara blundered after the chief. Since acquiring an ass's head his nostril powers had developed a thousand-fold. He could not only sniff traces of the chief's perfume amidst the stench of human fear and burning rubber but he could also smell the station. A sort of familiar, slightly sanitised odour. As O'Hara went towards the smell he was almost trodden on by the library which was fiercely bashing the station with its reference wing. Feeling he had a score to settle, the sergeant stooped, picked up a hardback novel and threw it at the looming silhouette of the library. Antagonised by this tiny assault, the library fired back its entire children's hardback collection at O'Hara and he was knocked flying by thousands of colourful illustrations.

As he lay almost buried by ripped and scrawled-on books, he saw Sandra Bottomley sprawled beside him. She'd been severely wounded when the library had fired a filing system at the police station and missed.

"You should've listened to me," she croaked, opening a black eye and seeing an arm with three stripes on it. "I told you to arrest me before I caused any more disasters. Now look. Armageddon. And you've been turned into a donkey. Serves you right for being so stubborn."

O'Hara dragged her up the broken steps of the police station.

"Are you arresting me at last?"

"I'm saving you!" shouted O'Hara.

"I'm beyond redemption! Arrest me and save the world!" she wailed as he set her on a waiting room bench.

O'Hara ignored her; the smell of the chief's perfume was overpoweringly near. Running unsteadily through a building that swayed and shuddered under devastating blows, the sergeant staggered into the front office. The chief was trying to revive the conjuror whose ginger hair was matted with blood.

"*Chief!*"

She recoiled at the sight of her desk sergeant encumbered with a donkey's head.

"O'Hara! You're a … Oh never mind, help me." Between them, they heaved the conjuror across the floor. He felt like a Guy Fawkes full of wet cement. "We've got to get him to my office."

"Don't worry, folks," the man babbled, "This has already happened. We're just witnessing an immutable occurrence in a fixed dimension."

"Guy? Who hit you?" asked the chief as she and O'Hara dragged the conjuror along a corridor. "Bass? Studds?"

"Some modern composer."

The threesome staggered and fell against a wall as the station dodged one of the library's more extravagant blows. O'Hara was winded.

"He's delirious!" wept the chief. "Guy! Guy! You've got to get us out of here! Can we risk the road? Guy?"

O'Hara suddenly smelt the chief's office. An unexpectedly sweet, sweet smell. She backed into the door, turned on a light and then, with O'Hara's help, pulled the conjuror through. She slammed the door and locked it.

"Cyrano. Get him behind the desk. He needs to be able to see the controls."

"Hey?"

The chief recklessly cleared her desk with a few swipes of her arm. Like a mannequin, the conjuror was propped up in a chair, head lolling.

"You realise, of course, that bleeding is fun," he mumbled.

The chief ripped a cover from the desk, revealing an array of lights, dials and switches that looked more confusing than a sound engineer's mixing desk.

"Guy? Can you work it?"

"What?"

"The desk?"

"No. Somebody's been playing Prokofiev on my head with a hammer."

"Guy! Concentrate. We're going to be arrested unless you get the three of us out of here. How do I start this thing?"

O'Hara looked at the desk and asked, "What thing?"

The conjuror looked at the buttons without comprehension. "I need to lie down."

Taking the conjuror's blood-smothered face between her palms, the chief squeezed till his mouth went oval.

"Guy. You can't lie down. I need you. Are you there?"

Someone thumped on the door.

"Sergeant? Sergeant O'Hara? Let me in."

It was Fanny's voice.

O'Hara and the chief looked at each other in desperation. Fanny's voice said, "If you don't let me in, I'm going to shoot off the lock. Cyrano? You might as well give up. You can't go anywhere. There are officers all over the building. Don't bother protecting *her*. She'll just get rid of you when she doesn't need you anymore."

O'Hara looked over at the chief. Her blonde hair was wild. Her blue eyes wide as oceans. Grime streaked and besmirched her skin. Yet she was utterly, compellingly beautiful. O'Hara could no more hand her over than surrender a fawn to the local butcher. He knew that the only man the chief really cared for was bleeding to death in her arms. And that she would probably sell him to the first donkey mart she went by. But so what?

Whilst Fanny's voice left O'Hara unmoved, it seemed to electrify the conjuror. He sat bolt upright and stared at the controls in front of him. He pressed a series of switches. Weird noises augmented the cacophony of buildings slugging it out.

"Don't worry," said the conjuror to the chief. "Everything is an illusion. Even illusions are illusions."

Fanny's voice shouted desperately, "Cyrano! Cyrano! Open the door!"

A screen appeared on the wall facing the desk. Through it, the donkey-headed sergeant saw a road. Lights swam in the office as if it was a bad disco and O'Hara had the nauseous floating sensation of a lift dropping several floors. Then, as the office began to slide with uncanny speed down an unlit highway, he almost started towards the door, for he heard

Fanny give a drawn-out scream of terror. Moments later the sergeant saw why. A large contingent of undead councillors eerily elbowed their way through one of the walls. O'Hara reeled as a stench of maggoty flesh assaulted his highly sensitive nostrils. Zombies in suits crammed into the room chanting, "Guy Brinkman! We're here to haunt Guy Brinkman!"

# Chapter 50

Staggering, as if drunk, Eric tried to find his locker. He had a torch but it wasn't much help. The police station seemed even more jumbled up than usual. Eventually, he discovered some lockers hiding inside one of the cleaning cupboards. They were trembling. Eric's torch beam picked out the word, "Eric". He knew it was his locker because someone had scribbled, "Useless twat" underneath his name. He shoved a small key into the lock. From inside what had once been a tortoise's cell, he extracted the high explosive, wires and plunger that he'd confiscated at the swimming baths. The wire was coiled into a roll. Making sure the connections to the explosives were still in place, Eric unrolled the wire and walked unsteadily backwards out through the cleaning cupboard door and down the corridor. After doing this for fifty yards, he realised he'd been watching too many films because he was intending to blow himself up as well. It would actually be better and quicker to be right near to the blast. So then he rolled the wire back up again. Neatly. After nearly half of it was back on the spool, he realised that this didn't matter either as all the wire was going to get blown up as well. So Eric sat in the corridor trying to connect the wires to the plunger. The torch kept being jolted out of his hands by the motions of the building. The fact that the building was crashing about and showering him in loose plaster made it almost impossible to get the fiddly wires in place. After several frustrating minutes, he took a deep breath, took hold of the plunger and thought of his mum. He loved his mum. It broke his heart to do this to her. He saw her standing in floods of tears at his funeral repeating, "Oh, Eric. Why did you do it? You weren't a bad lad."

Eric said out loud, "You don't understand, Mum. This place had to be finished off forever. So it couldn't hurt any more people. Any more living creatures. That's what it made me do. It has to be destroyed for good reasons. I'm not doing wrong."

He saw tears coursing through the fingers that covered her face.

"Come on, Mum. I was just doing my duty. Like you would have wanted. You should be proud of me."

In his imagination her tear-streaked face came out of her hands and looked at him.

"Who am I going to love, Eric? Who is there left to love, if I haven't got you?"

Eric took his hands off the plunger. Tears started dripping over his eyelids. Then he saw O'Hara in his imagination saying, "You've got to toughen up, lad."

He *couldn't* toughen up. He wasn't tough. He should never have joined the police force. Eric wondered if there was anywhere in the world that would actually be delighted to employ a wet lettuce. Somebody as tough as a newborn lamb. Eric decided that maybe if he talked it over with his mum, she would help him change career. Help him find a profession in which being pathetic was an advantage. Eric decided he wouldn't blow himself and the police station into tiny bits.

Unfortunately, at this moment a drunken, deaf music teacher wearing a stolen uniform and carrying a bloodied tuning device staggered into the corridor.

Moore was running out of heads. He'd brained the conjuror and half a dozen other policemen during his rampage round the station but the supply of constabulary victims had begun to run out. And still his rage had not dissipated. Stumbling upon a naked figure kneeling in a gloomy passageway, he raised a piano tuning cosh and asked, "Are you a policeman?"

Unable to lip-read in the dark, he snatched the torch and shone it into Eric's astonished face.

"Are you a policeman?" he shouted ferociously.

Although Eric didn't plan to be a bobby for much longer, he nodded. A few moments later, he was lying unconscious on the floor, blood pouring from his skull.

Moore shone the torch on the plunger then on the wires. Following the unwound cable to the cleaning cupboard, he discovered the bundle of explosives and shouted, "Stravinsky!" as others might cry, "Eureka!" With immense satisfaction, he went back to the plunger, took hold with both hands and with all his strength, pushed down.

# Chapter 51

In the chief's office — a quantum car — there was standing room only. Seventy-five stinking councillors were squashed shoulder-to-shoulder. So much so, that several heads came off like lids from squeezed tubes of toothpaste. O'Hara found himself forced against a wall by the press of rotting visitors. It was like being in an extremely busy mortuary lift.

"Out of the way! We need to see!" shouted the chief, finding the throng was obscuring views of the warped motorway.

"What the hell's going on?" whinnied O'Hara, gasping for breath.

"We are the undead. We cannot rest in this world until we have justice," droned Alvin and his cronies.

Trying desperately to see over the crush of zombie politicians jammed up against her desk, the chief expostulated, "Look, what happened with the cupboard was an accident, alright? We were trying to build this very road, to open a holiday link to another more corrupt universe and you were getting in the way. *Like you are now!*"

Veering all over the road, the quantum car gathered speed. The conjuror was studying the panel of controls with fixed concentration. The chief's hand was on his, steering a joystick as she continued, "So we thought we'd send you on a warped vacation early. Guy just made a bit of a mess of it and you died in transit. *We're* going to die in transit, too, if you don't get out of the way. We can hardly see."

Alvin spoke menacingly, "You cannot leave this world until we have sorted out our spiritual documentation."

"We're leaving *now*," said the chief. She shouted towards O'Hara, who was still pressed, gagging, against a wall, "We may not make it. Guy's in a state and with this lot standing in the way …"

"Then stop this thing," he hawed.

"We *can't* stay." The chief's face took on a look of ruthless determination as she shoved at an undead body that was folding over onto the desk. "Prison's for innocents. We're all going to a further warped world. A *perfectly* warped world. Maybe it will be the next one along. Where people who've done nothing wrong get put in jail. Where only warped blind people hold power. And they run the police and the government. Where corruption is normal and 'goodness' is an aberration."

"That's *here!*" wailed O'Hara, sandwiched between what seemed like sacks of bursting rotten flesh. Nauseated by the stench of putrescent people, he felt a sensation of panic and tried to wriggle and worm free from the weight of decomposing bodies.

"Where's the door?" he retched.

The chief screamed, "*Guy!*"

The conjuror had collapsed over the control desk. Blood was trickling over the switches and lights.

"You cannot yet leave this world!" intoned the councillors.

Unable to stand the crush of fetid flesh against his face, O'Hara began a frantic struggle towards the door. The office shook and whined hysterically, as if taking off, just as the sergeant turned a key and the door burst ajar. O'Hara fell into nothingness. There was a sensation of floating through space like a drifting spore. His long ears heard a divine voice calling, "Cyrano! Cyrano!"

Sinking through timeless emptiness, he expected to see dead bodies floating all around him. Instead, he felt and smelt fresh tarmac. There was a small taste of eternity before O'Hara heard footsteps and saw torchlight flashing towards him. Somehow, he knew instinctively — call it bobby's intuition — that it was Fanny Fetherby.

# Chapter 52

Moore expected to hear an explosion. Then remembered that he was deaf. Still, he *should* have been blown into lots of little splashes of blood and stewing-sized lumps of meat. Obviously, a connection was loose somewhere. His fingers fiddled with tiny screws and wire. But, before he could press the plunger a second time, Moore heard something. In fact, he heard rather a lot. As if he was wearing a hearing aid the size of Jodrell Bank. With appalling loudness he heard the police station barging into the library. Moore listened to every gritty crumb of concrete disintegrating. Even more strangely he heard the station's high voice squeaking, "Come on then, son! You haven't got another hit left in yer!"

Moore winced at the noises made by a thunderously collapsing library. Its thin voice wailed, "Shiiiiiiiiiiiiiiiiiiiiiiiiiiiiiiiiiit!"

The corridor shook and a large piece of plaster broke over Moore's shoulders. It was then that — ten feet away — he saw a glowing skeleton dressed in Shakespearean garb. A transparent old man's face superimposed on a skull grimaced and its bony shoulders shrugged at Moore.

"Oh dear. I'll just have to tell them I can't do it," said the vision and vanished.

Unaware that he had been transmogrified and that from the shoulders up he was now a collie dog, Moore forgot about blowing up the police station. The encounter with

Farmer Fogarth was strange enough to be sobering. Filled with incredible relief at the return of his hearing, Moore's anger drained away. The man laughed and wiped sweat from his brow. Then, in wonder, felt a cold, wet nose, furry triangular ears and a long tongue that slavered over his chin.

I'm a dog!" he whispered.

Convinced that the trauma of losing his hearing had undermined his sanity, Moore panicked, barked, howled and went round and round in circles, before panting, "Home! Home, boy!"

Shining the torch before him, he hurried along the corridor. In his slightly canine state, Moore reasoned that if he got home and listened to His Master's Voice, everything might return to normal.

Then he stopped and listened, ears cocked to one side. The building's aggressive movement and noise had ceased. But somewhere nearby, in the stillness, Moore heard somebody crying. With all the stealth of a border collie at a sheep dog trial, Moore opened a door and looked down a passage lined with cells. His eyesight in the dark had improved too. The ex-teacher and police impersonator reflected that being a dog wasn't at all bad. From the cell in which he had been kept, No 7, he heard Esmeralda sobbing.

"You have such a cold heart."

"I haven't got a heart. I'm a cupboard."

"Refrigerated shelves then. Please let me out. You know what they'll do to me for starting all this. They'll demolish me. With the yellow crane. And a large swinging metal ball. I only did it to rescue you. Because I thought they would hurt you."

The lost property cupboard replied, "Esmeralda. I'm sorry. There have to be rules in the world if we're all going to get along together. If you break the rules, you have to be punished. It's the same for everyone."

The attic bedroom burst into a fresh torrent of sobs. Tears gushed through the peep hole.

"And I don't even hate you. I love you. But I don't understand. How can you do this to me?"

"I'm sorry, Esmeralda. You'll just have to wait until they send an officer to deal with you."

At this, Moore stepped from the shadows. He knew only too well what went on in these cells.

"Ah!" said Moore. "The visitor's ready for interrogation, is she?"

"Yes, sir," said the cupboard. "Hey! You can hear me?"

"That's because I'm a police dog.

"Oh yes." The cupboard had heard of those.

"Open up, Constable Cupboard. She's to be taken to the main office to be charged."

The cupboard felt proud — he'd been called, "Constable."

"And maybe you could wait in the cell till she comes back?"

"Yes, sir. I mean, dog."

Esmeralda and the cupboard changed places. A key turned.

In all the smoke and chaos, nobody noticed a policeman with a dog's head leave the station with an attic bedroom.

# Chapter 53

After watching undead councillors and his fellow ghosts troop up the police station steps, Horace the Coachman paused to grumble, "Bloody messing about. Tie 'em all in a sack and drop it in a lake I say." Above him, the burly building suddenly lurched ten feet to one side to nut the library in its vitals. The modernist, concrete eyesore shuddered and keeled over sideways with an almighty crash, defeated.

Through clouds of smoke and dust, Horace went wafting up the steps of the police station in the wake of his fellow-dead, still disgruntled.

"I'm tuckered out," he moaned, catching up with the other ghosts as they glowed along dark corridors. "What about a sit down?"

"Shhhhh" hushed Ada sternly.

Horace decided he'd had enough of uppity women and elongated eco-warriors. He gave a grunt and tiptoed towards a wall, slipped inside it and went to sleep.

Meanwhile, up ahead, Jonathon had stopped abruptly. Some of the ghosts following behind walked through him before noticing that the murky legion of undead councillors were queuing in the corridor at the shoulder of a female police officer.

"Cyrano! Cyrano! Open this door!"

Feeling and smelling that something was wrong, Fanny Fetherby slowly turned. Confronted with the sight of decomposing undead councillors, she backed away with a shriek then watched in fascinated horror as the councillors slid through the walls of the chief's office. Moments later, the room shot off, wrenching free to leave a hole in the corridor walls. All that was left was a road stretching down into darkness. Fanny Fetherby switched on a torch and went running along the tarmac shouting, "Cyrano!"

Left stranded in the corridor, the ghosts of Grethwick graveyard turned to one another in shimmering green perplexity.

"I suppose this means …?" said Ada and Jonathon in unison.

Then Fogarth popped up, "*There* you are! Where's Lady Sturridge? I can't do this donkey business."

"*Fogarth!*" Harriet remonstrated as a policeman with a dog's head trotted past escorting a large attic bedroom. "You've turned half of Grethwick into farm animals."

"Yes, yes, yes. I was just practicing. Some of them didn't quite come out as I intended. Though …"

Ada appeared in front of the canine Moore.

"Excuse me, sir."

Moore stopped and growled.

"Please allow my farmer friend to put your proper head back on. Fogarth!"

Ada was surprised when Moore stepped away from her, holding on to his head and barking, "No. I don't want it changed. I like it just the way it is. It's a tremendous improvement. Please leave me alone."

Fogarth explained.

"No, sir. You see, I was trying to turn you into a donkey and …"

Moore interjected, "No! Not like that one kissing the faerie in cell number one. I'd rather be a dog any day! Leave me alone!"

Moore ran off before he could be re-headed. The speechless ghosts exchanged curious looks, then vanished. A few moments later they were taking it in turns to peep through the grille of cell number one where Titania was getting in death what Byron failed to give her in life. Jonathon sighed. The world was overpopulated enough, without dead people breeding like flies. Then Ada Brackenbury tapped politely on the cell door.

"Mr Bullfinch? Lady Sturridge?"

There was a hasty rustling, then two dead lovers came through the door.

"Ah! So you found our new rehearsal rooms? Well done everybody," said Lady Elizabeth unconvincingly.

Ada said, "As our graves have been vacated at last, Your Ladyship, it seems we can almost certainly return to rest in peace."

The old Grethwick ghosts vanished back to their graves. Except … Horace.

The ghostly coachman, who had fallen asleep in a wall, was woken by voices shouting, "Here's another one for the ambulance."

A torch blazed. A guy with a donkey's head bawled almost in his ear, "It's Eric!"

"His pulse is still going," said a woman police officer in a deerstalker.

Eric lifted his broken, bloodied head and croaked, "Sarge. You look like a donkey."

"Get him out of here," the woman urged.

Horace reflected that the bricks he was resting on were not particularly comfortable and moreover were situated in a corridor that was uncommonly rowdy. Yawning, he stepped out of the wall and scratched his skull. Wondering where the other ghosts had gone he noticed a small box nearby with a sort of shooting stick poking up out of it. To Horace, this appeared to be an ideal seat on which to perch his bones until his companions returned from their tiresome mission. He lowered his fragile frame. Imperceptibly, more slowly than an eye could see or a ghost's bottom could feel, the seat sank. Millimetre by millimetre his skeleton began to depress the plunger to its lowest position. In fact, the ghost had just settled into a light doze when there was an almighty explosion and an assortment of his ribs, tibias, pelvis and other bones were blasted hundreds of feet into the sky.

O'Hara and Fanny Fetherby were loading Eric into the ambulance when the blast hit them. Fanny Fetherby found herself lying over a bloodstained woman who choked, "You should have listened to me. You should have arrested me and none of this …"

O'Hara crawled from beneath a pile of rubble beside the ambulance in a daze. He stared wonky-eyed at a large smoking space where the station had once stood. Nothing was left. Only piles of smouldering bricks and … and … and … a cupboard! Unscathed. Standing isolated and alone like a sentry box. *That bloody cupboard!*

# Chapter 54

The Battle of Grethwick was over. Nice houses and people had won. Sort of. The flats had retreated in a rabble of rubble. The library was lying on its side — stone dead. Surviving citizens poked their heads out of hiding places, or stood brushing dust off their pyjamas.

Of course, the evening's events were far too sensational to be included in the morning newspapers. The tabloids wouldn't have touched the story, knowing that English people like to keep themselves to themselves and not poke their noses into other folk's business. The few editors who even considered a couple of lines about Trotskyist flats in Grethwick decided against publication on the grounds that covering the story might intrude on the lives of those who had already suffered enough. Journalists agreed that probably the last thing the people of Grethwick needed after all their suffering was hacks descending to pick over the story like vultures at a wake. So reporters avoided the area out of respect for other people's privacy. One or two sent notes of condolence. Consequently, the outside world — which wouldn't have been that interested anyway — never heard a thing about the uprising of Grethwick's low rise flats.

But that's not to say that nothing was learned from the experience. A few weeks later, after evicted victims had been placed in temporary accommodation, strange conversations sprang up between townspeople as they went about their shopping.

"Oh, yes," said Mrs Gobshaw, the cleaner of Old Grethwick Church to her friend Gladys, a white-haired ex-librarian, "Housing, from now on, should be made conducive to humanity's spiritual wellbeing."

"You're right, Mrs Gobshaw. It's no good just looking at budgets and cutting corners where building homes is concerned. That sort of short-term thinking leads to … well …"

The two women joined a queue to get money from the back of a Securicor van — Grethwick's temporary bank.

"The poor should never again have to suffer life in square, ugly flats," Gladys maintained, "The new councillors that have been voted in should see to it that they only build elegant, enduring, imaginative houses that are designed to fit each individual owner's needs and tastes."

"That's me," said Jeremy, the ex-town hall clerk who happened to be standing beside the two women in the queue.

"Come again, dear?"

"I'm one of the new councillors," said Jeremy proudly. "After what happened to the last lot, not many people wanted a go, so …"

"Yes?"

"Well a group of us are off to study the Taj Mahal next week. Then Gaudi's Parc Guell in Barcelona."

"Is that using public money?"

"Yes."

Jeremy sounded defensive.

"Good. That's what we need. More public money being thrown at things. Glorious waste can lead to very exciting results. That was what we were just saying, wasn't it, Gladys?"

"Oh yes."

Jeremy beamed.

"We're all full of enthusiasm for listening to local people, consulting about their needs and creating buildings that are curvaceous, brightly coloured and humorous on the outside while warmly embracing on the inside."

Of course, none of this subsequently happened. Architects *were* brought in, builders *did* raise two fantastical houses on the derelict site of Langley Farm Drive Estate. But, within days, the stained glass windows were all smashed. The roof slates were pinched. Graffiti was immediately sprayed all over the brightly mosaiced walls. Some of the slogans said, "Arty houses up your arses. The working classes say, '*No!*' to middle class culture!"

Wretched Eric walked up the temporary high street of Grethwick, stopping to buy an apple from a barrow. As usual, he was not wearing a uniform. But this was not because he was stark naked. He had handed in his notice. He was never going to not wear a uniform when he should have been wearing one, ever again. It was a relief. His mum had seen a job in the paper and Eric was going for an interview. Cheerily, and a little nervously, he went into Waterstones, which was sited in an old library bus. He moved sideways through an uncomfortable crush of people and rooted out a likely volume. After paying, he set off through the open market that had replaced the old high street. After half an hour of sitting on a letter "F" which had once hung over Grethwick's Friends of the Earth office, Eric decided he had read enough of *Raising Toads — A Tadpole Tutor for the Eco-Conscious.* He snapped the weighty tome shut and made straight for an outsized shelter nearby. A provisional dwelling that looked rather like a large tortoise.

Eric knocked on the hulky shell of willow and tarpaulin. His hand made a slithery dull thud. A flap parted and Wacca's face peered out, blinking at the harsh natural light of the outside world.

"I've come about this advert me mum saw in the Old Grethwick District Herald. Warden for Toad Sanctuary."

"Better come in."

Inside the dome of mud and branches, dozens of wax-dribbling candles were giving off yellow light. Eric saw a desk, filing cabinet, solar powered photocopier and a wind operated kettle. He also saw dozens of little brown things hopping about and making noises that were nearer a belch than a croak. A toad dropped onto his shoe and said, in toad language, "Giz a worm."

Eric sat on the floor with Wacca.

"Have you had any previous experience with animals?"

"Er, yes. Tortoises. I've kept tortoises before."

Wacca brushed at some dirt that had dropped on his suit. "Well, the job's 400 quid a week plus relocation expenses."

"But I already live here," Eric assured him.

"Yes. You have to relocate the toads."

One of the amphibians leapt onto Eric's lap and belched, "Giz a worm, ya stingy get."

"Will that be very costly, relocating them?" Eric asked.

"Depends if they're relocated to some expensive hotel," said Wacca.

"But shouldn't they be let loose somewhere muddy? A pondy sort of place with flies and stuff?"

"Normally, yeah, but these ones ..."

Eric looked at Wacca in puzzlement. The eco-warrior admitted, "Well, these ones think they're human, see. I rescued them from this graveyard. There was going to be a road through there and ..."

"Now there isn't."

"Yes. But they won't go back. I've taken them out in the car boot loads of times. Next morning, they're all hopping about at my front door, croaking like mad for worms. Fifty of them. The landlord's pissed off. It makes other potential tenants think the place is damp."

Eric stroked the hungry toad which was lying in his lap and looking up expectantly with big bulbous eyes.

"You see," said Wacca, "I didn't have anywhere to put them when I rescued them from the wild so I let them hop about my flat. Now they won't leave. They like it too much. They like watching all my National Geographic videos and they play tiddlywinks into my bed every night when I go to sleep. Landing on me like cruise missiles with warts whenever I lie down. Then they all start croaking their heads off for worms four times a day. I've got to set out fifty saucers heaped with brandlings and lobs to keep them quiet. Along with thimbles of tea to wash them down."

Wacca's face looked haunted and pale but Eric stood up beaming. His head bumped the low tarpaulin roof.

"Sounds just the job!"

"You'll do it? Look after them? Carefully? Properly? No flushing them down the bog and taking the money. There'll be weekly checks over their adoption."

"Honestly. Being a Toad Warden is my calling in life."

"Have you got a new location in mind?"

"Definitely," enthused Eric. "The perfect place."


An hour later Eric arrived home, pushing a small greengrocer's barrow. Strapped to this handcart were two large cardboard boxes which seemed to be belching loudly. Opening his front door, Eric shouted, "Mum?"

A voice from upstairs replied, "Did you get it?"

"Yes."

"Oh good."

The sound of her footsteps coming downstairs grew louder. Then she stood in the hall and asked, "When do you start?"

Eric gave an embarrassed cough as he carefully brought in the first box.

"Now."

# Chapter 55

Having trashed his record player, Mr Moore remembered that in the loft there was an antique gramophone. One that was wound up by a handle with a metal funnelled speaker. He rummaged it out and brought it down. After blowing the dust off, he set it up in the living room and slipped a vinyl record out of its sleeve. This was placed gently on the turntable. Moore cranked the wooden handle. The sound system crackled somewhat but that couldn't take away from the ecstasy of hearing Bach with new ears. Moore opened a tin of Pedigree Chum for his dinner and forked it onto a plate. The sweet aroma of dog meat filled the air. Disposing of the fork, Moore just gobbled the meal straight from the plate. Then he looked up. He saw the incorporeal form of the Reverend Dylan was watching him.*

"You?" woofed Moore. "A ghost of you, anyway."

"Yes. I've brought you a confession."

Dylan's transparent hand held out a note.

"It's from the two constables that killed me."

Moore took the paper in his mouth then dropped it onto

---

* You may be wondering how this could happen? How could an ordinary person see the ghost of a murdered victim? It's because dogs can not only hear frequencies of a much higher range than humans but also see the spirits of departed beings. It's another reason why our four legged friends sometimes stand up in a silent empty room and cock their heads staring at nothing. Had the guests at Macbeth's banquet all been wearing flea collars and chewing slippers, Shakespeare's plot would have been an awful lot shorter.

a table.

"Take a seat?"

"I'll hover. If you don't mind."

Moore was feeling hospitable. "Bowl of water? Chewy stick?"

The vicar's ghost looked impatient. "No, really. Thanks. This confession, it should ensure that your innocence is established beyond doubt."

Moore read the note.

"Hmmm," he said, tongue lolling out happily, "This is very nice of you. Though, to be honest, I wouldn't be so very bothered about prison now. So long as I was allowed to listen to my record collection. In fact, the idea of having somebody look after me, take me for walks in a compound, feed me regularly, shut me up in a sort of kennel — well, if I'm honest, the whole thing seems rather attractive. So …"

The vicar protested as Moore crumpled the confession and flicked it into the fire.

"You idiot!" The vicar was flabbergasted. "That confession proved your innocence and that I was murdered and …"

Moore panted sympathetically.

"Yes, yes, yes. I'm sure it was very important but listen to this fascinating rendition of Bach's *Fantasia and Fugue in G minor*. You see, with canine ears …"

Moore stopped because he saw that the vicar was starting to vanish into the floor. His spirit was going round and round at top speed. It was being sucked down into the floor like water going down a plughole.

"Arrrrrgggggghhhhhhhhhhhh!" screamed the reverend's voice.

"Funny man," said Moore, his collie's head cocked to one side. "And I forgot to ask him if he had a spare dog collar."

The Reverend Dylan found himself in an office where dust was heaped like sand dunes. A grey, mummified creature stared at him from black holes in rotting bandages.

"Good. You received our summons."

"What the hell's going on? I was really getting to grips with that haunting stuff. Now you've thrown me out of my stride."

The mummy scrutinised sheaves of paper.

"The Reverend Dylan."

"I *was*, yes."

"I regret to inform you that there has been an administrative error. Somebody filled in your "For office use only" part of the form wrong. You don't have to haunt people. You should have got eternal sleep instead. We're extremely sorry for any inconvenience we may have caused you. These things happen. We deal with billions of dead people, you understand. There's always going to be a little confusion in a place as big as this considering the vast numbers involved."

"Well, actually, I was quite enjoying not turning the other cheek so, if you don't mind …"

The black holes in the mummy's eyes stared with infinite vacancy, "It's most regrettable. You *weren't* murdered, you see."

"What?"

"It was filled in wrong. Routine clerical error. Apparently, you fell on your knife."

"I didn't. I was pushed!"

"I'm sorry, you fell. We've been over the video evidence several times from a number of different angles and you definitely fell after taking a slash at that policeman's throat."

"I didn't mean to slash his throat. It was dark. I was just making a few broad swipes to keep the bastards back."

"I'm sorry, sir. I've got down here, 'Video evidence reviewed. Not murdered. Asked for it.'"

"Asked for it?"

"Yes, let's see … 'Selling drugs to teenagers. Resisted arrest. Drew knife in van. Threatened police officer. Struggled with said police officer. Tried to kill said police officer. Fell on knife in struggle.' Sounds like you were asking for it to me."

The vicar exploded with indignation, "What sort of illiberal regime are you running down here?"

The mummy placed a paper clip on the vicar's papers and laid them to one side.

"Sorry sir. It's a pair of wooden pyjamas and eternal sleep for you."

"But …"

"Between you and me — and this is strictly off record — you may like to know that the two policemen who arrested you *were* murdered. In fact, they're next."

The mummy rang a bell. Two ghostly turkeys came into the room. Turkey Studds said, "I'm getting a bit tired of this. *They* won't have us in the animal underworld. *You* won't have us in the human underworld. You dead bastards should get your friggin' act together."

The mummy's eyes grew even emptier.

"Turkeys Studds and Bass. Interesting case. It's filling out your forms that's giving us difficulty you see. And of course now, with it being just after 4th July, there are big queues and waiting lists in the Turkey Department. They don't really want to accept responsibility for you and it's difficult for us to do so in your present condition. A condition which is now fairly immutable in spiritual terms. You're anomalies. So you'll have to get used to lots more tramping about before you get settled. Now the first thing to do is … Oh. Mr Dylan. Sign here and you can go."

Dylan signed. The mummy almost smiled through its bandages: "Thank you, Reverend. Rest in peace, as we say. Have a billion winks and, if you do wake up, bang your skull on the tombstone three times. That usually sorts it out."

"Christ," said the vicar.

"Yes. I remember him," said the mummy. "Interesting case. Didn't know if he was dead or alive either. Up and down like a yo-yo before he got settled."

The Reverend Dylan reappeared by his own mock marble tombstone.

"Here lies the Reverend Thomas Dylan," read the inscription. Some miscreant teenager had already sprayed with aerosol underneath, "Another dead fucker." Which actually cheered the vicar up a bit. He wondered when the occupants of the Old Grethwick graveyard would be transferred into his field and crossed the road for a quick chat before settling down in his plot of earth.

The ghosts of Old Grethwick had returned to their churchyard and, finding it a mess of broken tombs and uprooted trees, had spent some time restoring order. They were just putting the last flags back on the cemetery path when the vicar appeared.

"There isn't going to be a road," Preacher Bullfinch informed him. "So none of us will be moving anywhere."

"You mean I'm going to be left all alone in that field?"

"You'll have plenty of elbow room. You can't complain about living space. Or rather dying space. Loads of it."

"But you'll all be having parties over here and ..."

"We'll be sleeping," said Bullfinch.

"Most of the time," added Lady Sturridge pertly.

"Unless those infernal teenagers ..."

Ada Brackenbury butted in, "But Mr Dylan. There may be some space freed up in this graveyard."

She looked innocently at Lady Sturridge. Elizabeth said boldly, "Mr Bullfinch and I have decided to move in together. To shack up — as they seem to say in this day and age. I have donated my large and opulent crypt to those who were less well off than myself in life as a gesture of goodwill."

"Me, Horace, Bob and a few others are going to all go and be dead in it together. For a laugh. So you can have one of our graves if you want."

The peasant bowed, "Have mine, sire. It be cosy and broken in. And the fleas is all gone now. Left centuries ago."

"Or there's my grave," piped up Fogarth. "Harriet and I were always on top of each other when we were alive. Why change things just cos we've decomposed?"

Horace who had managed to locate most of the bits of him that had been blown up by an exploding police station said, "Or maybe you'd like to come and be dead in Lady Sturridge's communal crypt with the rest of us, Reverend? If you don't find the idea too sacrilegious?"

The vicar perked up considerably.

"Quite the opposite in fact," he said, "I'm sure we could find a great deal in the scriptures to support the idea if we looked hard enough."

As the ghosts drifted off through the graveyard to discuss this, Ada Brackenbury stepped into her grave and sat down saying, "And what about you, Jonathon? Are you going to curl up for the rest of your death, all alone?"

"Well, the trouble is, I'm so big. Do you think you could get comfortable with me in your grave?"

"It would be much more ecologically sound. Think of the space that would be saved."

He looked thoughtful.

"And I suppose we could lie down with a couple of handfuls of acorns each and try to germinate them through our ribs?"

"It would be like having children."

# *Chapter 56*

Inside a suburban house, Fanny Fetherby and Sergeant O'Hara were in bed — almost naked.

"Do you have to wear that bloody deerstalker and smoke a pipe when we make love? It puts me off."

Fanny blew out a plume of smoke.

"Would you rather I played the violin?"

"But you don't have to do all that Sherlock Holmes stuff now. You don't have to pretend to be some middle-aged, crime-mad spinster now I know who you are."

"I like pretending. Being head of a police corruption investigation unit is not as interesting as being Fanny Fetherby."

"What *is* your real name by the way?"

"Agnes."

There was a silence.

"Okay. Keep the hat on. Wasn't it a bit corrupt of you to investigate a situation by seducing me?"

Fanny blew out another long trail of smoke.

"If you want to find out what's going on in a police station, get into the undies of the desk sergeant."

There was another small silence. Then O'Hara said, "And isn't it a bit corrupt, not arresting me?"

"What for?"

"Corruption!"

Fanny sucked vigorously on her pipe to keep it going, then

asked, "You mean for the biros?"

"How did you know about those?"

"You talked about biros obsessively in your sleep. However, biros can't be stolen. They can only be borrowed indefinitely. Like books."

"But I slept with the chief," confessed O'Hara.

"I'm prepared to overlook your lapse of taste," Fanny said icily. "Especially because you won't be able to do so with her again."

"I helped her escape!"

"And I shall pretend I didn't hear you say that. I'm in a pretending mood."

Another silence opened up. O'Hara closed it by saying, "I wonder what happened to her?"

"Presumably, if we take the brochures on illegal transworld immigrants found in her home at face value, she must have made it to another, more warped parallel universe. Displacing herself and a chief engineer in a world very like our own but worse. Even more distorted, disfigured and corrupted."

"Is that possible?"

"It's hard to imagine."

"And you and me in that world are ..."

"Yes. At this very moment. Only wearing a bigger hat and smoking opium in the pipe."

"So I *should* be arrested, Fanny. For letting her get away with it."

"Nonsense. It's arguable whether any crimes were committed at all."

"What? What about the councillors?"

"Well, by her own admission, their deaths were an accident. It was manslaughter at worst. And some might say the killing of seventy odd politicians is a public service."

"But the dead councillors probably displaced the live councillors in the other world."

"That may improve it. Probably will. Besides, other universes are beyond our remit and jurisdiction."

"But she was using public money to build a superhighway there."

"Oh I know all that. Abuse of public funds is the reason we were called in by the councillors in the first place. They wanted us to investigate their seventy-five suspicions. But the more I think about it, the more I feel bound to conclude that nothing *very* criminal occurred. The quantum roads were destroyed in the bomb blast. And, sure, public money was wasted. But there's not enough wastage of public money. It's too accountable and penny-pinching. Nothing interesting ever gets done when purse strings are so tightly knotted."

O'Hara sat up in bed. "I can't believe I'm hearing this! You can't acquit the Grethwick constabulary of corruption! What about Bass and Studds? Murdering the vicar and braining that teacher?"

Fanny grew thoughtful. Philosophical even. "You know, sometimes — only sometimes — I think the universe and fate get together and bring out their own set of weights and measures. Bass' and Studds' heads were found beside the remains of two roasted turkeys. In the evidence I accumulated privately there can be no doubt that the Reverend Dylan *was* selling drugs to young people and resisted arrest. Vicars shouldn't carry flick knives, you know. Not with their own names emblazoned on the handle."

Her pipe had definitely gone out. She laid it on a bedside table and continued, "And the Hillman Imp used by the man who brained a policeman, stole his clothes and then used the disguise to clobber half of Grethwick's police force, including Eric, belonged to Mr Moore. Maybe the guy was innocent of one thing and guilty of something else. Two wrongs don't make a right. But a wrong and a right sometimes cancel each other out."

"Well, the very least you could do is arrest the houses that caused the riot. Hundreds were killed and injured."

Fanny suddenly looked a little paranoid. In sign language, she indicated that he should keep his voice down. Then whispered, "Actually, I wouldn't dare. The cupboard in all probability is innocent. It only ran away because it was aghast to have been used for such unlawful purposes. And it was locked up well before the riot was incited. The attic bedroom, who almost certainly started the whole thing, is nowhere to be found. But even if she *was* — would it be safe to arrest her? It might spark more housing riots all over the country. Better to let the dust settle and hope it doesn't happen again. Besides ..."

Fanny whispered even lower, right into O'Hara's ear, "In the middle of it all, just after I'd watched you and the chief run off, I thought I caught a glimpse of *this house!* Throwing bricks at the station. I recognised the paintwork. The same number was on the door."

O'Hara looked around Fanny's darkened bedroom in some alarm.

"And I couldn't arrest it anyway. Not when I want to rent it for at least another couple of months."

"You mean so we can …?"

"Yes."

"So you don't mind my nose then?"

"On the contrary, it's the most beautiful nose I've ever stroked. So soft and cuddly and smooth. The silvery greyness of it is bewitching. I can see exactly what Titania saw in Bottom."

She kissed his donkey's head and a renewed bout of heavy breathing and grunts took place. A few minutes later O'Hara rolled on his back with a little bray of satisfaction. Fanny moaned, "Oh! I think that's the first time I ever felt the earth move."

"Me too."

As Fanny toyed with his long grey ears, O'Hara asked, "There's one thing *really* puzzles me about all of this."

"Yes, my darling?"

"Why did all those naked people keep appearing with stolen umbrellas?"

Hatless, pipeless and still in some ecstasy, Fanny said, "Well, at first I thought it was because Grethwick's annual rainfall was higher, causing more people to get soaked and remove their drenched garments, whilst also causing a higher incidence of people carrying umbrellas. Then I realised …"

"Yes?"

Fanny had stopped at the vital moment.

"Did you feel something?" she asked.

"You realised *what?*" said O'Hara in exasperation.

"Oh. That it was all just mass coincidence."

"Mass coincidence?" O'Hara repeated incredulously. "You surely don't believe in ... Whoooaaaahhhhhh! Arrrrrrrrggggggghhhh!"

The two lovers screamed as the bed suddenly tilted sideways and slid across the room. They were thrown into the air and flew in a tangle of naked limbs out of an open upstairs window. They landed squelching in a marshy field.

"Ow!"

"Jesus! Cyranooooooooooooooooo!"

"Oh my arse!"

They were left sprawled together naked in a large, dark bog.

"My house!" shouted Fanny, rising unsteadily to her feet. "It's dumped us and run off!"

She tried running after it for a few foot-sucking steps.

"Urgghh. I'll never catch it. Bastard building!"

"I can't believe this!" said O'Hara.

"And I thought the earth had moved!"

O'Hara could see Fanny dimly in the murky light, her hands resting on her hips. She snorted, "At least the bugger could have left us some clothes!"

Holding hands, they slutched and slopped through the foul-smelling field.

"Ow! A fucking thistle!" said Fanny grimacing and holding her foot as they came out of the bogland.

"Allow me."

O'Hara ate it.

Shivering only slightly in the midsummer night's air, O'Hara and Fanny found a gate and clambered over it. They jumped down onto a road. Almost immediately, a lorry came roaring out of the night with lights blazing. O'Hara tried to flag it down.

"Stop! We need help! Help!"

The driver of the lorry, seeing a naked man with a donkey's head, accelerated for all he was worth and almost crashed as he went round a corner. As the lorry swerved and tilted, something clattered off the back of it and into the road.

"It dropped something."

The two of them went over to look. O'Hara stooped by the verge and groaned as he picked up two long pointed objects.

"Umbrellas!" He handed one to Fanny. "Do you think they're stolen?"

"No. They just fell off the back of a lorry."

Fanny opened her umbrella as a car came round the corner from the other direction, catching them both in the full glare of its headlights.

"Stop! Help!" she begged, from behind the segmented circle that shielded her.

They both heard the car drop a gear and scream off even faster. With opened umbrellas to the fore and rear, the two lovers stuck out their thumbs and walked, wincing, along the road back to Grethwick.

Had they paused for one moment and turned to look at a

sky haunted by moonlight, they might have glimpsed two angular silhouettes embracing on a distant hilltop. The kiss lasted only seconds. Then the moon crept behind a purple veil of clouds. Fanny's house and an attic bedroom vanished into the night.

# CULT FICTION

*'This book is an abomination! It must be banned at once!'* – The Archbishop of Roxborough-Wells (possibly).

Some people read stories because they offer an escapism that cannot be found elsewhere. Some people read stories because there's been a power cut. You should read this story because it is very important. It is the story of Stephen Moore. It is also the story of a bench and a fire called Malcolm. Above all, it is the story of the birth of that great religion called Mooranity.

## ABOUT THE AUTHOR

Ardie Collins is sometimes hungry and rarely late. He has spent half of his life inhaling and near enough the other half exhaling. He can almost speak one language which is only partly contributable to the fact that he is in the middle of making one up. In between these other commitments he has managed to write a small book. It's this one, by the way.

# *Cult Fiction*

Some people read stories because they offer an escapism that cannot be found elsewhere. Some people read stories because there's been a power cut. The reason you should read this story is because it is very important and I will guide you through it in the pages that follow.

It would be unfair to presume, however, that all those reading are familiar with the idea of a book. Even though it is likely that, to have come this far, one must understand the concept, it would be most undemocratic to make such an assumption. It really is very important for everyone to be able to read everything in this book, so if those that are fine with the idea could be patient for the next paragraph or so, it will really make this whole process a lot easier and we can all set off on the right footing.

Firstly, we shall establish how you gained possession of the book. There are several options, but some of the accepted ones are below:

You bought it.
It was a gift.
You are borrowing it from someone.
You are just scanning it to see if you want to buy it.

You found it perched lovingly underneath a drainpipe.
You stole it.

If your possession relies on the first five categories then I must insist that you stay with me to the end. This is purely because this is all so very important. I can assure you now that it will be extremely worth it. It might not seem like it now but it all gets very exciting. Even by the end of this chapter you will have met the main protagonist, his dog and a destructive fire named Malcolm. If you have stolen this book then I am contractually obliged to encourage you to take it back. But, to be frank, I am always slightly impressed by thieves. It takes guts. And it is somewhat of a skill. Like juggling.

Now we come to how you are to use this book. The basic idea of a book is to be read and the more complex idea of a book is to be understood. We will leave the latter up to someone else for now, although, if you find yourself in such a position then well done, you. Simply make sure that you follow the words left to right along each line, moving down a single line at a time. When you reach the end of the page simply turn it over to reveal a fresh set of words to read. Do remember to remember the first part of each sentence at the end of a page because that sentence will, most likely, continue on the other side of the page. You must understand that I do not intend to be patronising, I just want to make sure we are all on the same page. Luckily, that's this one.

Now then, at the beginning of a story a setting must be established. The setting for the beginning of this particular story is a house. Though this may not seem like an overtly interesting setting, I assure you that the level of interest will increase, perhaps due to the fact that it will burn down very shortly. It was the house of a good and kind man. He's bound to be, at the very least, your second favourite character in this book and if he isn't then I really cannot understand why because he was very pleasant indeed. This man's name was Stephen Moore.

The first thing you must understand about Stephen Moore is that he was very suggestible. The second thing you must understand about Stephen Moore is that he was a Christian. He prayed every night that a man in the sky would aid him through his troubles. This was quite an easy task because he didn't tend to have many troubles. The fact that he did nothing except go to work or church really made the man in the sky's job very easy. And I'm sure he would be eternally grateful. Literally.

Stephen attended his collective every Sunday where they sang to the man in the sky and his son, who is also himself, who once came to Earth, and then died to save us all from ourselves, only to come back to life. It is a gripping tale but I do not have the time to tell it right now as I'm digressing from Stephen's story which, I'm not sure if you are aware, is extremely important. Stephen and his collective sang about all the wonderful things He has done and all the wonderful things He is able to do. Stephen had always felt a certain warmth there amongst all of those people singing about the same thing. But it was not long until the warmth that Stephen enjoyed so much drifted away and left him standing alone and seemingly knowing nothing but cold.

Stephen Moore lived with a dog. He also had two bookshelves, one television set, a DVD player, one computer, seven kitchen cupboards, one cooker, a queen-sized bed, eight pairs of trousers, thirty-two T-shirts, sixteen jumpers, forty pairs of boxer-shorts, forty-two and a half pairs of socks, five pairs of shoes, two suits, three coats, a guitar, a sofa, an alarm clock, a telephone, a CD-player/radio combo, a Frisbee, one-hundred and twenty-four CDs, one-hundred and twenty-three books, fifty-two DVDs, a bottle opener, a can opener, a bag of rice, a bag of pasta, several sauces, a loaf of bread, some chicken, some mince, some butter, some ham, some cheese, some salad leaves, some apples, some dog food (obviously these pieces of food were variable depending on what day it was as Stephen tended to eat his food and then buy more) a kitchen table, two sinks, one toilet, a shower, and a certain amount of carpet of which I have been unable to ascertain the exact amount. But that doesn't really matter anyway, because all of these things are almost definitely going to be burnt to cinders very soon indeed.

Now that I feel you have gained at least a small understanding of these possessions, I will introduce their owner to you. As is the case with stories, I will not literally introduce him to you. Firstly, I don't know when you'll be reading this and it would be very difficult to guess where you'll be at the time. Secondly, this would be entirely impossible.

Instead of this I will write about him and you may feel as though you have been introduced to him. Perhaps you would like to, metaphorically, stand in the corner of his living room and watch him as he enters through the door. Don't worry, he can't see you.

There he is, walking in through the door. His house was quite cosy, if a little bland. Some people have suggested that Stephen suited his home perfectly. Stephen was a reasonably tall man who wore a tidy side-parting when at work and church and a messy side-parting at other times. His dark hair lay on top of a cheery-looking face that suggested everything was going to be okay, even if it wasn't. He tended to wear suits, except when he bathed, apart from the one time he forgot to take one off. In his leisure time he would also wear clothes.

You can decide what clothing he is wearing at this particular juncture. Make sure you have a good, long think because it is very important and could make the whole story not quite fit into place unless you pick the right outfit. I am almost definitely lying, of course, but 'it's nice to create a bit of tension now and again' as Stephen's mother used to say.

On his arrival home, his small dog, Elijah, would shake his tail vigorously and leap towards Stephen with a certain look on his face that suggested a deep understanding of the concept of an emotional relationship but was actually excitement for the prospect of food.

'It's okay, boy, I'm home now,' was almost always Stephen's response. This would make Elijah's stomach much happier. Stephen would go to the toilet but you don't have to watch that bit. He would then put together some kind of dinner for himself, give Elijah some dinner as well and settle down in front of the television set. He would invariably fall asleep, to be woken up by Elijah licking the small portion of his remaining dinner from his cheek. Stephen would then go to bed, read a small amount of the Bible, rustle up a small prayer and go to sleep with Elijah at the foot of the bed, safe in the knowledge that he would, most definitely, be going to heaven if he happened to die in his sleep.

There is a small amount of irony in this because one night he very nearly did die. And there is almost no way on God's green earth that heaven actually exists, which would have been a nasty shock for Stephen.

So far I have been talking about typical evenings. Let us, instead, move to a definite day of the week. It was a Tuesday. Well, it was very early on a Tuesday. It was actually the night of a Monday but the morning of a Tuesday in that awkward transition point where people don't really know where they are time-wise. Even though it cannot be denied that it was officially a Tuesday as far as the owners of calendar shops are concerned, if you happened to be awake at this time it would not be unreasonable to consider it still part of your Monday.

It's a small period of time where some feel quite alone and others are drenched in an immense feeling of freedom. Various studies into this small period of time have suggested that this is to do with the fact that this is a time when a country's leader is almost definitely asleep. Therefore, those that are fond of their leaders or leadership generally are worried about what might happen over the next few hours. They prefer to tuck themselves up in bed and avoid the whole horrible process of dealing with the thoughts that will begin to form inside their heads about what might happen when the invasion begins. Others, that aren't quite so fond of their leaders or leadership in general, find this an emancipating period of time and use it wisely by running through fields, taking up bewildering hobbies or skinny-dipping in their baths.

This aside, Stephen found himself asleep in the early hours of Tuesday morning, very much and unavoidably minding his own business when, downstairs, a very warm glow was burrowing its way through the house. This warm glow was spreading like wildfire. This was mainly due to the fact that it was a fire called Malcolm and it was spreading rather wildly. He was creeping his way through the household, up the stairs and being generally disruptive along the way. Stephen awoke in a splutter of smoke with a barking dog at the foot of his bed.

Stephen turned on the lamp next to his bed and suddenly sat up, rather rigidly, at the sight of all the smoke. After taking this sight in from a rigid sitting position he thought maybe he should consider it from a standing position. He decided to take forward this idea by standing up very quickly. At first he just stood there, staring oddly at the smoke seeping under his bedroom door. He wondered briefly whether this was a dream. If you were to ask me how I know this then that would very much undermine my position as the narrator. It is essential that you accept that I am aware of, near enough, everything that is going on. There is a two-way trust system occurring here. You must trust me that I am telling you the truth, and I must trust you that you are paying attention. This is mainly due to the fact that this is all very important.

Attention was one of the only things Stephen was capable of at this time as he stood with a gaping mouth while his rather unhelpful mind was asking itself whether it was dreaming. But his wandering, wondering mind which had started to drown out the distant, roaring sound of Malcolm rushing through his house was brought back to consciousness by Elijah's incessant barking.

Once he had returned to the situation, he leapt into action. He quickly grabbed Elijah under his belly, plucked him from the ground and ran to his bedroom door. He opened it and was greeted by a vision of being truly trapped. The roar grew louder and the smoke billowed through the doorway that it had been attempting to seep through for the past few minutes. Malcolm was outside his door and he was very angry. Stephen could see no way around the furious blaze before him and it was up to him to find another way out of the situation.

With great, spluttering difficulty he closed his door and put down his little dog. He scurried over to his window, propped his fingers underneath the groove at the bottom of it and lifted it as wide as possible, staring down into the night's darkness below him. This darkness was his only hope now. He removed his mattress violently from his bed and forced it out through his bedroom window, hearing a sound that would best be described as the sound of the word 'plump' as it struck the floor. He grabbed Elijah, who had been barking rather unhelpfully throughout this whole situation and made his way back towards the gaping window.

Stephen placed one foot onto the ledge and began to force his way out before his better judgment kicked in and told him to stop. He listened briefly. That is, until his even better judgement reminded him of just how angry Malcolm was and just how behind a wooden door he was. His even better judgement was struggling to overpower his better judgement until his best judgement emerged to clear up the whole situation. His best judgement addressed the squabble by explaining that he would definitely die if he stayed in the bedroom and that mattresses are fairly soft and welcoming. It was this judgement that got things to go its way and Stephen felt himself jump out into the cold, night air.

His stomach lifted out of him as he plummeted towards the mattress. This caused an incomprehensible noise-word to escape from his mouth. The two seconds of falling through the air were the most exciting of Stephen's life, which caused a mixture of distress and shame that Stephen didn't really have time to address right now even though he really, really wanted to. Elijah let out a little whimper as they grew closer to the ground. They found a safe landing on the mattress which they had been sleeping on only minutes before that moment.

Stephen simply lay there for a bit, trying to take in exactly what was going on. Once he realised what there was to take in he thought that perhaps now, more than ever, was the time for a little bit of action. His best judgement agreed so he stood up very quickly from the mattress for the second time in as many minutes. He found his way onto his feet and stepped onto the grass surrounding his house. His feet became instantly entrenched in the cold, wet, dew-ridden grass but this did nothing to make him hesitate. He tried to evoke the sense of being assured as he began walking across the night ground. He forced his hasty breathing to slow gradually as he walked round to the front of his house but soon the situation engulfed him once more and his breathing sped up to an uncontrollable rate when he saw the consuming blaze in front of him. Malcolm was completely and unashamedly ripping apart his house. He began to pace back and forth with his hands gripping various parts of his head entirely unsure of what he should do.

I will be the first to admit that Stephen does not seem to be portraying the qualities of a typical hero but just you wait; he really pulls it out of the bag. He remained there for another minute, though. His bewildered look persisted. His eyes were transfixed on the blaze before him. He was watching Malcolm viciously consume his only home. Billows of smoke slowly wafted into the darkness of the night sky as Stephen's gaze moved up towards the stars.

At this point I have chosen to end this chapter. I find it a sufficiently dramatic moment to make such a decision. Many people like to stop reading at the end of a chapter and take a small break. Others can manage many at once. Other others are quite happy to stop during a chapter and enjoy the challenge of trying to remember the story so far. So you may have already stopped. Other other others (which is the category I fall into) try to take this challenge further and enjoy stopping during a sentence to see how they will cope in two days' time. There are some that enjoy stopping mid-word but those people are quite strange. I would not, however, refuse one round to dinner as I'm sure their minds are fascinating places that I would very much like to explore.

**Cult Fiction by Ardie Collins can be purchased from all good bookshops.**

**RRP: £7.99**

**ISBN: 978-1-908134-03-5**